The second before the door closed, he called her name. "Hey, Tana?"

"Yes?" She waited, hand on the door, looking concerned.

What? What are you going to say? He just couldn't get the contrast between her and his sister-in-law out of his head. Every woman deserved to be as happy as his sister-in-law had been.

"Since I'm the first person in Masterson who knows you're expecting, I get to be the first person in Masterson to congratulate you on the big news." His smile was sincere, not forced. "Congratulations, Montana McKenna."

"Thanks." It took a moment, but she smiled. It started small, but she ended up beaming at him. "Thanks. Really."

Happy. Beautiful. That was how she should look, even if it blinded him.

"Good night," he said.

"Good night." She stepped back and shut the door.

He started the engine, but he didn't back out of his space until he'd watched her cross the street safely, open the etched-glass door of the pub and disappear inside.

"Goodbye, Montana McKenna."

* * *

MASTERSON, TEXAS:
Where you come to learn about love!

Dear Reader,

When I was a child, I loved the movie *The Wizard of Oz*, but I thought the ending was so very sad. Dorothy got her heart's desire by returning to her home and family, but she lost her very best friend in the process. The scarecrow stayed behind in Oz, and the two never saw one another again. You see, I had no idea that Hunk, the farmhand in the black-and-white ending of the movie, was the same actor who played Scarecrow.

As an adult, I can appreciate that this gives the movie a happier ending, but it does not change that heartbreaking moment in the Land of Oz when the scarecrow lets Dorothy go, although he will miss her for the rest of his life. It's the most selfless act of love.

I was not consciously inspired by that scene while I was writing this book, but now I can see how that one movie moment shaped my perception of how a real hero should put others before himself, even if it costs him the person he loves most. However, a lifetime of reading romance novels has taught me something equally important: love is worth fighting for. A happily-ever-after ending is always possible, if the hero and heroine are determined to make it happen. And that, dear reader, is what you'll find in this book.

I'd love to hear what you think. You can find me on Facebook easily, or you can contact me through my website, www.carocarson.com. I look forward to hearing from you.

Cheers,

Caro Carson

The Slow Burn

CARO CARSON

HARLEQUIN
SPECIAL
EDITION

HARLEQUIN®
SPECIAL EDITION™

Recycling programs for this product may not exist in your area.

ISBN-13: 978-1-335-89481-6

The Slow Burn

Harlequin Enterprises ULC
22 Adelaide St. West, 40th Floor
Toronto, Ontario M5H 4E3, Canada
www.Harlequin.com

Printed in U.S.A.

Despite a no-nonsense background as a West Point graduate, army officer and Fortune 100 sales executive, **Caro Carson** has always treasured the happily-ever-after of a good romance novel. As a RITA® Award–winning Harlequin author, Caro is delighted to be living her own happily-ever-after with her husband and two children in Florida, a location that has saved the coaster-loving theme-park fanatic a fortune on plane tickets.

Visit the Author Profile page
at Harlequin.com for more titles.

This book is dedicated to Gail Chasan, my editor,
with heartfelt thanks for loving my writing
and
with heartfelt apologies for driving her crazy.

Chapter One

"Which one of us is going to invite the hot fireman to join us at the pub?"

Tana McKenna heard the question, sort of, as she frantically scrolled through the calendar on her phone. Urgency made her all thumbs.

A too-long, too-silent pause made her look up from the screen. Her friends were all staring at her.

"What?" Tana grasped for the last thing she'd heard. "Something's hot?"

"Not something. Some*one*." Ruby, an executive assistant at Masterson University, lowered her voice and leaned a little closer. "Wait until you see who is teaching the CPR class tonight."

Next to Ruby, the university's diving coach giggled

like a Shirley Temple GIF. "Oh, my goodness. For once, I am so happy that we have to get certified every year."

A third member of the Masterson University faculty lowered her voice, too, leaning in as if they were conspiring together in the hallway of the academic building. "We should all flunk this evening. Get him to come back next Friday, too."

Tana kept what she hoped was a polite expression of interest on her face while trying to add nine months to today's date. Her brain wouldn't work. Her stomach was in knots.

The diving coach giggled again. "We can tell him we need extra tutoring during happy hour to prepare."

Everyone was smiling. These women, Tana's new friends at her new job at Masterson University, were making the effort to include her in their conversation. Tana didn't want to be rude, so she nodded along on autopilot as her brain raced.

It was September. Tana glanced at her phone's calendar. October, November, three, four, five… June. She would be nine months pregnant in the broiling heat of Central Texas in June. Just thinking about it made her mouth feel dry.

The conversation flowed around her, "What a sweetheart," followed by "I can't believe he's not wearing a wedding band." Then, in a tone of agreement, "Someone needs to put a ring on that, fast."

I'm pregnant. Not possible.

Well, it was possible, of course. She and Jerry, her boyfriend for the past year and a half, did have sex. But Tana had been an athlete all her life, always in tune with her body. Two weeks ago, when she'd noticed tiny changes, a little fatigue, a bit of bloating, she'd done a home pregnancy test. It had been negative. She'd been relieved. Jerry wasn't ready to settle down.

One week ago, because she was the Masterson University swim team's new coach, Tana had made her way through a doctor's office assembly line for the routine physical that cleared all the athletic staff and student-athletes for participation in this year's sports. A blood pressure check by a nurse, a quick once-over by the doctor with a stethoscope, a blood draw for some standard labs, no big deal. She'd waited in the lobby for two dozen freshmen swimmers to finish doing the same.

Five minutes ago, the doctor's office had called. *Coach McKenna? Your team's results are in. Everyone looks fine, but one person tested positive for pregnancy.* Tana's heart had sunk as she foresaw a difficult conversation with a student and her parents. That physical had been taken by the team's freshmen. Eighteen was such a young age for motherhood. Which girl?

Before she could ask, the doctor had chuckled over the phone. *Fortunately, that person is you, but you knew that, didn't you? Congratulations, Coach.*

"Such a babe, but he's funny, not just handsome," one of Tana's new friends said. "He'll be fun to drink a Guinness with."

"You have to invite him to come to the Tipsy Musketeer with us after class."

Nine months. Another expectant pause pulled Tana's attention from her phone's calendar and its blurring numbers.

"Me?" Tana looked from one woman's face to the next and the next. They grinned and nodded at her enthusiastically, as if she would start grinning and nodding, too, while her life imploded. This year was supposed to be the year of her redemption, finally, in the eyes of her sport as well as her family. For the team doctor to call her just now—just *no*.

"Yes, you." This was from the giggling Shirley. "I'm married. I can only be friends. I'll focus on his personality while you all focus on whichever other parts you like most."

"Be a sport and ask him," Ruby said. "Then we can eat some Irish stew and feast on the eye candy."

The thought of Irish stew made Tana feel slightly seasick. *Pregnant, pregnant—no wonder I haven't been able to eat all day. Or yesterday.*

"Poor Tana. We've all gotten to enjoy an hour with him already. He had us in stitches for the first-aid training. I actually feel sorry for you that you didn't have to take the first-aid class with us."

Pay attention. These nice women are speaking to you. You need to make friends.

"Um…first aid? I'm certified already. Just need to do the CPR class today…" Tana's appetite had been off for two weeks, so that meant she'd already been pregnant in August, even though the store-bought test she'd done at home had been negative.

Heart pounding, she recalculated. August, September, October… April. She'd be due in April. Which meant she'd have to coach the Masterson Musketeer swimmers through the NCAA finals in March while she was massively pregnant. A lifetime ago—one decade ago—one of the trainers for the Olympic team had missed the Games because the airlines wouldn't let her fly close to her due date.

Tana had to fly with her team to the NCAA finals this March. She simply had to, because she was the head coach. The *new* head coach. She couldn't lose this job. She had something to prove.

Now, she would have someone to provide for.

"You won't regret it, I promise you." Ruby bumped her with her shoulder and smiled. "Ask him after class."

"Who?"

Ruby frowned. "What the heck is so interesting on your phone?"

Tana focused on Ruby's friendly face. She'd liked Ruby since meeting her during her first day on campus. That meant she'd known Ruby for six weeks, which made Ruby her oldest and closest friend in the entire town of Masterson, Texas.

Tana needed a friend to confide in, but her assistant diving coach was standing right here—Shirley Tarkington, not Temple. The other woman Tana barely knew, but she was part of the evening's plan to go out to dinner together after the CPR class. There was a man in suit and tie by the vending machine, too, and he was probably close enough to hear them. Tana had to keep her shattering news to herself.

"Nothing," she said. "I'm fine."

"So, you'll invite him? To the pub?"

Tana didn't want to ask *who* again. "I'm already dating someone. You know that."

"Jerry." Ruby said the name with disapproval—disgust, even. "Jerry, who is leaving you for Peru. It's time for you to upgrade. I've got a hot fireman who is perfect for you."

Shirley squeezed Tana's arm. "Look. He's right over there."

Tana looked.

Okay…*wow.* By any objective measure, the man was indeed hot. Strong jaw, short hair, walkie-talkie on the belt of his firefighter uniform. He looked tall, even while leaning back against the wall. He had his arms crossed over his chest, and the bulk of his shoulders and the bulge of his biceps weren't really beefy, just simply…strong. Eye candy, for certain.

Who needed eye candy when the entire world had been flipped over like a flimsy card table? Not Tana.

But just as she was going to shrug and turn her back on him, the firefighter bent forward, practically doubling himself over, because the tiniest grandmother in the world had started speaking to him. She was known as Granny Dee around campus. Her job was to check student IDs at the entrance to the campus dining hall, but she was legendary at Masterson University for hugging every student who needed a hug at breakfast and lunch, before a test or after a heartbreak. She'd been doing so for two generations. Ten years ago, she'd given Tana hugs to congratulate her, when Tana had been the star of the Masterson swimming program. Granny Dee was an institution in herself.

She was very concerned, very animated about something. The firefighter listened until Granny Dee fell silent, then he answered her seriously. Granny Dee beamed at him as she held out her arms, and that hunk of a man pushed himself off the wall, still bent in half, so that Granny Dee could throw her arms around his neck. A chuckle, a pat on her back—he turned his head toward Tana—their eyes met.

Her stomach flipped.

Just eye candy. Tana couldn't quite pull off an uncaring shrug, but she turned back to her friends. Ruby gave her an arch look.

"What?" Tana asked, feeling thirstier than ever. She hadn't eaten much in two days, but she could buy herself a bottle of water out of the vending machine. She patted the pockets of her khaki shorts. No cash or cards. Only her van's keys.

From behind her, the firefighter made a general announcement. "All right, CPR time. Let's get started."

Tana knew it was him, because it was exactly the kind of masculine voice that one would expect a man who was that masculine to have. The dozen or so people in the hall obediently headed toward the classroom.

Ruby held Tana back. "Ask him to come to the pub, okay?"

"I can't ask him out."

"Sorry, but we elected you to do it."

"I'm dating someone. So are you."

She and Ruby and their guys had double-dated last weekend, when Jerry had driven up from Houston to see her. Jerry was still on the faculty at the much smaller Houston City College, where they'd both been working for the past two years. Tana had resigned her coaching position there for this more prestigious position, director of the aquatic program at Masterson University.

Redemption.

She'd wondered if Jerry would leave Houston and relocate to Masterson for her. If not, would absence make the heart grow fonder? Maybe he'd pop the question at the end of the semester.

She'd gotten her answer. He'd been planning to leave Houston and her, both, on a research trip he'd gotten funded an entire month before Masterson had started interviewing Tana. *Only for a year*, he'd said. Jerry, whom she'd been dating for eighteen months, hadn't realized she was hurt.

Ruby, her friend of six weeks, had. "I don't see a ring on your finger. Are you two supposed to stay exclusive while he's off to do whatever it is he's leaving you to do?"

I don't know.

Tana had been too chicken to ask. Jerry was going to communicate through letters while he was on his remote field study. She'd thought maybe they'd both find it easier to write about their feelings, since talking usually led to uncomfortable silences, but she was going to have to ask now. She was going to have to ask him not to go to Peru at all, in fact. A year from now, they'd have a four-month-old baby. Five months old?

She and Jerry had said their goodbyes over the phone last night, but his flight to South America wouldn't depart until midnight. She had time to reach him. She closed the calendar screen and opened her text messages. Jerry hadn't sent her one message.

That was fine; he'd told her he wouldn't. Jerry hadn't wanted to deal with any strong emotions today while he was tying up all his loose ends and heading for the airport.

Yesterday, Tana had been flattered by that. It meant she wasn't a loose end to be tied up. It meant she was a person toward whom he had strong emotions.

Ready or not, she was about to give him a reason to feel even more strongly about her. The phone trembled in her hand as she typed. Please call me ASAP.

She waited a moment. He'd reply, because she was important to him. *Even though he is willing to leave me to spend a year in Peru. Even though he never asked me to wait for him or to be faithful to him...or to marry him...*

It wasn't necessary, it really wasn't, but as she drifted toward the classroom, she added another text: This is important.

She sensed a warm presence at her shoulder a moment before an equally warm voice spoke by her ear. "You must be Montana McKenna."

The fireman was holding the door for her. He was quite...something...close up. He had a Texas-summer tan, like an outdoorsman, so the blue of his eyes was almost startling in contrast.

"I go by Tana. Coach Tana McKenna." Her response was automatic. So was the way she held out her hand to shake his, as though he were the father of a swimmer she wanted to recruit. It was awkwardly formal for this situation. She was merely the last straggler in the hallway, and he already had one hand on the door.

He looked a little amused, but he let go of the door to shake her hand. "Lieutenant Caden Sterling. I go by Lieutenant, Caden or Sterling. Take your pick. I saw your name on the roster. No first-aid training. Just the CPR?"

"I renewed my first-aid cert in June at—at my old job. In Houston. I'm here now." *Text me back, Jerry.* "I mean, I'm here at Masterson now as a coach, not that I'm here at your class now, although I guess I'm that, too."

Stop for a breath, already. She was still holding the fireman's hand. Her cheeks were warm, as if the heat from his palm had transferred to hers and rushed upward to make her blush.

She let go. "Sorry. I'm distracted. I'm waiting on an important call. I hate to disrupt your class, but it's critical that I take it. I'll slip out quietly. I promise you, I've been certified in CPR so many times, I'll be able to pass the test, even if I miss your instructions."

He was listening to her as attentively as he'd been listening to Granny Dee, looking directly at her, as if she were saying something that mattered.

She tried to return that respect. "If you'll let me take the test, that is. I understand if you don't want to pass someone who didn't participate in the entire class. I don't really have a choice about the phone call, but if you'd rather me not take the class tonight, that's your right."

"You have to do what you have to do, Coach. Take the call. We'll work it out."

"Thank you. Really." She dropped her gaze from his

ocean-blue eyes as another wave of dizziness threatened to pull her under. She brushed past him to find the nearest chair in the classroom and dropped onto the hard plastic seat. At the next break, she was going to get some money out of her van and get something to eat out of the vending machine and choke it down, nausea be damned. She looked at her shaky phone screen. Nothing.

She managed to pay attention to the fireman's CPR introduction for an entire minute before she peeked at her phone screen again. This time, Jerry had answered.

I'll send you an address once I'm settled. Write me about your important thing. It will be the best way for me to focus on your problem. Today is my day to focus on the logistics of my journey.

Tana's head swam.

Another text came in: As you already knew.

"Are you okay? Can you hear me?" The fireman asked the questions loudly, urgently.

Tana looked up, but he was speaking to the CPR dummy, the mannequin upon which they would all practice and then be tested. Students would have to try to rouse the dummy as if it were a person they'd found unconscious. The fireman was demonstrating the proper steps by shaking the mannequin's shoulder.

"Are you okay?" he repeated.

No, I'm not.

But she was no mute mannequin, and she didn't have time to play along with Jerry's elaborate designs for how and when he could best focus on her problem. He'd best communicate with her *now*.

"When there's no answer," the fireman said, "call for help."

Tana hit the call button next to Jerry's name as she slipped out the door.

Chapter Two

There went Montana McKenna.

True to her word, she left silently, managing to close the door behind herself without so much as a snick.

With a name like Montana, Caden had been expecting not only a man, but one of the ubiquitous cowboys who lived and worked here in Central Texas. A man like himself, a man who felt most comfortable in jeans and cowboy boots when he wasn't on the job.

Montana McKenna was not a man.

Caden Sterling could not be happier about that.

He'd heard people talking about hitting the Tipsy Musketeer after this class was over. He'd glanced over to see three of the women from the first-aid class, plus someone new, standing with her back to Caden. She was fairly tall and wore modest khaki shorts that revealed her legs—long legs, toned legs, legs for days. Just about the finest pair of legs he'd ever seen on a woman. Then she'd turned around.

One look at her face—brown-eyed, beautiful, serious—and he'd known he needed to get her name.

When she'd headed toward his classroom, he'd realized he already knew her name. She was the extra person on his CPR roster, the unknown Montana. He'd learned more interesting things, too, as she'd shaken his hand. A coach, she'd said. But which sport? She was tall, but not basketball tall. Maybe volleyball. Golf. Soccer, with those legs? He looked forward to finding out over a Guinness after class.

"What's next?" Caden asked the class. "This is a total stranger lying in front of you, not responding. They can't tell you what happened."

The suggestions came quickly. "Should you look for a medic alert bracelet?"

"Check their wallet for their ID?"

"Check their phone and see if they put their own contact info in it?"

Caden was glad they were so actively participating, but it was his job to teach them the right priorities. "Does it matter what their name is?"

The beat of silence was broken by the only man wearing a suit and tie. He'd informed the class that he was a law professor, and so far, he'd been a know-it-all, lecturing the class whenever he could. "Proceeding without knowing their wishes could result in punitive legal action."

Like now.

Caden corrected him. "This isn't a patient in a nursing home or hospital bed where you'd expect his resuscitation wishes to be known. This is a stranger you found unconscious, here on campus. You are a bystander doing your best to help. Good Samaritan laws protect you from being sued."

Those laws didn't protect Caden. He was both a paramedic and firefighter. Legally, he had a duty to act—as if he'd ever need a legal reason to help somebody who was helpless—and to act with the skill expected of someone with his experience and credentials.

He turned back to the room at large. "You've tried to get a response from him, but you got nothing. You don't know what happened. You don't know who he is. But the most important thing that matters is whether or not he's breathing. It's the only thing that matters."

"But what if they have diabetes or something?" Ruby asked. "Or they overdosed on a drug?"

"They need oxygen no matter what their blood sugar is. They need oxygen no matter what drugs are in their system. If they don't have oxygen, they die, and it won't matter what their medical history is."

The class was silent. Somber. This was good. It meant they were listening to him, really listening, so if they were ever under the intense pressure of being faced with an unresponsive human being, they'd remember that oxygen was their primary goal.

Caden had his own personal goal, which was to motivate people to jump in and help, not to scare them, so he smiled. "Fortunately, as you look at this person, you are breathing. You're going to be able to get this person the oxygen they need, because you are going to be an expert by the time you leave my class. So, step one, try to rouse the person. Step two, check to see if they're breathing."

Caden demonstrated how to do so, then how to give the first two lifesaving breaths. Then he stood back as each person practiced. The smell of alcohol wipes was strong in the air as the dummy's mouth was wiped clean between students.

The classroom door remained closed as they moved on to chest compressions. Coach McKenna was missing this chance to practice, but she'd been so confident in her ability to pass the test that Caden doubted she needed it. Ruby, the friend who'd told her to invite him to the pub, stepped up to the dummy.

"Are you okay?" Ruby enjoyed her role, shaking the dummy. "Yo! Buddy! Are you okay?"

It hardly mattered whether or not her friends convinced Montana to ask Caden to go to the pub. The Tipsy Musketeer was a good hangout for the adults of Masterson. It never sold cheap beer by the bucket, and it was known for checking IDs, which meant it was one of the few places in this college town that was not overrun with students. Caden and his crew often met there for a little R & R when they were off the clock. He'd show up there tonight and strike up a conversation with her naturally enough. Better yet...

He leafed through the certificates, found Montana's and slipped it to the bottom of the stack. She'd be the last to leave that way, and with his last professional obligation fulfilled, he'd beat her to it and ask *her* if she'd like to grab a bite at the Tipsy Musketeer.

She was distracted by a business call at the moment, but he had no doubt she'd be worth getting to know. She was well liked by a group of likable women. She had confidence—*I'll be able to pass the CPR test*—an interesting career, a warm handshake—

And legs that went on for days.

Yeah, if things went the way Caden hoped they would, tonight would only be the first of many evenings spent with a woman named Montana.

Jerry wasn't answering.

Tana refused to try him a third time. She resorted to texting once more. If I say it's urgent, it's urgent. Answer the phone.

She counted to ten, took a deep breath—and took a seat on the concrete bench near the door, because her legs felt like jelly. She dialed Jerry again.

He answered. "Tana, enough. This is getting to the point of being harassing. I can call you in a couple of hours, when I'm in the taxi on the way to the airport. I'll have twenty minutes then."

"This is important. I got a call from a doctor's office just, I don't know, just fifteen minutes ago." But any further words stuck in her throat. She couldn't swallow, couldn't breathe. This was it, ready or not—and she was not.

"You know I've set a strict schedule for myself. Wait a couple of hours. Precisely two. I'll give you what advice I can on the way to the airport."

"No." The word exploded past the constriction in her throat, and with it, a certain fury came pouring out, as well. "You do not get to live your life all calm and oblivious for the next two hours while I'm freaking out."

There was a moment of silence. Then, Jerry spoke again, and annoyance had turned to a sneer. "How much more dramatic is this going to get?"

Tana knew the exact facial expression that went with that tone, the way he rolled his eyes in impatience when he believed he was going to be imposed upon by somebody.

Ready or not...

"Jerry, I'm pregnant."

At his silence, she closed her eyes and leaned her head back against the brick building.

"You're certain?" Jerry finally asked. "Those grocery store tests can't be infallible. People misread the results, or they do them wrong."

"This was a blood test, done by a laboratory. I didn't pee on a stick incorrectly." Her words lacked any bite. She was slumping against an unfamiliar building in an unfamiliar town. She didn't feel angry. She felt lonely.

She shouldn't feel lonely. There were two of them involved in this, two reasonably intelligent adults who would work things out together. "I'm sure you're overwhelmed at the moment. I've known for fifteen minutes longer than you have, and I still can't wrap my head around it. What are we going to do?"

He hesitated briefly. "There's nothing for me to do. This pregnancy will proceed with or without me."

"But—but this is your child. The father cuts the

umbilical cord in the delivery room and—and other things." She thought of other people's pregnancies, the things that coworkers, male and female, were usually excited about. "Things like hearing the heartbeat, right? You'll be there for the sonogram. I guess we'll need to decide if we want to learn the gender early or not. We'll need to decide—"

"You'll decide. You're the one who is pregnant, not me. If you are pregnant."

"If?" She was truly baffled, as if Jerry had turned into some kind of alien species who didn't understand the way the world worked. "Do you think I would make up something like this?"

He sighed the sigh of a man who believed he shouldn't have to explain himself. "You might, if you thought it would prevent me from going to Peru. It won't work. I need this year to myself. It's important."

"You know what else is important? The woman who is pregnant with your baby. She's important." Tana supposed she sounded brave, but she was sitting on a concrete bench with her eyes closed.

"She's also very self-sufficient." Had Jerry always had this mocking undertone in his voice? "She's healthy. She has a good job."

"For this season only. What if I lose that job?"

What if I let down the forty-two kids I'm supposed to coach? Her team included two swimmers who were Olympic hopefuls. Her former Team USA coach had recommended her for this position because he thought she'd be able to mentor them through the pressure. Why he thought she could advise them, she didn't know, given the way she'd caved under pressure ten years ago, but she wanted to prove his faith in her wasn't misplaced.

"They can't fire you for being pregnant."

"They also don't have to renew my contract at the end of the season if I don't perform well as a coach. I can't remember seeing a pregnant female coach at the NCAA finals. I don't know if it's doable or not."

"You're hardly a helpless damsel in distress, Tana. This is beneath you, to beg for reassurance about your abilities."

"I don't need reassurance." But as soon as she said it, she knew that was exactly what she needed, yet Jerry sounded so remote. "We really should be talking in person. I could head your way now. I'll be there in three hours—"

"I'll already be through airport security. My flight leaves in four hours. I'll be on it."

"But—"

"Think, Tana. I can't *not* go at this point. The research center is expecting me. The plane ticket is nonrefundable. It would be a waste of the research grant."

Was he an alien or was he speaking logically? To be fair, he was being logical. She could be, too.

"All right, go. But that research assignment is for three months. You were going to freestyle your way around South America after that. You could come home instead. I'll be four or five months along. We'll have time to…time to… I don't even know what. So much is going to change. So much has to be decided."

"Look, Tana, assuming the paternity test works out

the way you want it to, I won't fight you if you take me to court for child support. It's only money. If you want to take it from me, then go for it. But this is my time. My year. It's priceless. It's what I *need*. You can't take this away from me. I won't allow it."

"Paternity test? You can't think there's a chance this baby isn't yours." The world swam behind her closed eyelids. She was going to throw up. "How could you say that to me?"

"Stop with the drama. You win. I'll assume the baby is mine, although we've lived apart for six weeks, haven't we?"

"But—I assumed we— Have you been sleeping with other people?"

"I'm willing to assume this was an accidental pregnancy, and this phone call was not intentionally timed so that you'd think I'd be required to make some dramatic gesture like rushing from the airport to your side."

"I didn't expect that." She could hardly follow his logic. He really was an alien.

He laughed. He *laughed* at her. "You forced me to watch enough chick flicks this past year. I know what you expect."

I expect to fail.

So far in her life, she'd failed her parents, failed the Olympic team, failed the whole damned USA. This was no different. Failing was what she did.

She thunked the back of her head against the building. With her eyes closed, her entire future came into focus.

The NCAA finals were in March. She'd be unable

to coach her team through them. Unable to prove her talent hadn't been wasted. Unable to justify her coach's faith in her. He'd taken a second chance on her by recommending her for this position, and she was destined to let him down again.

I'm sorry, Mom. Dad. I tried. I almost got it right this time. Almost.

She opened her eyes and was blinded by the setting sun. She blinked and lowered her gaze to the cars in the parking lot. Sunspots blotted her vision, but she could see everything now, all the things about Jerry that every person in her life, from her parents to her old coworkers to her new friend Ruby, had seen. Jerry would never alter his life for her in any way, for any reason. He'd never alter his life for anyone, not even his own child.

She was shocked. She was the only person in the world who was shocked.

Jerry continued outlining all the assumptions he was willing to make about her, but his voice was just a dull pounding in Tana's ear. She stared at her well-used van. It wasn't sexy or sporty, but its rows of extra seats held swimmers who needed rides to practices and meets, year after year, from city to city. There was a bucket in the back, full of the goggles and flip-flops that got left behind by some swimmers and used by others. So much history. There it was, parked neatly in the row with the other cars that also had faculty parking stickers on their windshields.

And here she was, part of the Masterson University faculty. For now, this was her life, and while the facade she'd built around Jerry had just collapsed, her life hadn't. Not yet. But in nine months' time…

She couldn't think nine months into the future. She had a job to do, a job she wanted to do. That job required her to renew her CPR certification. Right now.

She stood. As Jerry continued his monologue about everything that mattered to him, she went inside and walked past the vending machines. She had her hand on the doorknob as Jerry hung up on her. She walked into the classroom and returned a handsome fireman's smile.

"Your timing is perfect," the fireman said. "The last person just finished practicing chest compressions. Do you want to practice before the testing starts?"

"No, I'll take the test." She walked up to his side, turned to face the dummy, then smacked it on the shoulder once, twice, three times. Hard. "Are you okay? Are you okay?"

The fireman raised an eyebrow at the way she dove in, but he didn't interrupt her.

She shook the dummy, shouted louder. "Can you hear me?"

"No response," the fireman said.

She looked him in the eye and pointed at his strong chest. "I want you to call 911. Stay on the phone, stay beside me and help me."

Then she got to work and tried to salvage a stupid dummy's life.

Chapter Three

"Pass."

As Tana nodded at the fireman and headed for the nearest chair, he added, "Good job."

Yes, she had a good job at this university. She was going to keep it. Somehow.

But how? In the past hour, just taking a deep breath had become impossible.

The professor in the suit and tie wasn't pushing hard enough on the mannequin's chest. He argued with the fireman. "If I pushed harder in real life, I could break a rib."

"Look at it this way," the fireman said, all calm authority. "The worst has already happened. They aren't breathing. Their heart isn't beating. The patient is dead." He turned to the rest of the class. "Let that make you fearless. I want all of you to jump in and try, if you find yourself in this situation. It's impossible for you to make the situation worse. Anything you do can only make it better."

The worst has already happened. The words swam around Tana's foggy brain. She was dimly aware of the professor pushing hard enough to grunt with each compression, making the green indicator on the dummy's chest light up.

"Pass."

The worst had happened. She was mere months away from letting down a team of hopeful swimmers who were looking up to her. Mere months from destroying her reputation in the swimming world for once and for all. Months from her parents' crushing disappointment. Their scorn. The situation couldn't get worse, but she was far from fearless.

"Oh, I don't think I can do this." The famous Granny Dee sounded distressed as she looked up at the fireman.

Me, neither. I can't, I can't, I can't...

"I'm in my eighties. I'm five feet tall. Do you really think I'm going to be able to inflate that mannequin's chest?" She fluttered one hand toward the three lights that were implanted on the dummy's torso. "I couldn't make that little yellow dot light up, let alone the green one during practice. It's frustrating to be old and frail and—" her hand fluttered between the fireman and herself "—and small."

The size difference between them was laughable, but the fireman didn't laugh. "You're not helpless, even if the person is twice your size. Suppose you find me unresponsive. What's the most important thing you can do to help me?"

"You said to call 911."

"Exactly."

As Tana listened, she breathed in deliberately. She needed oxygen, just as the fireman had said. There was something so positive about him. Lieutenant Something.

"Could you tip my head back to open my airway? Could you sweep your fingers in my mouth to clear out anything that might be blocking my airway?"

Granny Dee started nodding along with his questions.

Lieutenant Sterling, that was it.

"I'd like to say you'd find that I'd collapsed in the middle of eating a healthy apple, but it's just as likely I was chowing down on a chocolate-chip cookie." Lieutenant Sterling flashed a charming smile.

Granny Dee smiled, too. Tana almost smiled herself at the little scene. It was clear the fireman had a soft spot for the elderly. Tana breathed in one more time.

"You could start looking for the nearest AED box," he added, referring to the automatic defibrillators located throughout the campus.

Granny Dee patted his arm, as if she were consoling him. "I could and would do all that, but I know I wouldn't be able to breathe hard enough or push on your chest hard enough to have any effect."

"Maybe not, but let me tell you now, while I'm healthy and conscious, that I'd sure appreciate it if you'd try. You have nothing to lose, and my life to gain."

Granny Dee looked down at the mannequin and

sighed. "I feel silly, but I'll try." She pinched the dummy's nose shut and gave it the ol' college try.

The green dot did not light up.

"Fail." The lieutenant pronounced the grade gravely. Maybe that soft spot wasn't so soft.

"I knew I'd fail," Granny Dee said, a little reproachfully, before she started to head back to her seat.

Lieutenant Sterling stopped her. "You failed because you didn't do all the steps."

"Watching me attempt this is a joke. You know I can't do it."

"Trying to save a life is never a joke. I think you can do this." He stepped back and put his hands behind his back. "Begin at the beginning."

She sighed, but then she smacked the dummy on the shoulder. "Are you okay? Are you okay?"

"No response," Sterling said.

"Who can call 911?" Granny Dee asked, turning toward the class.

Tana raised her hand without thinking. "I'm calling 911."

"Is there an AED?" Granny Dee called to the classroom in general. "Somebody look for a box on the wall that says AED."

Ruby raised her hand. "I'll start looking."

Granny Dee put one hand on the dummy's forehead and pulled out the chin to open the airway. She put her ear toward the dummy's mouth and pretended to listen for breathing. Then she took a deep breath, pinched the nose shut and blew with all her might.

The green dot did not light up.

Granny Dee looked at the lieutenant, who remained as he was, standing with his hands behind his back, expressionless. She turned away, irritated, frustrated—flat-out angry—and she jabbed her finger at the man in the suit and tie. "You. Come here. I want you to blow two hard breaths into this person's mouth. Then I'll show you where to place your hands so you can do chest compressions."

"Pass." Lieutenant Sterling clapped his hands together in a single, loud clap of satisfaction. The room erupted in applause and laughter. "That is the kind of fierce determination that can save a life. Pass. Absolute pass."

Fierce determination.

That was what Tana was going to need. She'd had that, once upon a time. She'd made an Olympic team on fierce determination. She knew what it took.

Person after person shouted at the dummy. The little green dot lit up over and over.

Tana could handle this pregnancy, Jerry or no Jerry. She could coach her team while she was nine months pregnant in the middle of the NCAA finals. She would.

She had no choice.

Her vision swam. Dimly, she realized she was no longer hungry, no longer thirsty. That was good, wasn't it?

The fireman's calm voice was addressing the group. *The worst has happened*, he'd said earlier. *Fierce determination*, he'd said. She wanted to know what he was saying now, but as he placed a new mannequin on the table, the world suddenly began whooshing past her.

She held on to her desk, disoriented, and stared at the new mannequin.

It was a baby, a baby-sized mannequin, which they were all going to pretend was dead. It was the baby's fault she felt so dizzy...

It really was an actual baby's fault she felt so dizzy...

The sunspots came back. Tana blinked, and then the world went black.

Class was nearly over.

Every one of Caden's students had passed. Montana had, true to her word, been the ace student, passing with flying colors. She'd given those chest compressions sharply, forcefully—entirely appropriately—yet he couldn't help but feel she'd been using the CPR as a little stress relief. He'd bet her urgent call hadn't gone well. They could talk it out over a beer later.

Or sooner. All that he needed to do now was explain the difference between adult and infant CPR, pass out some diplomas, then head for the Tipsy Musketeer. He didn't think he'd ever looked forward to a beer more.

Caden put the adult mannequin away and unzipped the bag that held the next mannequin. "You can stay in your seats. This part is not tested. I just need one person for this demonstration. Granny Dee, are you willing to be the guinea pig?"

She joined him at the front of the room. He laid the pediatric mannequin on the table.

Granny Dee recoiled from the infant-sized dummy. "Oh. Oh, that would be horrible."

It's a nightmare, and it will reappear in your night-

mares every once in a while for the rest of your life, even when your CPR was successful.

Caden glanced around the circle of students. Everyone's expressions were suddenly serious. The law professor looked repulsed. Montana looked ashen. Surely, she wasn't going into shock at the obviously fake mannequin, but he kept an eye on her as he turned his attention back to Granny Dee and the rest of the class. "You're right. It would be horrible, but it would be even more horrible to stand there and have no idea what to do. An infant doesn't require nearly as much force as an adult. Ready to save a life, Granny Dee?"

They went through the steps. He turned to the class and asked if there were any questions. Montana was looking at him, staring right at him, brown eyes big in a too-white face. Her color was off, really off. He took a step toward her. "Are you okay?"

Her eyes rolled up into her head.

Damn it.

He was fast, but not that fast. She crashed into the desk next to her on her way down, sliding from her chair into a crumpled heap on the floor as metal desk legs clattered against linoleum.

Everyone made an exclamation of some kind. Somebody screamed for a mercifully brief second. But nobody, not one of the students to whom he'd just taught first aid, moved to help.

Or maybe they did, but Caden was there first, kneeling over her. "Montana. Can you hear me?"

Ruby landed on her knee on the other side. "Tana!"

"She didn't fall far. Nothing's broken, she's not

bleeding, she's not having a seizure, and she is breathing on her own, so what do we do?" Speaking out loud as he assessed the patient was automatic, a given in the medical world, particularly when there were rookies around, but Caden didn't wait for them to answer with the right steps. "We make her comfortable."

He shoved a chair out of the way, and Ruby helped him straighten out her legs. "We elevate her feet."

Another woman jumped in to help, taking off her light sweater and rolling it up to put under Montana's head. A nice gesture, but—

"Feet," Caden repeated mildly. He pressed on the artery on the inside of her wrist. Her pulse was rapid, somewhat faint, but it was regular. This was a simple faint.

"Oh, Tana," Ruby whispered as she smoothed her friend's hair back. Again, nice gesture, but—

"Open your eyes." Caden wasn't going to slap Montana awake, but he tapped her cheek with the back of his hand. Ruby had called her Tana. Tana had told him herself she went by that. "Open your eyes, Tana."

The woman who had made a pillow of her sweater was from the pub group—Shirley. She moved to Tana's feet, sat on the floor, then picked up Tana's feet and put them in her lap. Caden nodded at her. *Right thing to do.*

"Open your eyes, Tana." He tapped her cheek again. "Somebody bring my medical bag here. The black-and-red bag."

It was second nature for him to put the stethoscope in his ears, a practiced move to slip his thumb under the tubing to keep it from rubbing against her skin and making noise. He tucked the chest piece an inch under her shirt collar. He listened to her heart from first the left side, then the right. He listened for long seconds: no obvious arrhythmia. Again, a simple faint.

"Should we call 911?" Ruby asked, sounding breathless herself.

Caden slid her a look.

"Oh. I guess 911 is already here."

Caden winked at her, so she'd relax. This was no emergency to panic over, but it wasn't good for anyone to lose consciousness, either. He moved the stethoscope to Tana's lower lungs, although he knew he'd hear no sounds of pneumonia. It was the proper order of things. The practice of medicine was one giant set of methodical procedures, so that nothing would be missed, even if the provider's feelings were involved.

I should have known she was too pale. I should have caught her before she hit the floor.

Ruby watched him. "Doesn't she need an ambulance?"

"We'll see. She's coming to." There was no traumatic injury that required the advanced equipment offered by an ambulance. He'd take her in his truck if she wanted to go to the ER. He knew everyone there, so he'd walk in with her. They'd take special care of her for him. *Like what? Like she's your girlfriend?*

Her eyes fluttered open.

He smiled at her, maybe more than his usual professional smile. "There you are."

She scrunched her face into a frown as he slid his hand and the stethoscope around her side to listen to her lungs from her back. He heard her breath in his ears, felt her ribs expand under his palm.

Ruby smoothed her hair some more. "You fell out of your chair. You must have hit your head on the way down, because you were out like a light."

Tana frowned. "My head?"

Caden slung his stethoscope across the back of his neck and moved to cradle the back of her head in his palm. He didn't feel any swelling, and she didn't respond as if he were touching any tender spots. "I don't think you hit your head. I saw you go down. Does your head hurt?"

"No, my stomach."

With his other hand, he immediately pressed her abdomen, feeling for an enlarged spleen or liver, for the telltale signs of appendicitis, for anything unusual.

She wrapped her hand around his wrist, so he paused, but her abdomen felt perfectly normal. Better than normal. Her flat stomach didn't come from starving herself; she was all sleek muscle. Whatever her sport was, she must still play it. Often.

"I'm hungry," she mumbled to him. "Let's go to the pub. You said you wanted dessert. Didn't you say that?" She looked a little confused at her own question.

"Oh, honey," Ruby said, "I think we need to go to the emergency room."

Tana frowned at Ruby. "No hospital. I'm just hungry. I haven't eaten all day, because—because I wasn't hungry, but now I'm starving."

Caden pulled his wrist out of her grip to tap his stethoscope. "I thought I heard your stomach growling."

"Ha ha ha." Her retort was said in a voice that was still weak, but she was definitely regaining her sense of orientation. She looked around at the people clustered over them, then back at him with a grimace, a little wrinkle to her nose that he shouldn't have noticed was so cute on a patient. "I'm sorry."

"For providing everyone with a real-world case? It was a good test." *Which most of them failed.*

"Sorry for disrupting your class. I promised you I wouldn't."

"You kept your word. Class was over." He was smiling at her, because she was smiling at him. With his hand cupping her head, this felt almost…personal. Intimate.

Unprofessional.

He let her head rest on the sweater once more so he could get his glucometer out of his bag.

Tana moved to sit up. He stopped her with a hand on her shoulder. "Not yet. Let's check your blood sugar. Only takes a second."

"I can tell you it's low. I meant to get myself something from the vending machine earlier. Should have done that, huh? This is so embarrassing."

Granny Dee was hovering with the rest, so he asked her to distribute the CPR certificates for him, so the class could leave, and Tana wouldn't feel so self-conscious.

He held up an alcohol wipe and a lancet. "You gonna let me prick your finger or not?"

"I have a choice?"

"Always." He pulled on disposable gloves. "But the right answer is yes."

"Fine." She held her hand up. He had the crazy impulse to be a gentleman, to bow his head and kiss her fingers.

He pricked one with a needle instead. While he squeezed a drop of blood onto the test strip, the class took their diplomas and left one by one, except for Ruby and Shirley.

He whistled at the low number on the glucometer. "I think we know why you fainted. You don't have hypoglycemia or diabetes, do you?"

"No. I swear, I just didn't eat today."

"Let's have you chew up a couple of glucose tablets, and we'll test it again. I bet you'll feel good as new." He dug in his medical bag for them.

Shirley still had Tana's feet in her lap. "She didn't know if she'd invited you to the pub or not. Isn't that a sign of a concussion?"

"Confusion can be a sign of low blood sugar, too. Or dehydration." He found the tablets and looked down at Tana. "I don't suppose you remembered to drink today, even if you weren't hungry?"

"Um… I had a cup of coffee this morning."

"Not good."

"I know."

"But you're in good shape. If you start drinking right now, you'll hydrate yourself pretty quickly." He turned to Ruby. "Can you get her a drink out of the vending machine? Not a soda. Water or a sports drink would be good."

Ruby took off.

"Let's sit you up so you can enjoy these glucose tablets. They're delicious."

"Sure, they are."

Shirley let go of her feet, and Caden moved to put an arm around her shoulders to give her a boost, but she threw both of her arms around his neck. It was unnecessary, but he wasn't going to complain. They were practically cheek to cheek as he lifted her to a sitting position. Her hair had a little bit of a flowery scent.

She whispered in his ear, her words rapid and urgent. "Nobody knows, but I'm pregnant."

He froze.

"That's why I couldn't eat. In case that matters."

Pregnant?

No. She wasn't wearing a wedding ring—he'd looked. Damn it, he'd gotten his heart set on getting to know her, starting tonight. Starting now.

Pregnant.

She already belonged to another man. *In case that matters.* It was the only thing that mattered, the only thing that could stop him from asking her out himself.

Tana dropped her arms and shifted herself to sit up with those gorgeous legs crisscrossed. The glucose tablets were still in his hand.

"Should I eat those now?" She cleared her throat. "They're safe?"

Caden knew she was asking if the tablets were safe during pregnancy, the secret he was now bound by confidentiality laws to keep. He would've kept it, anyway, because she'd asked him to.

"They're safe. You shouldn't cross your legs, yet.

It's harder on your circulation. Have you been vomiting today?" He meant morning sickness, of course. If so, she might be more severely dehydrated than she appeared to be.

"No, I just didn't want to eat. But I'm starving now." She crunched down the tablets.

Disappointment weighed him down. Pregnant? Her abdomen had been flat, as toned as her legs. She couldn't be far along.

As if that mattered. His dashed hopes were the second secret he had to keep. There was no reason he wouldn't still be the friendly paramedic, as far as she knew. He forced himself to smile at her again.

Ruby came back in with a bottled drink. Tana chugged it like an athlete on the sidelines, then got off the floor to sit in a chair with no clumsiness, another sign of recovery. When he checked her blood sugar again, it had risen significantly. She spoke to her friends without any confusion.

Shirley retrieved the rolled-up sweater from the floor and shook it out. "I'm so glad you're feeling better. You'll get way better food at the Tipsy Musketeer instead of the hospital."

"Is that okay?" Tana asked him, looking at him with those beautiful brown eyes. He would've liked to have her looking at him for something besides medical advice. *Not going to happen. She's taken.*

"It's okay," he answered, "but you should stay away from alcohol."

She bristled at his advice. "I wasn't planning to drink."

He hadn't meant it as pregnancy advice.

"Because I'm driving myself," Tana added belatedly, with a glance at her friends.

"Because alcohol will keep you dehydrated." Caden gave her another excuse besides pregnancy. "Water and juice for the rest of the night." *For the next nine months.*

"I don't need to go to the ER?"

"You could go, if you wanted to. They'd be able to give you fluids through an IV. It might hydrate you more quickly."

"But...do I need that?" She sounded skeptical. He was certain that she wouldn't have asked at all if she weren't pregnant.

He held out his hand for hers again. Her palm was warm against his, but he slipped his away until he was holding only her fingertips. With his thumb, he pressed the nailbed of her index finger until it turned white, then he let go. It turned pink again quickly. "I don't think you do. You're rehydrating quickly."

She shook her hand out. "Between the pricking and the poking, I don't think I want to give you my hand again."

"Understandable." *And I probably shouldn't take it again.* She had feminine hands, soft hands, short nails, no polish. He wanted to know what she liked to do with her hands when she wasn't coaching or executing perfect CPR moves. Did she ride horses or play the piano? Did she race motorcycles or do embroidery? All of the above?

It didn't matter. She was taken.

Caden hoped his smile didn't look as forced as it was. He stood and picked up his bag.

"You're coming with us, right?" Ruby asked him. "Apparently, Tana had a vision of you saying yes while she was knocked out."

I would have asked her first. I couldn't wait to ask her.

Tana stood, too, steady on her feet. "I would love it if you could come, Lieutenant Sterling. I definitely owe you a drink. I could buy you a beer, and you could watch me drink cranberry juice. Sounds like a thrilling Thursday night, right?"

It had sounded thrilling, actually. It still did, because the heart was a senseless organ.

Shirley joined in. "My husband will be meeting us there after a while, so you won't be stuck with three women all night."

"I've got no problem with joining three women for a drink. I'm sure your husband would agree. He might not be all that excited that I've joined you."

Shirley's giggle was as infectious as a baby's. "Goodness, no. He'll be thrilled to have another guy to talk football with. I try to pretend I care who will be this season's quarterback, but we've been married seven years. I can't fool him. You follow Musketeer football, don't you?"

"Sure."

They were a nice group. He'd be a jerk to turn down such a genuine invite for a beer and the chance to make a few new friends. He let himself look at Tana for a second.

Just friends.

Her boyfriend or fiancé or husband would probably join them, too. Seeing her happy with the father of her coming baby would kill any lingering regrets, and Caden would be able to move her into the friend zone in his mind. Easily.

"Thanks for the invite," he said. "I'll meet you at the pub."

Chapter Four

Alone in the classroom, Caden started loading himself up to leave. He threw the strap of his medical bag over his left shoulder, the bag that held the adult dummy over his right shoulder, then he picked up his clipboard full of the inevitable paperwork in his left hand, the bag for the infant dummy in his—

"I'll get that."

The woman he didn't want to keep thinking about beat him to it, startling him in the bargain.

"Sorry," she said. "I wasn't trying to sneak back in. These shoes are quiet."

He nodded at her shoes, some kind of sporty little loafer with a rubber sole. "No wonder you could leave the class so quietly for your call." *Do not look at her legs.* "Aren't you going to the pub with the rest?"

"It didn't seem fair to leave you with all the cleanup."

He reached for the bag she'd taken.

"I've got it." She lowered her voice, although they were alone. "A pregnant lady should be able to carry a baby, right?"

"You fainted less than an hour ago. Give me the bag."

She lifted the bag a few times like it was a barbell. "This isn't even ten pounds. I got it."

He grabbed the handle and took it from her. "Sorry, but it violates every man-code out there to let a pregnant patient be my pack mule."

"Former patient." But Tana stuffed her hands into the pockets of the modest khaki shorts that revealed such sexy, sleek legs and followed him obediently…for about two steps. Then she jogged ahead of him to get the door with a smirk. "You didn't say I couldn't be a doorman."

He shook his head. "Stubborn?"

"As a pack mule."

"Well, then, lock the door behind you while you're at it."

She jogged ahead of him and got the door for the main entrance, too. The sun had set, but the sky was still a lighter shade of gray than the parking lot asphalt. Only two vehicles remained, his pickup truck and an older-model van. It must have been hers, but she trailed him to his truck in silence.

Caden wasn't sure what she wanted. "Planning on getting my truck door for me, too?"

"I wanted to thank you. It was very nice of you to let me take the test even though I skipped out on most of your class."

He reached over the side of the truck to set the smaller dummy in the bed, then shrugged the heavier, adult one off his shoulder. "You were a pro. I'd be willing to bet you're a CPR instructor yourself."

"It's been a long time since I taught it, but my lifeguard cert is current."

"Lifeguard? That's pretty cool." *Do not imagine her in a red bathing suit. Do not.* He put the medical bag in the truck bed, then opened his own door, just in case she was under the delusion that he'd stand by and let her do it for him.

"Not as cool as a firefighter, but thanks. My old job required me to be certified. That way, they didn't have to hire a lifeguard for swim meets. I coached at Houston City College."

"Again, pretty cool." He stood by the open door of his truck. He couldn't climb into the cab and shut the door on her, but she made no move to leave him.

Caden had intended to have a getting-to-know-you conversation with Montana McKenna over a drink, with the hope that it would lead to more. That hope had been crushed, but he found himself having that conversation in a parking lot despite himself. "You're coaching the women's swim team, I take it?"

"I'm the director for all the aquatics. Men's, women's, diving."

That sounded impressive to him. What an interesting woman…to be just friends with.

She'd turned her attention to the sky. He watched her watching nothing.

She noticed the silence after a moment. "Don't tell

me you're struck speechless at the thought that a woman is leading the men's team?"

"Not that you're a woman. Just that someone as young as you has such a senior position. Congratulations."

"Thanks, but I'm over thirty."

"Like I said, you're the youngest head coach I know. I'm right there in the thirties with you, but I'm not the city's fire chief."

"Yet?"

He shrugged. He'd been moving up the ladder at a good enough pace. He was in no rush to reach the point where he'd spend more time pushing papers on a desk instead of going out on calls. It would happen when it happened. As a lieutenant, he was in charge of his team, but he was still part of the action, part of every call, every shift. He enjoyed being a firefighter and paramedic.

Speaking of being a paramedic…she was still his patient, as far as he was concerned. "We should be having this conversation while you eat something. Do you feel okay to drive to the pub?"

"I was going to walk. It'll take fifteen minutes to get there on foot, or fifteen minutes to drive there with all the stop signs and one-way streets. At least if I walk, I won't waste time circling the block, looking for a parking spot for the swim-mobile." She nodded toward the van.

The Tipsy Musketeer was just off campus, but she'd been laid out on a classroom floor not very long ago.

"It would be better if you didn't walk it. You need

to be putting calories in, not burning them off. I can drive you over, if you don't want to move your van. Hop in." He gestured toward the passenger side, keeping things in the friend zone. He was not going to escort her around the front of his truck. He was not going to get the door for her as if they were on a date. She was taken. Pregnant. Really, really, already taken.

He kept sports drinks and nutrition bars in his truck, part of the set of gear he always had on hand for his go-bag, because there were no lunch breaks while a fire burned out of control. He unzipped the duffel he stored behind his seat and took out a bottle, then climbed into the cab and handed it to her. "Sorry that it's not cold. Drink it anyway."

She took a swig. "At this rate, I'm not going to eat anything at the pub, because I'm going to be running to the bathroom every five minutes."

"That'll be a good sign. If you don't have to go, then you're not drinking enough."

He glanced at her as they waited for a red light. He was accustomed to talking about bodily functions with patients all the time, so he talked about it too easily. He probably needed more of a filter when he was off the job.

Tana didn't seem offended. She looked good in his truck. She smelled good as she held the drink between her bare knees, pulled a ponytail holder off her wrist with her teeth and pulled her hair up and back. He caught the smell of a flowery shampoo again.

That was irrelevant, again.

"That was my free medical advice," he said. "You know what that's worth."

She laughed. "Aren't pregnant women famous for having to go to the bathroom all the time, anyway?"

She had a nice laugh, not a giggle, not a guffaw. They'd be at the pub in a matter of minutes. He'd shake hands with the lucky man who'd seen her first, drink a beer, go home and be absolutely no worse off tomorrow morning than he'd been this morning, even though he now knew what her laugh sounded like.

"It's going to make coaching a fun challenge this year. The locker rooms aren't that close to the pool. The big meets are crowded. Multiple schools, men's, women's, diving all going at the same time. I might have to throw a few elbows to get from the pool deck to the locker room."

He sneaked another peek at her as he drove. She had a faraway look in her eyes as she watched the town go by. She was saying all the right, light things, but she looked a little lost.

He was imagining things. She was a bright woman with a great job and a baby on the way. "I bet you can throw an elbow like no one's business. You'll make it work."

She drew in a deep breath, held it, let it go. Maybe that was a swimmer thing.

"It's going to be so weird." She slowly shook her head. "I can't even imagine this season anymore. I don't know how pregnant I'll be."

"One hundred percent pregnant." It was an old joke.

Her smile was fleeting. Forced, too. "I'm not sure when my due date will be."

There was absolutely, positively no way he was going to ask her the question he'd asked dozens of other female patients in dozens of medical situations. *When was your last period?* No way in hell.

"Drink up," he said.

"Sorry." She downed half the bottle. "You probably don't want to chitchat about pregnancy with some woman you just met. It's just that you're practically the only other person in the world who knows about it. You, me and the doctor. I found out today, during your class."

"That was your phone call?" He remembered his sister-in-law's face when she'd made the big announcement over a family dinner. She'd been beaming with happiness. Even before the announcement, Caden had known something was up, because she'd been as antsy as a kid trying to keep a secret at Christmastime.

Tana hadn't looked very happy about anything while she'd executed those chest compressions on the CPR dummy.

"I'm sure your friends will be toasting you with cranberry juice tonight."

Tana flinched a little. "No, keep it secret. Please."

"Well, *I* wasn't going to be making that announcement. I didn't have anything to do with it." He laughed through a prickle of some somber emotion. "You don't want to tell your friends?"

She didn't laugh at all. "No. They're super nice, but they're also my coworkers. Shirley coaches diving and reports to me. Pregnancy and a new job aren't the best combination. Technically, an employer can't discriminate against you, blah, blah, blah, and all that, but I intend to have my plans squared away before I break the news to anyone at the university. I need time to prove myself first."

Caden pulled the truck into a spot on Athos Avenue, the historic main street of the town, and killed the engine. The silence made the cab feel too close for the distance he was trying to keep.

"Your secret is safe with me, even if I didn't already have to follow patient confidentiality rules." He didn't want to watch her guy arrive at the pub, didn't want to see the way she'd take him aside to tell him the good news privately, but she deserved to have her moment of bursting with happiness. "You've got to tell someone the good news."

She raised an eyebrow and pointed at his chest.

"Someone besides the paramedic who keeps telling you to drink more. Will the father of the baby be coming tonight? Do you have family around here?"

"I'll head back to Houston this weekend. Some news should be given in person." She sounded pretty grim about it. She chugged the rest of the bottle, then she opened the truck door and stepped down to the curb.

"Tana…" *Shut up, Sterling. Shut up.*

She looked up at him in the last of the gray twilight, all big brown eyes in a too-pale face once more.

"Are you okay?" he asked as gently as he could ask a friend. "Usually, having a baby is a good thing, but… Is this not good news, maybe?"

She held her breath again.

He held his.

Then she exhaled, and he swore some of the tension left her shoulders. "No, you're right. A baby is good news. My parents aren't going to be too thrilled, that's all. They have a very rigid idea of what things should be done in what order, but we thirtysomethings are adults. We can do things in whatever order we want to, right?"

"Right."

At least she hadn't said the father of the baby would be unhappy with the news. Her thirtysomething adult of a man better stand by her side when she told her parents. Caden would, if he were him. A woman like Tana didn't come along every day. And if she were carrying his child?

The idea gave him another odd prickle of jealousy or wistfulness or something. This evening was going nowhere good.

"Let's go get some food," Tana said.

"Actually," he began, then stopped to clear his throat. "Actually, I'm going to have to take a rain check. I start my shift at dawn tomorrow. I've got to get some stuff done at my house tonight."

It was a flimsy excuse, and judging by the way her smile slipped, she knew it.

"I wish you could stay."

Her sincerity killed him. She was something special— and she was going to head down to Houston to tell a man in person that he was going to be a father.

"Thank you for everything," she said. "The test, the glucose tablets, listening to me talk about pregnant women and locker rooms. It was really nice of you. All of it. You're a—a really nice guy."

"I'll see you around." He probably would, too. Masterson was a big college but a small town. Nine months was a long time to not run into somebody.

She stepped back and put her hand on the door that would shut them off from one another. Her frown had returned.

The second before the door closed, he called her name. "Hey, Tana?"

"Yes?" She waited, hand on the door.

What? What are you going to say? He couldn't get the contrast between her and his sister-in-law out of his head. Every woman deserved to be as happy as his sister-in-law had been.

"Since I'm the first person in Masterson who knows you're expecting, I get to be the first person in Masterson to congratulate you on the big news." His smile was not forced. "Congratulations, Montana McKenna."

"Thanks." It took a moment, but she smiled. It started small, even shy, but she ended up beaming at him. "Thanks. Really."

Happy. Beautiful. That was how she should look, even if it blinded him.

"Good night," he said.

"Good night." She stepped back and shut the door.

He started the engine, but he didn't back out of his space until he'd watched her cross the street safely, open the etched-glass door of the pub and disappear inside.

"Goodbye, Montana McKenna."

Chapter Five

"Hello, Lieutenant Sterling."

Tana tapped him on the shoulder. He had his back to her as he stood in front of the white display of milk and eggs and yogurt, but it was definitely him. Those navy blue firefighter slacks and dark T-shirt on that big frame had drawn her attention the moment she'd headed down the huge grocery store's aisle, and she'd been more certain with each step that he was the one firefighter in town she knew by name.

He turned around. "Hi."

"Happy Halloween." She shouldn't feel as startled to see his face as he seemed to be to see hers, but she'd somehow forgotten in the past seven weeks just how attractive the man was. Most of that emotional tsunami of a day was a blur in her mind.

"Nice to see you…" He dipped to look under the brim of her pointy witch's hat. "Montana?"

She flipped back her cape and got lightly choked by its black ribbons, which she'd tied into a bow at her throat. "I guess my costume isn't much of a disguise. It's just Tana, by the way."

"It's a great costume. The black lipstick threw me for a minute." He put back the gallon of milk he'd been holding as if it didn't weigh a thing. With arm muscles like his, it probably didn't.

Eye candy. Trick or treat.

"And it's just Caden, Tana."

His smile was warm. That was the one thing about him she'd remembered the most clearly, more than the strong body, more than the contrast between those light eyes and his dark hair. She remembered being taken care of by a firefighter who had smiled at her as if her world was not actually going to hell in a handbasket. *Congratulations*, he'd said, and she'd believed he really meant it.

She didn't need eye candy, not for the rest of her nine months. But she'd wanted to say hello to Caden. He was, so far, the only person who'd acted like her pregnancy was something to celebrate. Jerry had informed her she would not ruin his sabbatical, and during her first prenatal visit, her new doctor had been all business about calculating due dates and prescribing vitamins for her, before moving on to the next woman in the next exam room.

Nobody else knew. Still.

Ruby came up to them, her pink tutu bouncing with

every step, her hands full as she carried a party platter from the supermarket's deli. "Well, hello there! Remember me? I remember you."

Tana could tell the lieutenant was both amused and clueless. Ruby had dark circles under her eyes, blood dripping from her lips and her hair teased into a rat's nest.

"This is Ruby," Tana said. "She was in the CPR class with me."

"Ruby, sure. Nice to see you again." He turned right back to Tana. "How have you been? Are you able to eat now? No more—"

"Fine. Just fine." She should have warned him that her pregnancy was still a secret before Ruby joined them, but she hadn't, so she smiled too brightly and spoke too quickly. "Isn't Ruby's costume great? Can you guess what she is? It's a secret."

Caden and Ruby both looked at her.

"I mean, she told me what she was planning to be, but I've been keeping it a secret."

Caden gave her a nod so slight, nobody would have noticed it, but Tana did. He'd gotten her message. She was relieved—and embarrassed. He must wonder why she hadn't even told her friend yet. That CPR class had been almost two months ago. Seven weeks, to be precise. If there was anything pregnancy did, it made one pay attention to calendars.

"It's not a secret," Ruby protested. "It's so obvious. I'm a zombie ballerina."

"Right." Caden drawled the word. "Perfectly obvious. Everyone knows the zombie virus hit hard during *Swan Lake*."

With her hands full, Ruby bumped shoulders with him. "What are you? A hot fireman?"

"Just a fireman. I'd rather not be hot when I'm working. That would mean I'm in a burning building. Halloween is a busy enough night for us as it is."

"Aw, you're so cute."

Tana had to agree. He was warm and funny…and good-looking. Tana was glad she'd gone with a glam kind of witch costume. She'd used black eyeliner to give herself dramatic cat eyes. Thank goodness she hadn't used it to draw in frown lines and wrinkles, because…

It didn't matter, did it?

She was in a new phase of her life now. She was pregnant. Apparently, her hormones were still capable of responding to a man, despite the fact that the biological purpose of sex had been accomplished and she was beginning the second trimester. Things like flirting with men at costume parties were now in her past.

Caden picked up an egg carton. "We stopped to grab things we can cook up fast, before the night gets too crazy. Scrambled eggs and orange juice can keep us going between calls. We'll have a lot of calls tonight, guaranteed. All you witches and zombies are trouble."

"You poor things," Ruby said. "I guess a fire truck can't fit through the McDonald's drive-thru. You boys and your toys are just too *big*. Not that there's anything wrong with large boys' toys."

Caden shook his head and rolled his eyes. He winked at Tana after she rolled her eyes, too, but then he got serious with her. "We worked a call about a woman who'd fainted on campus a few weeks ago. I was glad it wasn't you, but I've been wondering how you're doing. Any more fainting?"

"None. I feel really normal, nothing…different." Which was odd. She would have thought being pregnant would be this momentous change, but so far, there'd been nothing after those first few weeks of feeling queasy.

"Drinking a lot?" he asked.

"So much that I have to use the ladies' room everywhere I go. That was memorable advice."

He grabbed the gallon of milk again. Really, the flex of that arm muscle was a thing of beauty. "The guys are probably waiting for me at the register. It was good to see you. You look great, black lipstick and all. Glad to see it."

"Hey," Ruby said, bumping Caden's shoulder again before he could turn away. She held her deli platter higher. "We're bringing this to a big party for the staff and faculty at the Treville Center. Everyone's bringing guests. There's going to be more food there than anyone knows what to do with. Maybe we'll see you there later?"

"Let's hope not," Caden said. "I'm on duty until morning, so if I showed up, it would mean—"

"We're in a burning building." Ruby sighed. "Well, a zombie girl can dream. Happy Halloween."

"You, too."

He had to go. Tana knew he had to go, and there was no reason to keep him, but as he turned away, something in her pleaded *Stay.* Here with him in the dairy aisle, she felt like she had an ally, one person who understood the subtext when she said she felt fine, the only man who knew it mattered if she ate, because there was another life depending upon her to stay healthy. This man not only spoke to her, but he smiled at her while knowing everything, and she wanted him to stay.

She blurted out, "Be safe."

He turned back and looked at her with serious blue eyes. "Thanks. You take care of yourself, too."

She knew what he meant. *You're pregnant. Drink and pee and don't faint.*

"I will."

She and Ruby both watched him walk away.

They kept watching, until he turned down an aisle and disappeared.

"Really," Ruby sighed in approval, "the view from behind is as nice as the view from the front."

New phase of my life. A handsome man with a firm backside and a confident, masculine walk was just a handsome man with a firm backside and a confident, masculine walk.

Tana turned back to the dairy display and examined the row of sour-cream dips. "Should we get ranch or French onion?"

"He is so into you, you lucky witch."

"No, he isn't."

"Then you must've cast a spell that forced him to act like a man who is really into you. He could not take his eyes off you."

"That's not true." Tana frowned at the cucumber dip. "It's just not."

"Hey, look at me." Ruby prodded her with the deli tray. "That man is totally interested in you. He looked you over from head to toe. He liked what he saw."

It was surprisingly painful to hear that. In another time, another situation, another Tana might've been thrilled if Ruby was right. But Ruby was wrong, and Tana didn't want to imagine otherwise. It would make her want things that didn't matter anymore.

She pulled the ranch, French, and cucumber dips off the shelf, all three, stacking the extra-large tubs on her palm. She slapped her other hand on top of the tower to hold them steady. "Trust me, he wasn't looking at me like that."

"You are blind."

"Ruby, I'm serious."

"You could have him with a snap of your fingers, I'm telling you. He barely knew I was here, he was so into you."

"No."

"Yes."

"I'm pregnant."

"What?"

The stack of dips and the deli tray kept them far enough apart that Tana couldn't whisper, but she looked over her shoulder to make sure nobody else was in the aisle. "I'm pregnant."

Ruby's mouth fell open, a zombie struck speechless.

"And he knows it, so he wasn't looking at me like that, okay?" Tana turned back to the cold, white shelves, her black cape swishing around her, tugging on its tie at her throat. She inhaled the refrigerated air through her nose slowly and deliberately. She wasn't angry at the situation, not bitter at all. "He knows."

"Why does the world's hottest CPR instructor know that? Is he—is he the father? Tell me he did more than give you a ride to the pub. Did you two have a little extracurricular activity? A little welcome-to-town kind of—"

"No! Jeez. No." After another quick glance around, Tana spoke quickly and quietly. "I was already pregnant when I fainted at the CPR class. I told him then, because, you know…fainting."

"Oh, Tana." The zombie makeup did nothing to mask the pure pity in Ruby's expression.

"So, if you saw him checking me out from head to toe, he was looking to see how far along I am, or if I look dehydrated or whatever. He wasn't flirting with me. He's just being a paramedic, checking up on a patient. Okay?"

"You've been pregnant since the start of the school year, and you're just now telling me?"

"I haven't told anyone."

"Why not?"

Because I hate failing. I hate admitting I failed.

She'd had seven weeks to think about it. She was pregnant because she'd failed to make her boyfriend use a condom correctly. Jerry had always slipped in a few strokes before begrudgingly donning a condom, telling her he just wanted a taste of how good sex could feel for him, if only Tana would go to the doctor and spend the money and put herself on the pill, if only she'd swallow one every single day to alter her body chemistry, so that when he spent the night a few times each month, he wouldn't have to wear a condom.

In retrospect, his attitude meant she'd failed to choose a decent man to be her boyfriend in the first place. Now, she was going to spend the most critical part of the swim season as a waddling whale who couldn't travel with her team, a coach who couldn't coach, and the odds were that she'd fail to get her contract renewed for a second season. She might never coach at the college level again, once her résumé showed that she'd lasted only a year at Masterson. She could coach high school, perhaps, but high schools barely paid even a thousand dollars a semester, not enough to live on, not enough for a baby to live on, not enough to hire a lawyer to make Jerry pay enough for a baby to live on.

She was scared.

She answered Ruby with a shrug.

"Is Jerry still in Peru? You poor thing. You should have told me, at least to have someone to sympathize with you. When is he coming back?"

He had not sent her his mailing address. He hadn't contacted her in any way, and it sucked to have to tell anybody that. Tana should have let Ruby go on and on about how much the fireman was into her.

"I have no idea where Jerry is," Tana said. "We're not a couple anymore."

"He left you? Oh, honey." Ruby set the deli tray on the bottom edge of the refrigerator case, freeing her arms to hug Tana despite the tubs of dip between them.

She squeezed Tana hard, knocking the tower askew, then released her. Tana juggled the dips back into place.

"Listen to me," Ruby said. "The rat will have to come back when you take him to court for child support. I hope the judge takes his last dime for running off to Peru when you needed him the most. Oh, I hate him."

It wouldn't change her situation at all. Jerry might grudgingly give her money now and then, when he was in the country, if the courts forced him to after the baby was born, after the paternity testing was done, after they'd waited to get on the docket to appear before a judge, but Tana could end up spending more money on lawyers than she'd ever receive in child support.

The cape's black bow was choking her, but her hands were full. She shouldn't have thrown the cape back while she'd been talking to Lieutenant Sterling. To *Caden.* In this costume, she'd felt confident, walking up to him without hesitation. He'd smiled at the glamourous witch who'd tapped him on the shoulder.

He'd stopped smiling to ask her about her health as a pregnant woman. Ruby wasn't smiling now, either. Their expressions were so similar when they looked at her.

Pity. Pure pity.

Anyone who knew pitied her. Even the doctor had felt sorry for her when he'd asked about the expectant father, and she'd said he did not want to be part of the pregnancy.

Poor thing, pregnant with no partner.

Ruby wanted to help. "If Jerry refuses to take a paternity test, I think the courts can order him to, if you can provide some reasonable evidence that you guys were together. I'll testify that we went on that double date. Please let me testify against that rat fink bastard."

Jerry hadn't pitied her. He'd simply not believed her. Tana was not going to beg anyone, not a judge and especially not Jerry, to believe her about the father's identity. She would not drag a baby through paternity tests and family court, just so he or she could be legally saddled with a man who didn't want to be a father.

"Sorry, Ruby. There won't be a court case, because there won't be a paternity test. Jerry's not a father, not by any stretch of the imagination."

"He's not? Oh, thank God." Ruby's whole expression changed from pity to relief to something else. Her zombie lips twitched in a mischievous smile. "I hope Jerry stormed off to Peru dying of jealousy, then. Let him eat his heart out."

Two things hit Tana instantly. First, Ruby had completely missed that Tana had said Jerry was not *a* father. As in, not a man cut out to be a father. Not fatherhood material.

Secondly, the pity wasn't for her pregnancy. It was for the circumstances, for the baby being an accident, for Tana being abandoned. If Tana hadn't gotten knocked up accidentally by a loser like Jerry, then she wouldn't be a loser, even if she was pregnant.

If only that were the situation.

The plastic tubs were starting to freeze Tana's hands. She said nothing as she started toward the cash registers.

Ruby snatched up the deli tray and walked down

the aisle with her, giving her one of her flirty shoulder bumps. "So? Who is it? You can tell me. Who's your secret guy? Can I meet him? Do I know him already?"

You misunderstood what I said. It's Jerry, of course. All of Ruby's pity would return. She'd apologize for having been so obviously relieved that it wasn't Jerry a moment ago.

"I—I don't know what to say." Tana only had the length of the cereal aisle to figure it out.

That last, awful phone call with Jerry had been playing on repeat in Tana's head for seven weeks now. *You're the one who is pregnant, not me.*

Those words hurt, but maybe she could use them. Maybe she could turn it around and *own* them.

"I'm the one who is pregnant, not him. The father is nothing more than a sperm donor. He's not important."

"He's not?"

"Once the sperm has done its thing, the man's existence doesn't affect the situation at all, does it? I'm the one who decided to have a baby."

That was true, in a way. From the doctor's first phone call, it had never occurred to her that motherhood wasn't her new future, ready or not.

"Wow," Ruby said. "Did you always plan to have a baby on your own?"

Tana had always planned to fall in love, get married and have a baby. She had imagined herself in love with one of her physical therapists while she'd been in training for the Olympics, so she'd married him when he'd asked, but she'd been far too young. She'd been married for less than a year, a huge mess of a failure that her parents would never let her live down. Ten years had passed since then. She had no love, no marriage, no baby—because no man had chosen her.

She stopped in front of the tea. "I hate that women are expected to wait around until a man decides whether or not he thinks they are good enough to be the mother of their children. We're supposed to live our lives single and alone until the day we die, unless some guy decides to get down on bended knee with a ring box while we're still in our fertile years. *Then* we're allowed to have a family? It's such bull."

She started walking again. The cash registers were only a few yards away. The sound of her high-heeled black pumps striking the hard floor sounded strong. She was wearing a cape. She had cat eyes, damn it.

"You're so badass," Ruby said. "What's your plan?"

"I'm not waiting for Prince Charming to show up."

Caden Sterling walked up to the cash register line. So did two other men in similar blue uniforms. Tana and Ruby would be standing right behind them in a matter of seconds. Caden would look at her with heart-stoppingly blue eyes that were filled with a professional kind of concern. He'd look at her with pity.

She spun away. "Chips."

Ruby scrambled after her. "What?"

"I got all these dips, but I forgot to get the chips. Maybe pretzels."

"I think someone else signed up to bring the chips."

Tana kept heading in the opposite direction of the checkout line, anyway. "I need you to keep this a secret, Ruby. I can't announce anything until I've figured out everything. Travel, maternity leave. Childcare, so I can come back next season. All kinds of things. It's a lot."

"Oh, you poor thing. I'll just bet it is, and you have to make these plans all on your own?"

Jeez, not more pity. Tana couldn't stand it, so she lifted her chin and ignored the ribbon tied around her throat, focusing instead on the fabulous flutter of the cape flaring out behind her. "My plan is to grab some chips. I'm going to go to a costume party and be your designated driver. Monday, I'm going to run swim practice, just as I did last Monday."

"What about your pregnancy?"

"I'm going to be pregnant while I do those things." She let go of the tower with one hand and tugged her witch's hat more firmly into place. "One day at a time."

"Load me up with chips, then."

Tana placed a supersize bag on top of the party tray, and they headed back to the checkout line. There were only two firefighters up ahead. Caden was missing.

Ruby spoke *sotto voce*. "Whoever the father was, I hope he gave you mind-blowing orgasms."

That surprised a laugh out of Tana, loud enough that the two firemen looked over their shoulders at her. The firemen looked at each other, then looked back at them.

Tana murmured, "If there'd been mind-blowing orgasms involved, then I wouldn't be talking about sperm donors right now, would I?"

"Maybe next baby, then," Ruby said under her breath, just before they got in line. "Hello, gentlemen."

The guys told them they liked their costumes, then told them to go ahead of them.

"Thanks. I like your costumes, too, by the way. You look like real firemen." Ruby smiled with her bloody lips and gave Tana's cape a subtle tug, so Tana forced the corners of her black-painted lips into a smile, too.

"Stay safe tonight," Tana said, after they'd paid for their party food. "Tell Caden I said goodbye."

Caden cursed himself all the way back to the dairy aisle. He'd remembered the eggs, but he'd forgotten the bacon. The guys had given him hell, rightfully enough, because bacon was the best part of the whole meal. He'd had to walk the entire length of the big-box store again. There'd been no sign of Tana along the way.

No sign of Ruby, either, but Tana was undeniably the one he'd been looking for. That sexy-witch look had scrambled his brains badly enough to make him forget bacon existed. Her skirt had been longer than the khaki shorts she'd worn in September, but her legs looked frigging out-of-this-world in sheer black pantyhose. She'd stood beside him in high-heeled, pointy-toed, feminine-as-hell shoes, and he'd totally forgotten for a moment that she was taken.

But she was.

He stared at the gallons of milk.

She looked fantastic, because her morning sickness had subsided, and her pregnancy was progressing without any problems. She looked happier now than she had at the CPR class. She was a happy, pregnant woman.

Taken.

Bacon—that was what he was here for.

Caden grabbed the first pound of bacon he saw and

headed back to the registers using a different aisle, but there were no further sexy-witch sightings.

Just as well. What kind of pervert made the effort to get a second look at a pair of legs belonging to a woman who was having a baby with another man? *She's taken.* If he repeated it to himself another thousand times, maybe he wouldn't forget it the next time he ran into her.

The guys, Keith and Javier, saw him coming and put the rest of their food on the conveyor belt. Caden tossed the bacon. It hit the milk jug and scraped along the metal bumper as the belt dragged the food toward the cashier.

"You just missed them," Keith said.

"Who?" Caden asked, but it was a stupid question.

"Some kind of dead ballerina and a totally hot witch." *She's taken.*

"Funniest thing," Javier said. "I was just thinking the witch seemed like she was exactly your type, and I was trying to think of a way to stall her until you came back, but then she says, 'Tell Caden goodbye.'"

Keith clapped him on the shoulder. "My dude. Well done."

"You're congratulating me on having a woman say goodbye?" Caden paid the cashier with cash from the kitty they kept to cover their family-style meals during shifts. "That's not an achievement in the dating world. I'll explain it to you when you get older."

Keith, as the rookie, grabbed the grocery bags, and they headed out to the fire engine.

"It means something when she says it like this." Javier wiggled his fingertips and batted his eyelashes and made little kissy noises.

Keith pitched his voice into a falsetto. "Tell Caden I said bye-eee."

I wish. But Caden knew Tana had said nothing flirtatious. She was friendly. Pregnant and friendly. She didn't look pregnant, but she was. Good for her. Really.

Javier and Keith were still carrying on.

"Give it a rest." Caden reached up to yank open the engine's shiny red door, then he hauled his six-foot-almost-two self into the cab and said the words out loud. "She's taken."

As lieutenant, he used the passenger seat. Javier drove. Keith sat behind them. They all buckled in and put on their microphone headsets, because the engine was too loud to speak over, even without running the sirens.

Nobody spoke.

At the first red light, Javier sat back from the massive steering wheel and looked back at Keith. "*Taken,* the lieutenant says. I didn't see a ring on her hand, did you? I'm betting she won't be taken for long. I'll put twenty on Caden getting her to say *hello-ooo* to him by Valentine's Day."

Caden snorted. "Bad bet. Don't take it, Keith. I'm telling you, she's not free."

Not for the next nine months, for certain. Or seven months, or however the hell much longer she had to go. She wasn't showing, not at all, but she was happy and pregnant and going to a Halloween party with some man who was luckier than he was.

Except there'd been no man with her. When Caden had driven her to the pub, she'd said something about going to Houston, because some news should be given in person. Maybe the lucky guy was on his way to meet her at the party.

If Caden had a girlfriend like Tana, he'd damn sure come up from Houston early enough on the weekend to drive her to every party they went to. If he had a girlfriend like Tana *and* she was carrying his child?

She wouldn't be his girlfriend, for starters. She'd be his wife, or he'd be doing his damnedest to put a diamond on her finger and make it a forever kind of thing.

His dad had that kind of thing with his mom. His brother and sister-in-law had it, too, plus two babies and counting. Caden wanted his own forever, someday.

Keith's voice came through Caden's headset. "I'm not taking that bet. The lieutenant's gonna make her his date for New Year's Eve, at the latest."

Their money was safe, because they were both going to lose and cancel out each other's bets. Caden couldn't tell them why. Just as he wouldn't poach someone else's pregnant girlfriend, he wouldn't spill Tana's secret to anyone.

The first call of the evening came in. A candle in a jack-o'-lantern had set a decorative hay bale on fire on someone's front porch. The structure—which meant the house, in this case—could become involved in seconds.

Caden hit the sirens, then he shrugged into his turnout coat and started buckling himself into the air tank that was always stored as part of his seat's back.

"And so, it begins," he said into his headset.

And so, it ends. The busy night ahead meant that he'd have no time to ruminate on a sexy witch, committing every detail to memory. She'd asked his crew to tell him goodbye.

Goodbye to you, too, Tana—for the second time.

Maybe there would be a third.

Surely, in a small town, he would run into her a third time. As soon as he thought it, he tried to douse a spark of anticipation. He wouldn't find his own forever-girl by obsessing over someone else's sexy witch. He knew that. He did.

But when they reached the house with the flaming hay bales, Caden still hadn't managed to douse that inner spark.

Putting out a real fire was easier.

Chapter Six

She'd had to buy new bras.

That was it, so far. Tana's breasts had gone up a full cup size, maybe more, but her stomach still didn't have the slightest bit of a bulge. It was bizarre to be four months pregnant, yet now have her sexiest figure, ever.

She toyed with her turkey and gravy. She wasn't showing, so why had she broken the news to her parents during Thanksgiving dinner?

There were only the three of them this year, tucked into the little house where Tana had grown up on the outskirts of Houston, so she'd thought it would be a positive, private family time for her announcement. Then again, Thanksgiving was always just the three of them. Tana had no siblings. Neither did her parents. No aunts, no uncles. Not one cousin.

"Please pass the mashed potatoes." Her mother pronounced every syllable as its own word: *Poh. Tate. Toes.* The extra emphasis on the *T*s meant she'd like to throw the bowl against the wall, probably.

Her mother would never do that. Tana kept a helpful smile on her face. "Would you like the gravy, too?"

"I did not ask for the gravy."

Tana should have waited until Christmas to tell them. Her second prenatal appointment had been two weeks ago. The doctor had pressed all over her abdomen, squishing everything. Tana had asked how much longer it would be before she'd start looking pregnant. Of course, she'd wanted to know how much longer she could hide her pregnancy. The Musketeers had won their first two swim meets, men and women, both. The men's diving team had won, too. Women's diving had lost by a mere point. Everybody was happy with the new director of aquatics at Masterson University, so far. Tana wanted to bank as many positive impressions as she could, before she had to lower everyone's expectations.

The doctor had been amused by her question, as if she were disappointed that she wasn't wearing maternity clothes yet. "Generally speaking, with a first pregnancy, you might not show for four months, even five, sometimes. The abdominal muscles haven't been stretched before, so they stay tighter longer. Could be quite a bit longer for you. I don't run across a lot of Olympians in my practice. Your abs are particularly strong, compared to my average patient."

And so, Tana had been forced to correct somebody, once again.

"I'm not an Olympian. I made the team, but I didn't go to the Games."

Because I fell in love, and I sacrificed everything else that mattered to me.

"But thanks for the compliment on the abs. I still swim almost every day." She'd patted her stomach good-naturedly, to show that it didn't bother her at all to bring up her failures.

As her mother scooped mashed potatoes with force, Tana took a quick bite of cranberry sauce, mostly because it was easy to swallow, so she could keep up her pretense that this failure didn't bother her, either. It was only an accidental pregnancy with a man who'd turned out to be even more selfish than her parents had warned her he was. They'd *warned* her, and they'd been right.

She swallowed more cranberry sauce. "The doctor said I'm due April twenty-third, plus or minus two weeks."

"NCAA championships are the last week of March," her father said—to her mother, not to her. "It's back in Indiana this year for the men. Georgia for the women."

"She won't be able to travel," they said, practically in unison.

It had taken her parents one second to pinpoint the issue that kept Tana up at night, the one fact that she couldn't change.

Stress and poor sleep weren't good for a pregnant woman. Fortunately, the doctor had already assured her that she could continue swimming throughout her pregnancy, up until the day her water broke.

She had only a vague idea of what that meant. The internet said it was a sign she'd be going into labor, but that it was unlikely to be a sudden gush of amniotic fluid. She might feel a trickle of water running down her leg, if anything. How would Tana know that her water broke if she was in the pool at the time?

Regardless, she planned to be using the pool up to the very last day. She would have gone crazy already if she hadn't been able to put her head down and drive through the water, where the only sounds were those her own arms and legs made as she propelled herself forward, always forward, lap after lap. She counted her strokes and took a breath every twelfth one during the first laps, then every tenth, until she was winded enough to need one every eighth stroke, then sixth. Numbers and air and water filled her mind until there was no room to worry about anything else—as long as she stayed in the water, head down, moving forward in her lane.

"Please pass the chestnut dressing." Mom was still doing the *T* thing. The ches*T*nu*T* dressing meant Mon-*T*ana was in trouble.

I'm a grown-up. They can't ground me for the rest of the holiday break.

But it sure felt like they could.

"The turkey is delicious, Mom." She shoved a fork-ful of turkey into her mouth. Lean protein was good for her. It had always been good for her, but now…well, she didn't want to wake from a faint on a hard floor again. Not even with a good-looking fireman cradling her head in his hand, smiling at her with the warmest of smiles. *There you are*, he'd said.

Tana tried again. "So, have you heard any interesting news lately? Any *other* interesting news, besides mine?"

Her mother looked up at her father mournfully. "Poor Coach Nicholls. After everything that man has been through…" She pressed her fingertips to her lips, pausing to maintain her composure.

Tana set down her fork, alarmed. "What happened to him?"

Her father drizzled gravy over his mashed potatoes, a very precise operation, given the petite size of the silver ladle they used only at Thanksgiving and Christmas. "My understanding is that he put in a good word for you, not only with the athletic director of Masterson, but with the president of the university. Despite—" he pursed his lips, as if the words he was thinking would taste bad if said aloud "—everything."

"He did, yes. But what has happened to him? Is he ill?"

Her father ladled another tablespoon of gravy. "You can't be unaware of the consequences for what you've done. Coach Nicholls convinced everyone to give you a second chance at a school which competes at the national level. He must be so disappointed in you. You've let him down again."

Nothing was wrong with Coach Nicholls, then. Tana was the problem.

"Coach Nicholls isn't disappointed in me." *Not yet.* "We beat the Longhorns last Saturday. They're the reigning champs. It was a huge upset. Coach Nicholls sent me an email to congratulate me, actually."

It had been one of the best days of Tana's professional life. "You should have seen it. We beat them off the blocks, almost every swimmer, every heat. I've been having the distance swimmers do block work like sprinters this month. They practically gained a second before the first breath on the first lap. It's so satisfying to try something new at practice and see it pay off like that."

"Coach Nicholls has no idea yet, does he?"

The knots in Tana's stomach were familiar. They were nothing like the odd queasiness of those first few weeks of pregnancy. These knots were an old and too-common sensation.

She picked up her fork to take another stab at the turkey, anyway. "Why would I have told him before you?"

She chewed. She waited.

Please act like normal parents.

But they never had, not since it had become clear that she was a prodigy in the pool. She'd been fourteen, a freshman in high school, but she'd broken every school record for girls' swimming in every event: butterfly, backstroke, breaststroke, freestyle sprints, freestyle distance. She'd broken the boys' record in three of those races, too, but the school hadn't put her name on the wall for that.

When Tana had broken the entire state of Texas's high school records for backstroke and freestyle events the next year, a renowned coach, Bob Nicholls, had shown up on their doorstep. With her parents' blessing, he'd taken her to Colorado, to see if she could compete on a national level with the right training. Her high school education had been completed with tutors while Tana added weight training and dryland exercises, physical therapy and nutrition classes to her life. Nicholls and his staff had wanted to see if she had what it took—that *fierce determination* that Caden Sterling had told his class they needed—to make the sacrifices necessary to become world-class in her sport.

Sacrifices? Her life had become enchanted. She'd spent all day, every day, in a pool full of her heroes: Olympic medalists, world-record holders. When she was twenty, she'd set one of those world records herself. She'd loved Coach Nicholls for making her dreams come true. She would always love him, but he was not her parent.

She swallowed. She broke the silence.

"Of course, I told you first. You're going to be grandparents. Coach Nicholls is not going to be any relation to this baby at all."

Her parents' voices erupted in a cacophony of exclamations. "The man put his neck on the line for you—"

"His reputation already took a blow from you once before—"

"—to help Shippers and Appelan make the Olympic team, but now—"

"—it would have been better if you'd stayed in Houston, under the radar—"

"—you'll leave his swimmers in a lurch when they need you most."

"—rather than get knocked up right when the swimming world was noticing you again."

"Oh, Tana."

In all of that, the most chilling thing was that her parents knew the names of the two Masterson swimmers who were the most likely to qualify for Team USA, Shippers and Appelan. Tana's father was a bus driver, and her mother was a teacher's assistant at the local public middle school. There was no reason they should know the names of the nineteen-year-old intercollegiate swimmers whom Coach Nicholls was scouting.

Her parents had been checking up on her. They must have called Coach Nicholls themselves to ask if her performance was meeting his standards. They'd done that often enough during the years she'd swum for him, until she'd fallen in love with one of the team's trainers and eloped just before her twenty-first birthday.

Just before the Olympics.

That had been more than ten years ago. They had no reason to call Coach Nicholls and check up on her now.

"How do you know who Shippers and Appelan are, Dad?"

Her father maintained determined eye contact with his roll as he buttered it fiercely. "Since Nicholls recommended you for this position, we thought maybe he had forgiven you for the way you ran out on the team. Dara Torres returned to the Olympic stage at age forty-one. She pulled in three silver medals. You're only thirty-one."

"A single gold medal would set you up for life," her mother said. "We had that soup commercial lined up for you. A million dollars you could have had, if you'd only won a gold medal."

"Now that you're back at Masterson, you could train up and start competing again. Thanks to Coach Nicholls, you're at the same pool where you set your NCAA records. Naturally, we suspected that he had this in mind for you. You must have been thinking it, too. You've been keeping yourself in shape for years now. You must have some reason."

For my sanity. Every twelfth stroke, every tenth, head down, moving forward.

"So, we called. Coach agreed that if anyone could stage a comeback after ten years, it would be you."

Tana heard the note of hope in her mother's voice. Not scorn; hope.

It crushed her.

"Oh, Mom. Dad. I'm not in that kind of shape. I don't have the time to get into that kind of shape again. Not while I'm coaching."

They all fell silent for a moment, all three of them holding forks in their right hands, all three of them not eating. She looked at their faces, at their genuine misery, their dashed hopes.

Tana had failed them, then and now. But even when Tana had screwed up, she'd always had another goal to strive for, and she did have another goal. She hadn't voiced it to anyone yet, but she offered it to her parents now.

"I can see myself at the Olympics as a coach. Coach Nicholls didn't say anything to me about training myself to compete. I really think he wants me at Masterson to train others, because I'm—I'm a good coach. I love coaching."

"There are no soup commercials for coaches," her father said.

Her mother set her fork and knife down, precisely parallel to each other on the top of her plate. "That doesn't matter now. None of it matters now, not even this coaching thing she's been doing. She can't run a college program when she's due to give birth in March."

I can so. You'll see. I'll show you.

"April twenty-third. I'm due April twenty-third."

"Pregnant." The way her father spat the single word, there was no doubt it meant *failure*. "You have a God-given talent, Tana, but you keep squandering it on all these idiot men you think are Prince Charming."

All these men? There'd been only one. Her Prince Charming had been a trainer, one of the physical therapists who kept the bodies of the elite athletes working at their peak. He'd soaked Tana's aching muscles in ice water. He'd taped up her tender triceps on the pool deck, minutes before she'd set the world record in the 100-meter backstroke. He'd sneaked her away from the training facility in Colorado and married her.

Whither thou goest, I will go, they'd vowed. He'd added that to their vows himself. So romantic.

Days after their clandestine wedding, he'd told her he was quitting, leaving Colorado, leaving the whole country, to serve as a physical therapist on a medical mission with a group of orthopedic surgeons.

He expected his wife to come with him. She'd set a world record, so what else did she have to prove? To

continue focusing on medals would be selfish, he'd said.
He'd seen a lot of Olympians come and go, a lot of records set and broken. Her kind of achievement was always temporary. Someone would come along who was
better than she was. She ought to believe him, he'd said.
After all, he was thirteen years older than she was.

Whither thou goest, I will go, he'd reminded her.
Vows were unbreakable.

He'd taken her with him, far, far from any pool. Tana
had kept her head down and moved forward in this new
lane. She'd done the best she could, for as long as she
could. It hadn't been long, only a year, but it had been
an Olympic year.

"You're letting yet another man take everything away
from you," her mother said. "Again and again and again.
When will you learn? Why couldn't once be enough?"

"Once was enough." Tana forced the words out as
if each one caused her pain. The memory of that year
couldn't possibly be as devastating as the actual year
had been, but pain was a tricky thing. Even the memory
of pain could be painful. Athletes would favor a knee
or a shoulder long after an injury healed, because the
memory of the pain made them fearful.

For the past decade, her parents' scorn was something she'd avoided at all costs. After the divorce, she'd
been determined to finish the college degree she'd
started prior to her ill-fated marriage. She'd still had a
year's eligibility left to compete at the collegiate level.
Masterson University had given her a full scholarship
to swim for them, and she'd given them four NCAA
records in return. With her bachelor's degree in sports

management, she'd dedicated herself to coaching, even running swimming clinics around the country when she had summers off from Houston City College.

In other words, she'd worked hard for her chance at redemption in the eyes of the competitive swimming world. She might have been a flighty swimmer for one summer, but she'd been a reliable coach for a decade. She wasn't the director of aquatics at her alma mater because Bob Nicholls had made a phone call. At least, she wasn't the director *only* because of that.

"I haven't fallen for another Prince Charming. Not in ten years."

"You fell for Jerry. We told you that he was not really in love with you. We could see it. Why couldn't you?"

I didn't go to Peru with him, she might have pointed out. She hadn't given up the opportunity to coach at Masterson to follow Jerry. She'd learned that much from her brief marriage.

"He's kept you dangling on a string for more than a year. You've gotten knocked up by a man who has accomplished nothing in his life, which now prevents you from accomplishing anything in your life. Again."

Tana could have defended Jerry. He'd earned a doctorate, after all, but why bother? Her parents were right about the only thing that mattered: Jerry did not love her, not enough to use birth control correctly. Not enough to change his travel plans. Because he didn't love her, she was going to have a baby—by herself.

A baby is a good thing. Congratulations. One person, and only one person, had said that to her, a fireman she barely knew.

She wished that memory wouldn't pop into her head so frequently. It made her ache for what she did not have. She had her ex's indifference, Ruby's pity, and now, her parents' scorn. She wanted more Caden Sterling—or rather, more people like Caden, people who would smile at her warmly and say *Congratulations*.

Her father finished the last bite of his Thanksgiving feast and tossed his napkin onto the table. "You haven't mentioned an offer of marriage. I suppose I have to get out my shotgun and make that selfish bastard do the right thing."

There was no way Tana could tell them what Jerry had said. *You're the one who's pregnant, not me.* But there was no way she'd ever tie herself to a man who thought his wants and needs were all that mattered in the world, either. She'd already done that at twenty, and as she'd just assured her mother, once was enough.

"I'm not going to marry Jerry. He is not part of this pregnancy."

Her father slammed his palms on the table. "Do I need to prod *you* with the shotgun, Montana Dawn McKenna?"

"You have to marry the father, so that the baby isn't illegitimate." Her mother threw her napkin onto the table, too. "It still matters. Times haven't changed that much."

Her dad piled on. "You can divorce your boyfriend later. Maybe this time you'll make it to your first anniversary."

Pain was a tricky thing. When it couldn't be avoided,

it made people desperate. Tana threw caution to the wind. "Boyfriend? You mean sperm donor."

"Don't be crude," her mother said.

"It's a medical term."

"You do *not* mean you got pregnant by a sperm donor."

Tana's laughter might have been a little manic, a little frantic, but it was better than crying. "Whether you like the term or not, I am pregnant by nothing more than a sperm donor." God knew Jerry had decided to be just that. "It's just me and this baby. No father."

But her parents exchanged a serious look. Her father sat up straighter. Her mother folded her hands on the table. "You decided to have a baby by yourself? On purpose?"

They looked almost like Ruby had at the suggestion that Tana had *not* gotten accidentally knocked up by an uncaring boyfriend. If Tana had intentionally chosen to be pregnant…

No pity from Ruby. No scorn from her parents. Maybe.

"Why would you choose such a drastic way to get pregnant?" her mother asked. "Is it because you're over thirty?"

Her parents had jumped to the wrong conclusion. Couldn't Tana just let them? It wasn't lying, not really.

"I chose to have this baby because—because—a baby is a good thing."

Her parents looked uncomfortable. "Well, of course, but…"

"This is *good* news."

"But, Tana, a sperm donor?"

She tried to remember what else she'd said to Ruby on Halloween. She'd never outright lied and said she went through artificial insemination, but Ruby had jumped to that conclusion...if her parents did, too, then...

"Why do I have to wait for a man to decide I'm good enough to marry and good enough to produce children for him? I was married. My husband wasn't a good man. You made it clear you don't think Jerry is, either, and I agree with you. We broke up months ago. I don't need a man's permission if I want to be a mother." She raised her chin. "The bottom line is that I'm not knocked up. I'm expecting. There's a difference."

Her father jerked his head back as if she'd taken a swing at him. "You know nothing about its father? You have no idea whose DNA is..." he waved his hand in the general direction of her stomach "...combining with yours, right this second? This is—"

"It wasn't sperm roulette, Dad."

"Do they give you a catalog? You just leaf through it until you see something interesting?"

Tana supposed that was how it was done, actually. Certainly, prospective parents were given basic information about the sperm donor.

"I know he's healthy." Jerry had been through a rigorous medical evaluation before being approved for his high-altitude jungle adventure. "He's six feet tall. He has brown hair and brown eyes, like I do. Primarily, a Mediterranean ancestry. Plays some sports. His level of education is a doctorate."

Her parents were silent. They were too shocked to realize she was describing Jerry. Shocked—but not scornful.

"The important thing here is that my pregnancy is going fine. The doctor says I'm healthy. It would be lovely if you said something nice now, like *congratulations*."

They were silent.

Please act like normal parents.

Her mother spoke. "You must tell Coach Nicholls immediately."

"For now, this is a secret. I care about my coaching career, and I especially care about my team. They're doing fantastically well right now, and it would be unfair to everyone to rock the boat before I must. I'll announce my pregnancy to my team, to my employers and to Coach Nicholls in my way."

Her father dismissed his only child's pregnancy with a single word. "Fine."

"It's not fine," her mother objected. "Have you even thought about how you'll manage after the baby is born?"

"Millions of women manage being single mothers. If they can do it, I can do it. I've always had a fierce determination to be the best at what I do. Coach Nicholls would back me up on that."

"Being the best unwed mother isn't something to brag about."

Her mother's disapproval, her father's dismissal, it all hurt. It would always hurt, always put these knots in her stomach and kill her appetite. But until April twenty-third, not eating was not an option.

You take care of yourself, her fireman had said. Staying at this table with her stomach full of knots did not feel like she was taking good care of herself.

Tana threw in the towel—or her napkin. It landed on the table next to her parents' napkins. "If you'll excuse me, I think it would be best if I headed home now."

Her parents did not object.

Tana picked up her plate and, out of habit, her parents' plates, too, and carried them into the kitchen. She kept moving, knowing from experience the pain would fade into numbness. She got her car keys and put on her jacket. *Everything is okay. I'll manage on my own.*

Her phone chirped in her jacket pocket. Ruby had texted her an hour ago. Hope your T-giving in Houston is good. Everyone's hitting the Tipsy Musketeer later. Will be fun.

Tana released the breath she'd been holding for who knew how long. Twelve strokes? Ten?

At the front door, her mother offered her a little plastic container. "I thought you would like to take your slice of pumpkin pie with you."

It was something of a peace offering. Tana had to bow her head to receive her mother's kiss. Tana had gotten taller than her mother at fourteen, the same year she'd gotten so alarmingly fast in the pool, but her mother still kissed her on the forehead, as she always had and always would. Her parents were so often unhappy with her, but they would never pretend she'd never existed. They'd never move to another continent and cut off all communication. That was something.

Tana raised her head. "I love you both. Good night."

Chapter Seven

"I love you so much."

"I love you, too." Caden smiled at the prettiest girl in Texas, who was cozied up beside him in their booth at the pub.

"High five!" she demanded, and Caden obligingly held up his hand so she could slap his palm with all the mighty force of a three-year-old.

Her momentum toppled her right into Caden's lap, where her little brother had been peacefully sitting. The baby wailed in protest.

"Whoa, there." Caden caught his niece under her arm, lifted her in the air and deposited her back onto the plastic booster seat, next to him in the booth. He bounced his knee a little to jostle his nephew. "It's okay, Max."

"It's okay, Max. Accidents happen." His niece could speak big words clearly in her little voice. Caden recognized the singsong lilt to that particular phrase. Little Abby could impersonate her mother, Abigail Sterling, to a T.

Abigail slid out of her side of the booth and scooped up the wailing Max. "I think this is our cue to get back to the ranch. What a long day."

As Thanksgivings went, this one hadn't been restful for anybody. It had been a good one, though. Caden had volunteered to work Christmas this year, so the guys with little kids could be home for Santa duty. That gave him Thanksgiving off. Of course, he'd gone to his parents' house. Caden's brother, Edward, had come down from his ranch with his wife, Abigail, and their two kids. His mother had both bragged and complained about the size of the turkey she'd put in the oven before dawn.

Mom had served the meal around noon, as she always did. The family had finished their seconds and were settling in to watch some football before diving into the pumpkin pies, which meant they'd all intended to catch a nap, sprawled out all over the family room in front of the TV, when a phone call had thrown the rest of the day into organized chaos.

Edward and Abigail allocated space on their ranch for horses who needed rehabilitation. Today's call had come from an animal welfare group that had been keeping tabs on a mare that was underfed and slowly starving. Since the law couldn't do much to force bad owners to surrender their animals, rescue groups had to persuade negligent owners to turn their animals over to them. The mare's owner had, perhaps in a fit of holiday spirit, finally agreed to allow the group to take the horse. The mare needed to be picked up immediately, because owners were known to change their minds on a whim, deciding to keep the animal just because someone else wanted it, or as a way to keep getting attention from the rescue group, as twisted as that was.

Little Abby and baby Max had been left with their grandparents while Caden, Edward and Abigail had headed an hour north to the ranch to hitch up the horse trailer. The three of them had the routine down pat. Abigail would charm the negligent jerk of an owner, praising him or her for being so smart to let the animal go. Caden and Edward would stay silent and try to look meaner than they were. Edward's ranching and Caden's firefighting kept them in better-than-average shape, so they'd stand behind the smiling Abigail like a couple of surly cowboy bouncers at a country-western bar. The combination of his sister-in-law's flattery and the brothers' brawn usually worked, and it had worked again today.

Watching the mare check out the small quarantine pasture on the Sterling ranch had made Caden's Thanksgiving Day. She'd rolled around on the clean ground, stretching her back out, now that she had a space free of rusting car parts and broken lawnmowers. That horse was a special horse, still spirited despite the neglect. She'd been worth every mile they'd driven.

They'd driven a few hundred, so far. Caden's parents lived south of Masterson. The ranch was north of

Masterson. The horse had been rescued fifty miles west of the ranch, brought back and settled in. Afterward, they'd had to drive back through the town to get the kids. Their parents had suggested meeting halfway in Masterson itself, here at the Tipsy Musketeer, to knock some miles off their journey.

"These kids are ready for bath and bed," Abigail said, swaying to soothe baby Max. "And so am I. We have to go now."

"I don't want a bath," Abby said. "I don't have to go now."

Caden tried not to laugh at her perfectly correct logic. It would only earn him a matching set of glares from his sister-in-law and brother. Instead, he got out of the booth and held out his arms for his niece. "Come on, kiddo. You gotta go when Mommy and Daddy tell you to go."

Max's tears were apparently contagious, because Abby's upper lip quivered. Her little voice wavered. "I don't want to go." She threw her arms around Caden's neck.

Caden blew one of her strawberry curls away from his mouth and raised an eyebrow at his brother. Edward was the stricter of the two parents. Caden was just the indulgent uncle. He wasn't about to get all hard-nosed with Abby. *Not my job, brother.*

Edward opened his mouth to say something firm and fatherly, but then he sighed and patted Abby on the back. "If we leave now, you don't have to have a bath, okay? You can eat pumpkin pie with me."

"Oh, goody," his wife murmured. "Bribery. Exactly how we planned to parent."

"I had pie at Gramma's house." Abby pouted.

Edward negotiated. "Was it good? Would you like another piece? I haven't had any yet."

Abigail turned the stroller toward the pub's etched glass door while baby Max kept fussing on her hip. She smiled sweetly at her husband. "You don't want me to witness this, honey, because I'll never let you live it down if I do. I'll meet you at the truck."

Edward shrugged a little sheepishly as she kissed his cheek and walked away. With a sigh, he held out his hands to Abby. "Come on. Time to go."

Abby strangled Caden and shook her head, getting more curls in his mouth. Caden didn't mind. It was always fun to see his big brother get bested by a tiny tot.

Edward pleaded with Caden. "I don't suppose you'd like to come back to the ranch with us and spend the night?"

"Can't. My shift starts at seven in the morning. Since my truck is still at Mom and Dad's, I'm going to sleep at the station tonight." Pretty much everything in Masterson was within walking distance of the pub, from the college campus to the fire station. The Tipsy Musketeer had *Est. 1889* etched in its glass door. It had been built first, back in the days of the wild, wild West. The rest of the town had grown around it.

Edward looked resigned to his fate. He'd have to carry Abby out of the pub as she protested all the way, but when he moved to pry Abby away, Caden held up a hand to stop him.

"Hey, Abby," he whispered. "Did Gramma give you whipped cream with that pie?"

Abby nodded.

"I think that's the best part, don't you?"

Abby nodded some more.

"If I were you, I'd go with my daddy, and when he got his pumpkin pie, I'd eat all of his whipped cream, really quick, before he got to. Then he'd have to put more on his pie, and I'd eat all that, too."

"I don't think she's fast enough to eat all my whipped cream," Edward said.

Abby picked up her head to give her father an offended glare.

Edward ignored her and spoke to Caden. "I guess I could race her, but there's no way she can eat as much whipped cream as I can."

In a matter of minutes, Abby was willing to be handed off from uncle to father in order to prove her ability to eat whipped cream.

"Do not ever breathe a word of this to my wife," Edward said to Caden under his breath. He carried his daughter out of the pub.

Caden sat in the booth to finish eating in peace. His Irish stew had gone lukewarm, but he was used to eating whatever food he could, when he could, while he was on duty. Since he was not on duty, however, he ordered an ice-cold beer after he'd polished off the sourdough rolls.

"You can't drink alone."

Caden looked up.

"Remember me?"

"Zombie ballerina. You look like you've rejoined the ranks of the living."

"Until next Halloween." Ruby helped herself to his sister-in-law's vacant spot as she gestured to the largest corner table. "Come join us. We've all been perfect little boys and girls with our families all day, and now we're having a drink to recover. There may be cussing and dirty jokes. I saw you with those little kids. Totally adorable, but if anyone needs to chill out now with adults who are not relatives, it's you, am I right?"

Ruby wasn't hitting on him, Caden was pretty certain. Not that there was anything wrong with being hit on by a friendly, attractive girl. Ruby was just...well, as much as he disagreed with Javier that he had a type, Caden had to admit that he didn't feel that kind of attraction to Ruby. They could be friends, though, easily. That was a good thing.

Caden checked out the folks at her table. He recognized another face from that same CPR class, but the one face he wanted to see, which was the one face he ought to avoid for his own peace of mind, wasn't there. No sexy witch tonight. That was a good thing, too.

A country-western DJ was upping the volume of the music, now that the family dinner hours were ending, and more couples and singles were showing up. The light from the pub's Victorian-era chandelier was dimmed, and the tables in front of the stage were removed to create a dance floor. The Tipsy Musketeer usually had live sing-along folk music. The music was known for being good, because this was a college town, and the owner was a smart man who hired the university's music majors. But, since this was a college town, all those student musicians were home for the extended holiday weekend, along with the faculty.

Like the swim coach.

He could hang out here with other Masterson locals, and nothing would mess with his resolve to forget about a witch with cat eyes and a lifeguard license.

Caden brought his beer over to Ruby's gang and said his hellos. He'd barely started debating football conference rankings with the woman next to him when he and the other men were pushed onto the dance floor by all of the women, and line dancing commenced.

It was a relaxed way to dance. The steps were the same for everyone as they formed a few loose lines. The ladies tended to throw a lot of hip-wiggle into it, but Caden and the other men just hooked their thumbs in the belt loops of their jeans as they kicked the heels of their cowboy boots against the floor. Heel, toe, kick, shuffle back four steps—

Tana McKenna walked into the pub.

Ruby squealed and grabbed her and hugged her. Tana was barely given a second to drop her purse on a chair before she was pulled onto the dance floor, too. The whole crowd turned a quarter turn, and Caden was intensely aware that she was somewhere behind him. Heel, toe, kick, shuffle—another quarter turn, and Tana was dancing beside him in the same line.

She gave him a little wave and a smile, and damn it to hell, he did have a type, and Tana McKenna was it.

Another kick and turn, and he was behind her for the final lines of the song. She still had on her light jacket, and she wore slacks instead of a skirt or shorts. It was her dark hair that caught his attention tonight, the way it fell loosely to her shoulders, catching the light from the antique chandelier. He remembered that her hair had smelled like flowers when she'd sat next to him in the cab of his truck and pulled it up into a ponytail.

At the last note, Caden headed off the dance floor and dropped into the chair in front of his beer.

Tana retrieved her purse and came over to the table. After a moment's hesitation, she chose a chair away from his.

She didn't look pregnant yet. That was the first thing he noticed.

She had arrived alone. No man had dropped her off, parked a truck, then come in a few minutes later to join her on the dance floor. That was the second thing he noticed.

She wasn't happy. That was the third thing he noticed, when their eyes met again. She smiled politely as they exchanged *How are you?* and *Good, thanks, how about you?* Underneath that, something was bothering her. She seemed almost embarrassed to see him.

He played it cool and turned to talk to the woman next to him, resuming their debate on which college teams should go to which bowl games over Christmas and New Year's.

It worked. When Caden casually looked her way again, Tana looked more relaxed. His first thought had been wrong; she was starting to look pregnant, after all. She had that glow about her, that super-healthy thing that Caden had seen in his sister-in-law during both of her pregnancies. Tana's face was a little fuller, just a little softer around the edges, sort of.

Maybe he was imagining it. Maybe he wanted to convince himself that she looked pregnant, because, whether she was softer or glowing or not, Tana McKenna was off limits.

Tana shook off her jacket and hung it on the back of her chair. She was bigger in the chest. A lot bigger. He was not imagining it.

That damn spark was hard to douse, but Caden knew a fire couldn't burn out of control if the fuel was taken away. He turned back to the football-loving woman. "You want to go dance?"

It helped, two-stepping in a lazy circle around the dance floor with a woman in his arms, but the song only lasted so long, and if he kept her out here for song after song, she'd start assuming he wanted more than he did. He walked her back to their group.

"Oh, you're a good dancer," Ruby said, before he could sit down. "My turn."

Back to the dance floor he went, but so did Tana, with another guy from the group. Caden and Ruby assumed the ballroom-style hold of the two-step. Next to them, Tana and her partner did the same. Caden felt things he didn't want to feel when he saw another man's arm around Tana's back, another man's hand holding hers out to the side.

The song ended before they could begin. The DJ started a country waltz.

"Oh, shoot. I don't know how to waltz," Ruby said, dropping her arm and stepping back from him.

Tana's partner was saying the same thing. Caden felt a little desperate. If Tana was going back to the table, then he wanted to stay on the dance floor, far enough away to not fan any flames.

"Waltzing isn't that hard," Caden assured Ruby. Unfortunately, Tana said the same exact thing at the exact same moment.

"Neither one of you is going to call jinx?" Ruby asked.

The four of them laughed, but Tana's laugh didn't sound any more genuine than his.

"It's just counting to three instead of two," Tana said to her partner. "I can show you how."

The guy had that trapped look about him, like he'd rather do just about anything than stumble through his first waltz right this second. Ruby grabbed him by the arm. "Come on, let's go to the bar. They can show us how it's done. We should order a round of shots for the table."

That was how Caden found himself with Tana in his arms, waltzing to a classic country-western song. She was a good dancer, which he appreciated, because he enjoyed dancing. She was better than good, actually, which shouldn't have surprised him. She was the woman of his—

She *could have been* the woman of his dreams.

Honest to God, Caden hoped he'd run into a woman just like her one day, this time *before* she was starting a family with someone else.

Tana stayed relaxed in his hold, moving lightly in whichever direction he turned them, trusting him not to steer her wrong or run into another couple. Her slacks and sweater were dressier than his jeans and plaid shirt, but the two of them meshed together effortlessly, her boot stepping neatly between his on every downbeat, *one*-two-three, *one*-two-three, and not once on his toes. She was both athletic and graceful—and entirely too soft in his arms.

Honest to God—how about meeting a clone of Tana one day *soon*? Soon would be good.

In the meantime, he might as well make friends with the original. Friends danced. Friends talked. So far, they had one out of two going.

He broke the awkward silence. "Don't worry. I'm not going to ask if you've been drinking enough. You must be. You look like you're feeling good. You're starting to look a little bit pregnant, just in your—"

"Chest. I know. It's so bizarre. My bustline is heading toward Dolly Parton territory."

Awkward didn't begin to describe that as a conversation starter. Caden had to laugh. "That was not what I was going to say."

"It wasn't? I thought it was so obvious. Isn't it?"

"No comment."

They were getting boxed into a crowded corner of the dance floor. Caden spun them in a full 360, just because he could when he had a partner as good as she was, then led them into a more open area.

"That means *yes*," she said.

"That means *no comment*. I have some manners, you know. I don't casually chat with women about their chest size, pregnant or otherwise. Jeez. How's the weather?"

"Sorry. Now I'm embarrassed." She bit her lip, but it looked like she did so to keep from smiling. "I guess I think of you as being a medical provider, so, you know…"

"Yeah. But no. I'm not your doctor. I'm your dance partner." He made their steps smaller, making the dance less challenging, so they could talk more easily.

"Got it. Sorry." Her apology was definitely playful now. "I'm going to go broke buying new bras every month, though."

"Stop."

"Guys have no idea how expensive bras are, do they?"

"I'm trying to be your friend here. Do you always torture your friends?"

"Only when it's fun." She laughed—*that* laugh, the real one.

He hadn't forgotten how perfect it had sounded that first night, when they'd been parked right outside this pub. He looked at her smiling face, felt the bustline in question brush against him as she laughed, and Caden gave up trying to think of her body as maternal. The fact was that he was dancing with a gorgeous, desirable woman, and this waltz was sweet, sweet torture.

"You've got me curious," she said. "If I hadn't interrupted, what part of me were you going to say looked pregnant?"

"Your face."

"What's wrong with my face?"

"Not a thing."

"Uh-huh. Sure. Friends tell friends when they have something on their face. Spit it out, friend."

"It's nothing bad. You've got that pregnancy glow going on."

She froze, just for a fraction of a second, just long enough that they stuttered a step out of sync. He caught her closer and got them back into the rhythm.

"I didn't know that was really a thing." She sounded more subdued.

He kept it light. "Sure, it is. My mom says pregnant women are radiant because their bodies are going full-out, operating at max capacity. Getting things done. Big things."

He hadn't thought that was a jaw-dropping thing to say, but Tana gaped at him in silence.

He turned them in another swooping 360.

She closed her mouth. Wet her lips. "You, ah, you talk about pregnancy with your mother?"

"Never. What kind of weird bachelor would that make me?"

"But…but you said…"

"*I* don't talk about it, but my brother? He's crazy in love with his wife. I've had to listen to him brag about how great his wife looks, what a goddess she is, every nauseating thing you can imagine, through two pregnancies now. That's eighteen months of 'glowing' discussions. Also, eighteen months of me reminding him that I don't want to hear all of my sister-in-law's personal details." Caden winked at Tana. "Like the amount of bras she has to purchase, or what they cost."

Tana smiled at his joke briefly, but she looked away,

brow furrowed as she thought about something that wasn't amusing to her at all.

Who is bragging about how beautiful you are, Tana?

Caden was afraid the answer would be nobody, if he could ask such a personal question.

He couldn't. This was a chance encounter, a casual night at the Tipsy Musketeer. He needed to keep it light and friendly, as anybody would with someone who was only an acquaintance.

The song came to an end. Caden raised their joined hands so Tana could twirl under them and away, because that was the traditional way to end a country-western dance, not because he wanted to let go of her.

The next song was a Christmas carol in three-quarter time. Another waltz.

Standing apart, holding hands at arm's distance, they looked at one another. *Shall we?* he intended to ask, but they stepped toward each other and resumed their hold without either one of them saying anything at all.

He had more important questions. Why was she here alone? Where was her baby's father? Why didn't she know how good pregnancy was looking on her?

Tana followed his lead smoothly, but she was lost in thought. Something about her struck him as fragile now, somehow. He felt entirely too protective of her once more—or still. The feeling hadn't really left him since the moment she'd fainted.

"Are you okay?"

She focused on him. "Just worried. Between the glowing and my bra size, I don't know how much longer I'm going to be able to keep this a secret."

"It's still a secret?"

Abruptly, she got all perky. "Yup. Wow, can you believe we're dancing to Christmas music already? 'Silver Bells,' and it's not even December yet. But Thanksgiving's over. I guess I can't really be outraged. It's not like when Christmas decorations are for sale before Halloween."

"I thought the faculty all took off for the whole week to go home like the students. Why are you in town?" He was fishing for information, and he knew it.

"This is the middle of swim season. The varsity teams have practice tomorrow."

"They don't get a vacation? That's some dedication."

"It is a lot to ask of kids, isn't it? The swimmers have to really want it. That's the commitment it takes to excel at this level."

"I take it your family is used to you missing Thanksgiving dinner with them."

"I went to Houston today. Ate the turkey."

Houston, where somebody lived who deserved to get the news face-to-face, she'd said in September. Caden turned them another 360 as he shoved the jealousy to the back of his mind. He'd kept the conversation light and friendly all evening. He could keep doing so until the end of this Christmas carol. How many verses to "Silver Bells" could there be?

"Couldn't he come back with you for the rest of the weekend? Is he a coach, too?"

"Who?"

"Your boyfriend. Fiancé. Husband?"

She gave him a dark look. "I don't need a husband, thanks."

She must have gotten in a fight with her man, then. Or maybe they'd had a fight a while ago. Had they broken up recently? Were they trying to make it work because they had a baby on the way?

Something was making her unhappy. Caden had known that all evening, and whether he ought to or not, he *cared*, damn it.

So, he did a 180.

"Tana, I've got to ask. Where is the father of your baby?"

Chapter Eight

Now *Caden* wanted to know where the father was, too?

A whopping four people in Tana's life knew she was pregnant, five if she counted the doctor, and every single one was so damned concerned about the father.

Jerry.

Jerry didn't deserve so much attention. He didn't deserve any attention at all, since he'd so effortlessly decided not to be a father. Men could do that: *I don't feel like being a parent. See ya.* Women were left to handle everything—and as they did, they were required to explain to everyone, every time, the reason they were alone.

She was not up for this conversation. Not again. Not twice in the same day. But Caden had asked, so Tana forced herself to laugh. "I have no idea where he might be. Does it matter?"

The song ended. She quit gladly, sliding her hand off Caden's shoulder—but he kept his arm around her and pulled her closer, as if she'd merely stumbled again, and he moved them into the next song.

It was a two-step, and she did stumble along for a few beats before she realized the rhythm had changed, *quick-quick, slow, slow*. The two-step was the most popular dance in every bar in Texas. It wasn't as athletic as a waltz. The hold was similar, but without big, swooping turns, couples could get as close as they liked. Some women even rested their heads on their partner's shoulders, like they were babies taking a nap, as they shuffled along, *quick-quick, slow, slow*.

Caden held her only close enough to speak quietly, no more. "Of course, it matters."

"No, it really doesn't." She forced herself to laugh.

The couple they passed looked at her. She'd sounded so unnatural, too loud, too shrill.

She moved closer, so she could speak into his ear, which made them dance practically cheek to cheek, but she wasn't whispering sweet nothings. She gritted out the truth through clenched teeth. "Everyone asks that as if he's important, but he's not. Nothing changes, no matter where he lives or what his name is. The DNA has been delivered, obviously. What does everyone think a man has left to do at this point? Hold my hand?"

Caden was holding hers out to the side at the moment, and she was squeezing it, hard.

She relaxed her grip. "Whether or not there's a man

out there to hold my hand is—it's—*irrelevant*. I'll have the baby, either way. The only thing that matters in this pregnancy is where *I* am."

Caden didn't falter. His arm stayed securely around her as they two-stepped with the crowd. She was dancing backward, but she didn't need to look over her shoulder. He was leading.

Instead, she glared at his ear, at his unnecessarily strong, perfect jawline. It was so annoying that the man was still taller than she was, despite her boots' heels.

Her rant had killed the conversation, but it hurt to hear Caden asking the same thing her parents had. It wasn't Tana's fault that she didn't know where the baby's father was. It was *Jerry's* fault. She shouldn't have to pretend she had it all together, that she'd planned this pregnancy, that she was taking it all in stride, *quick-quick, slow, slow.*

Caden was probably silent because, like most guys, he thought she was too much to handle, too driven, too bold. He would never go on a tirade like she just had. He was such a mellow guy. Friendly, always. A paramedic, a public servant, a caregiver—

"What kind of *son of a bitch* abandons the woman who's carrying his child?"

Tana jerked in surprise. He'd put more fury into that single line than she had put into her entire speech. Her anger came from a place of hurt and self-pity. Caden's anger had power behind it.

Power, strength—she'd had one hand resting on his shoulder for several songs now. His body heat had been warm under her palm, right through his shirt, as they danced. The muscle was rock hard, even when he was relaxed. If an angry Caden Sterling swung a fist, he'd deck his opponent.

It was impossible to imagine him picking a fight. Tana's first impression of him was too strong. He was kind to little old ladies. He was an encouraging, positive teacher. He'd used his hand to cushion her head from the floor, not to make a fist.

They turned at the corner. The momentum let her slide her hand along his shoulder until her fingertips brushed the back of his neck. He was a very, very strong man. It seemed at odds with him being a caregiver.

He's a protector.

The word resonated with her. Caden's hand spanned her lower back. If he wanted to protect someone with that hand, he could. He would. He *did*—he was a fireman. When someone was in danger, he jumped in. The arms that were holding her now also wielded axes and hefted ladders. That, she could picture.

Something fluttered, low in her belly.

"I'm sorry," he said quietly, gently, his voice low in her ear.

She wasn't that pitiful, was she? Her parents were disappointed in her for wasting her talent, and maybe Bob Nicholls was going to be disappointed, too, if he'd been hoping she'd make another run at the Olympics, but disappointment was different than pity. A pregnant woman with an ex who didn't give a damn about her? That was pitiful.

She tossed her hair back, but she kept her voice low, for Caden's ears only. "What are you sorry for? For cursing at some man who doesn't exist? I'm not an abandoned woman, carrying a man's child for him, as you put it."

But she was.

"I'm carrying *my* baby. For me."

Because she had no other choice.

Her confidence was paper-thin. She was facing the biggest of life events. Fear and anxiety threatened to swamp her. She wished she could rest her head on Caden's strong shoulder. Wouldn't it be nice to just give up?

She couldn't let herself do that. The one time she'd let a man take care of everything for her, she'd ended up in a dry, landlocked country. She needed to keep her own head above water. Trust no one's life preserver but her own.

"It's not like my situation is unique. Think about how many relationships go sour. People fall out of love all the time. There are a million single mothers out there who don't get any support from the father."

"Then there are a million sons of bitches out there, too." Caden sounded serious.

Tana wished she could laugh, but her father had addressed shotgun weddings just hours ago. "What should those men do? Marry women they don't care about? Should a woman be forced to marry him, if she doesn't want him?"

Caden gave her a *don't-be-ridiculous* look. "Even if you're no longer in love, you can still support the woman who's having your baby."

"Money?" Tana had first misled Ruby about sperm donors so that Ruby wouldn't push her to take Jerry to court for child support. "I'm the head coach at a university. I make enough money to support myself, and I can support a child, too. I don't need a man's money."

Not this year, but I have to prove myself this season, or else.

"There are other kinds of support." Caden stated it with finality, then he started to let go of her, his large, warm hand sliding off her back.

The song had ended. Tana held on to his shoulder more tightly, so he couldn't back up. "Wait. I want to hear this."

Caden sighed, but his hand returned to span her lower back, and they resumed their two-step to the new song. He kept a little more space between them, so they were looking at one another, not speaking urgently into each other's ears. "What do you want to hear, exactly?"

"I want to hear what kind of support you think a woman needs from a man, when he doesn't love her and she doesn't need his money."

He shrugged. "There's no set answer to that. Too many things factor in."

"Hypothetically, then. Let's say you knocked up some woman you don't really like. If she doesn't need or want your money, what else is there for you to do?"

"That's not ever going to happen."

Tana wanted to shake him in frustration. She didn't know why it felt so imperative, but she needed to know the answer. "No birth control method is one hundred percent effective. It could happen."

He seemed frustrated with her, too. "I meant I don't

have sex with women I 'don't really like.' It wouldn't happen like that."

"But you said—"

"I thought we were talking about people who'd once been in love, but the romance went sour?"

"Fine. You dated for a year, then, so you must have liked each other. You even said 'I love you.' Now there's a positive pregnancy test, and you find out she'd been planning on leaving you before the pregnancy happened."

"Then I'm pretty damned sad." He squinted a bit as he studied her. "Do I have a broken heart?"

"Does it matter?"

"Of course, it does."

He was being difficult. He probably knew there wasn't anything an ex-girlfriend could possibly need from him, just like Tana didn't need anything from Jerry.

"All right, then," she said. "You are not brokenhearted, because you've realized you weren't truly in love with her, either. This isn't about feelings, anyway. The clock is ticking. Nine months are going by fast. What kind of support is there for you to give this woman who never loved you, and you never loved?"

"I'm not her enemy, just so we're clear on that. We're not in love, but we're not enemies. We're going to be parents together, like it or not. We got along for a year. We'll find a way to keep getting along."

Tana imagined saying that to Jerry. *Look, you and I might never have been truly in love, but we got along for over a year, and now we're going to be parents. We shouldn't be enemies.*

She'd have to know where he was to say anything to him.

He'd cut her out of his life completely. He'd never sent her an address. She wasn't an ex-girlfriend to him; she was being treated like she didn't exist. Some of her guilt over misleading Ruby and her parents dissipated. What else could she do except pretend he didn't exist, either?

Apparently, Caden wouldn't cut off his hypothetical ex-girlfriend like that. "I want to give her whatever she needs so that we have a healthy baby."

"Like what? Be specific."

He shook his head, just an inch, at whatever he was thinking, then he pulled her a little closer. "We don't have to be lovers for me to give her a ride to her next checkup at the doctor's."

"She can't drive herself to the doctor's?"

He had danced them over to the edge of the floor when the conversation had taken its serious turn. They were marking time in place, out of the flow of dancers, so he didn't need to watch where they were going. He watched her instead.

She couldn't look away. His eyes weren't an icy blue. They were a warm blue, like a tropical sea, the loveliest water for a lazy swim.

"I would ask her, 'Do you need help assembling the crib?'"

His words shouldn't give her butterflies in her stomach. She wasn't a schoolgirl. He wasn't her hero. The way he'd asked that, though… She could imagine what it would feel like if he'd said it to her for real. It made her feel a little weak at the knees.

Weakness wasn't good in her situation. "She ought to be able to read instructions and operate a screwdriver. You wouldn't have dated a dummy, right?"

He didn't answer that, but the corners of his eyes crinkled a little in amusement. "Thanksgiving's over. Why don't I come over and get the Christmas tree down from the attic for you? Pregnancy klutziness is as real as that pregnancy glow. Anything else you need me to go up the ladder for?"

She blinked. She had an apartment. No attic—but it didn't matter, because he hadn't really asked *her* that. This was about a hypothetical woman. "She's got neighbors who can do that."

He didn't take his eyes off her. "I'll take the day off work for the sonogram. No neighbors allowed. It's a big day for both of us. We'll find out the baby's gender."

"No. Let it stay a surprise. It will give me something to look forward to during labor."

"Fair enough. Lady's choice." That little crinkling at his eyes looked good on him.

They were swaying now, like a couple of kids at a middle school dance. Her heart was beating harder than it had while they'd waltzed.

"I'll pick you up and drive you there," he said, "while you drink the ridiculous amount of liquid they require."

"They do?"

"'Fraid so. Abigail said they made her have such a full bladder, she could barely walk, let alone drive."

Tana's heart thudded. "Abigail?"

"My sister-in-law. The one whose pregnancies I know way too much about, remember?"

Tana nodded, but she had to look away from those blue eyes for a moment. This had been a terrible idea. Caden was showing her, too easily, the kinds of support she would not get, because Jerry was a terrible ex-boyfriend. Caden would have been a wonderful ex-boyfriend.

Had any woman actually broken up with this guy? If he was so thoughtful about ways to help out as an ex-boyfriend, she could hardly imagine what kind of boyfriend he'd be.

Let's not imagine that.

"Let's dance," Caden said, and the gentleness in his voice was a dead giveaway. He could tell she was sad. He was stopping their hypothetical conversation for her sake.

They two-stepped into the flow of dancers in silence. Tana had nothing to be sad about. Caden had done exactly what she'd hoped he would do. He'd proven to her that she was not missing out on anything by choosing to be a single mom. Jerry would never have done any of the things Caden had suggested. Jerry would never have thought of doing them in the first place. Therefore, although Jerry had cut her out of his life, it was no loss for her.

It was shocking to realize that she'd feel obliged to share her medical info with Jerry, if he still lived in Houston. He'd be a terrible person to have in the room during a sonogram. He'd make sarcastic comments about everything. He'd be bossy, and if he wanted to know the sex of the baby, it wouldn't matter to him if she didn't want to know.

She'd never been so grateful that Jerry had so utterly abandoned her. Thank goodness she was having this baby without him.

"Do you want to get some dinner?" Caden asked.

Tana scowled at him. His point had been made. "I don't think your ex-girlfriend is going to want to have dinner with her ex-boyfriend every day. She's still going to have her own life, you know. Her own friends. Her job. Being pregnant doesn't mean the rest of her life stops."

"I meant you, Tana. Let's take a break when this song ends. If you're not hungry, I'll buy you that cranberry juice you wanted back in September."

I don't need you to. I can afford my own drinks. I can walk up to a bartender and order anything I want, anytime I want.

But she didn't want to do any of that right now. She wanted Caden to be her ex-boyfriend, to be the man she'd gotten pregnant with, the man who would never be her enemy.

He wasn't.

She was on her own, and she had a fierce determination to be the best at motherhood. But while Caden kept his arm around her and held her hand, what she needed was a fierce determination not to cry.

Chapter Nine

He should never have started dancing with her.

Caden knew too much about her now. They'd laughed through one song, been serious through another, gotten testy with each other for a chorus or two. He'd called the father of her baby a son of a bitch. Not his best move, even if the man seemed to be a worthless piece of—

Well, that didn't matter. Since the worthless jerk was someone Tana had to co-parent with for the next eighteen years of her life, getting along with him did matter. Tana was obviously angry with her ex right now. Caden hadn't intended to throw fuel on that fire. That wasn't how he operated.

They moved in time to the music. Tana wouldn't meet his eyes, and he didn't know what else to say. He couldn't tell her that he'd be happy to assemble a crib, carry something heavy, give her a ride. *Her*, not a hypothetical ex. If she was busy coaching over the holidays, he could swing by the campus with something for dinner.

Or breakfast. He'd like to be the one who made this woman some breakfast while she sipped coffee on the couch, barefoot in her pajamas, her flowery-smelling hair still a mess from her pillow. From his hands the night before.

The clarity of that vision set off an internal alarm. He was going into dangerous territory there.

"I'm not thirsty," Tana said, with enough frost in her voice that he knew her thoughts were not running anywhere along the same lines as his. "We should probably quit after this song, anyway, before we give everyone something to talk about. When I start showing, that gossip could get uncomfortable for you. They'll assume... you know. That you're the father."

"Don't worry about that." With a woman like Tana, he'd take it as a compliment that anyone thought she'd slept with him in the first place. He'd be proud as hell to claim her as his.

That internal alarm got louder. He was letting too many feelings grow, too many fantasies take too firm of a shape.

The song was coming to its end. "I'm sorry if I hit a sore spot, talking about exes. I hope you two work things out." He meant it. She shouldn't be alone now.

"You don't work things out with a man who is nothing more than a sperm donor. I am sick of explaining that to my family. That's why I came here tonight, to get away from this exact conversation."

"A sperm donor?" Caden raised an eyebrow. He supposed that wasn't any more harsh than his use of *son of a bitch*.

She was silent for a moment, *quick-quick, slow, slow*. Then she tossed her hair back again and raised her chin, and all he could think was that she reminded him of that mare, the one with a spirit that couldn't be broken no matter how shabby her circumstances.

"You know, we're only acquaintances. I don't owe you an explanation of when or where or how I conceived any more than I owe my mother or my father one—my boss or my team—or—or anyone. I'm having a baby. Me. No one else."

In his experience, people got defensive when they were hurt and in pain. Her parents didn't sound supportive, that was for certain. Caden didn't want to be one more person criticizing her.

"You don't owe me any explanation. You're right."

The song came to an end. Normally, he would have stepped back and lifted their joined hands so she could finish with a twirl. Instead, they just stopped. Dead.

"Thank you for the dance." If she was trying to force a smile, she was failing. "I'm going to hit the ladies' room."

Caden touched his forehead as if he were wearing his cowboy hat, a silent cowboy *thank you* before she turned and walked away. *Stalked away* was more accurate.

"My turn." Ruby didn't give him a chance to say yes

or no. She put a hand on his shoulder and held out her other expectantly.

He couldn't force himself to smile any more than Tana could. Still, manners were manners, and he couldn't leave a woman standing on the dance floor with her hand in the air, no matter how poor her own manners were as she demanded a dance.

They two-stepped for less than two lines of the song before Ruby started talking. "You do know she's pregnant, right?"

Caden didn't answer. It was clearly not public knowledge, even among the small group around the table, but the zombie ballerina must be close friends with the sexy witch.

Caden two-stepped in a straight line, backward, so Ruby would be moving forward, the easier direction, in case she wasn't a good dancer. "I know she's pregnant."

Ruby studied him, openly skeptical. "Not a lot of bachelor dudes would spend their night out with a pregnant woman."

"We're just talking over drinks, all of us. Tana and I waltzed because we're apparently the only two people at the table who know how to waltz. Don't make it more than it is." That was good advice for himself, there. *Don't make more out of this, Caden.*

"It's just a little creepy for a guy to be hitting on a pregnant woman."

Caden glanced over his shoulder to make sure he wasn't backing into another couple. "I'm not hitting on her. She's part of the group this evening."

Ruby was a decent dancer, so he turned them at the

corner. Moving forward, he could return Ruby's glare with a deliberately neutral expression. *Nothing going on here, no major emotions to pick apart.*

"What is the message you want me to be receiving?" he asked. "If a woman is pregnant, I should ignore her? Does she stop being a real person? This is a night out with friends, and she's a friend."

"You're friends? She stormed off just now. You shouldn't piss off a friend."

Caden didn't need a lecture from someone who claimed to be her friend but who wasn't acting like it, not in his book. "And you shouldn't betray your friend's secrets. I knew she was pregnant at the CPR class, but if I hadn't known, then you would have just told me something I'm sure she asked you not to tell."

Next corner. Turn. Would this song never end?

Ruby didn't stay silent long. "I don't know if you know this, either, but…"

Caden didn't like the long pause, her effort to pique his curiosity. He wasn't going to play games where Tana McKenna was concerned.

"Don't tell me her secrets," Caden said tersely.

"You're pretty loyal to someone you've only met a few times."

Caden said nothing. *Quick-quick, slow, slow.* Surely this was the last verse of the song.

"So I'm not too worried if I say something you don't already know. You won't go blabbing about it." Ruby was watching him closely, wanting to get his reaction to whatever little bombshell she was about to drop. "But if you didn't know, there is no guy in the picture."

He kept his poker face in place.

"Just FYI," she added.

There was no guy in the picture? *Just a sperm donor*, that was how Tana had described him. It sounded like they'd had a pretty bad breakup.

Well, hell…

If the coast was clear…

He killed that idea before it could get going. Tana was not only on the rebound, she was on the rebound while pregnant. She had things to work out, a co-parenting relationship to form, if not a romantic reconciliation with her man before she gave birth. That would be the best thing for her baby. Caden could only get in her way.

"You two looked pretty into each other," Ruby said. "You seem like a nice guy."

Nice guys finished last.

Decent men didn't even start that kind of race.

Tana must have been suspicious that Caden was pushing the boundaries of *just friends* when he'd offered to buy her a drink. She'd probably been right, and she'd shut that down: *I'm not thirsty.*

"Obviously, there is a guy in the picture, or there recently was," Caden said. "They've got a powerful reason to work things out. The most powerful reason."

Ruby shook her head vigorously. "No, you don't understand."

"I understand plenty."

Tana had made it very clear that she didn't want his help. She didn't even want him to lend her a sympathetic ear. *I'm sick of explaining this*, she'd said.

The song ended. Caden raised their hands and gave

Ruby's waist a light push, too, so she'd twirl away a little more quickly. A little farther. He didn't care what the next song was, he was done dancing.

The DJ started "The Cotton-eyed Joe," a crowd-pleaser that filled the dance floor. Ruby got swept up by the incoming dancers, strangers linking arms as lines formed again. Caden headed for the table. There was only one other person there, sitting this one out. Caden nodded at him, sat and picked up his beer.

The song had an inappropriate but popular crowd response to the chorus. After each line, the crowd on the dance floor cheerfully shouted *bullshit* to the beat.

That fit his mood, but Caden wasn't going to go back out to the dance floor to shout it at the top of his lungs. He drank his beer and looked for Tana over the brown glass of his bottle, but if she was out there, she was lost in the crowd.

Not lost. She seemed like a woman who had a point to prove, either to the baby's father or to her parents. Caden couldn't begin to put himself in her shoes, but he could respect that she was a competent, successful woman, and she wanted to do things her way.

His beer was finished. Caden didn't want another. He could either sit here and stare at the crowd, or he could leave.

He headed for the etched-glass door. Tana had finished their conversation. She'd been fed up with his nosy questions, and he didn't blame her. There was no special spark between them, and he shouldn't try to start one.

They were only acquaintances.

The crowd stomped their boots and shouted, "Bull—"

Caden shoved the door open and headed into the night.

Chapter Ten

"Do you need me for anything?"

Caden grinned at the younger paramedic's obvious hope that the answer would be no. He finished his quick inventory of the medical kit. "Looks like I've got everything I need. Go."

"Thanks. I owe you." He took off, practically running, to go on a ski vacation.

Caden called after him. "Don't break your leg on the mountain. I'm not going to cover your shifts for six weeks while you laze around in a cast."

The new guy's flights had been changed at the last minute, so he'd called Caden in a panic, begging him to cover the last half of his shift, an easy standby at a sporting event. Every university athletic competition required an ambulance on site, so all Caden needed to do was hang out this Saturday, indoors and out of the cold.

Basketball? Courtside? Caden had asked. He'd at least get a great view of the game if he covered the shift.

No. Poolside.

Caden had said yes.

Coach Tana McKenna would surely be at the swim meet. He'd like to see how she was doing. Say hello, if they were anywhere close to each other. If not, that was okay. They were only acquaintances, after all, and Caden had any sparks, flames or burning desires under control.

It was the middle of January. He'd met a girl before Christmas at the town's annual yule log lighting. They'd hit it off well enough during dinner and a movie that they'd gone to another. He and Sarah weren't hot and heavy, but things were heading that way.

Keith had lost the bet that Caden would have Tana on his arm for New Year's Eve, of course. He'd had Sarah instead, and it had been nice to have someone to kiss at midnight. Sarah had looked good in her evening gown. Caden had worn a tie and jacket to her friend's party. There'd been no dancing, though. Maybe next date.

Caden shut the medical kit at his feet and leaned back against the natatorium's wall. So, this was Tana's natural habitat. The indoor pool was huge, fifty meters long, like the pools he saw on TV during the Olympics, but a massive divider split it in two today. In the far half, swimmers were randomly cruising back and forth, doing various strokes, warming up or cooling down.

This side had its red, white and blue lane lines running in the opposite direction. At the end closest to Caden, men in Speedos all stepped up onto diving blocks at the same time, shaking their arms out, pressing their goggles more tightly to their faces.

"Swimmers, take your marks."

A short buzzer blast sent them flying off the blocks into dives so shallow, they looked horizontal. They surfaced when they were already halfway across the pool and started butterfly strokes. Out and back, out and back, and it was over.

Caden looked up at the scoreboard. Forty-seven seconds? He'd barely had a chance to register just how much power was put into each stroke as the men scooped massive amounts of water out of their way. Televised swim meets hadn't given Caden a real sense of the amount of force involved. The winner pounded the water with his fist.

Cheers came from above Caden's head. The pool deck was for swimmers, referees and other people who had a reason to be there, including him. A balcony ran all the way around the building, however, with stadium seating for the fans. It was pretty full across from the diving boards and high-dive platform, which loomed over its own smaller, square pool, probably deeper than this one.

I'm the director for all the aquatics, Tana had said, on a September evening.

Caden was impressed. He'd been impressed then, too, but this was really something. The giant three-pool space formed a tiled echo chamber for buzzers, splashes and the school cheers he recognized from the Masterson football games. The noise level was as excessive as the amount of energy college students had to burn.

And their coaches?

Caden took a breath of chlorine-scented air and allowed himself to look for Tana. He'd *not* looked for at least five full minutes, because she wasn't the reason he was here today. He'd come to help out another paramedic and to hopefully *not* provide emergency medical care. That was all.

There she was.

She sat in a burgundy director's chair, clipboard in hand, her long hair held back from her face by a thick, burgundy headband. She was surrounded by young men in Speedos and young women in swim caps and goggles. The swimmers stood over her, listening avidly to whatever Tana was saying, as they dripped water on the deck in a semicircle.

Caden leaned a shoulder against the tiled wall and watched. Tana put her clipboard on a card table behind her chair, then held her hand out, palm down. The swimmers slapped wet hands on top of hers, building a tower on the foundation she provided. Caden could read Tana's lips easily as she said, "One, two, three." The swimmers shouted *Team*. The word bounced off the tiled walls, echoing all around, as the team broke their huddle and dispersed in all directions.

Tana reached back to retrieve her clipboard with a light smile on her face. Caden felt a smile tugging at his lips, too. This was a woman who was fully living, doing something she clearly loved to do, in a place where she wanted to be.

And she was beautiful, every bit as beautiful as she was in his memory of a waltz.

Honest to God, he wanted to find someone just like her.

Sarah was nice, though.

The splat of a body hitting the water, hard—like from the height of the platform diving board—echoed along with some worried *oh*s from the spectator gallery.

The diving looked a hell of a lot more dangerous than the swimming. He ought to station himself closer to that pool. He hefted the medic bag over his shoulder and walked past the row of starting blocks to the other side. He found a new spot on the wall to lean against. He was only a few yards away from Tana, but she'd have to look pretty far to the side to see him.

Caden decided to make it a point to say hello to Tana sometime today. It would be weird if he stood a few yards away and pretended he didn't see her. She was the coach. Hard to miss.

The racing lanes were empty. The diving must be break time for the swimmers, so this was probably the best chance he had to say hello to Tana without taking her away from her team. At the moment, one of her swimmers had all her attention, a tall girl in a swimming cap and a robe in Masterson's burgundy and black colors. He'd wait until they were finished. Watch the diving. Ignore the anticipation building in his gut.

"I know you didn't get the time you wanted," he heard Tana say.

"Reynolds beat me. I can't believe it. I lost to Reynolds."

"You did. You can't change that. It's time to get prepared, mentally prepared, for the medley relay."

"I went too deep off the starting block. I should have—"

"Cindy, listen to me."

Caden looked away from the diving to watch Tana.

"We'll analyze all that during practice. Right now, you have to compete. If you allow your brain to focus on a race you are no longer swimming, then you can't focus on what it takes to win the next race." Tana tapped her temple. "What's up here matters as much as anything else. Everyone loses sometimes. You have to put that loss behind you if you want to win again. That's a champion's mind-set. So, go find the other relay girls. Eat some fruit for energy. Keep your focus on your next chance to win."

"Okay, Coach."

"Before you do all that, give me a hand out of this chair." Tana held out her hand again, laughing, and her swimmer hauled her out of the director's chair.

Pregnant. Undeniably, visibly pregnant.

Caden couldn't have looked away if he'd wanted to. He didn't want to. She still had that athletic posture and energy from September, and she wore the same rubber-soled deck shoes, too. She hadn't lost that healthy pregnancy glow, but now she had a baby bump to go with it, a sweet little soccer ball under her loose-fitting top.

Something shifted inside him.

He got it. He understood his brother's near reverence toward his wife's baby bump, how he'd lay a protective hand on her belly when they talked. Pregnancy was a common, everyday thing, but Caden looked at Tana and realized it was extraordinary. How did women do it? They carried on as if there wasn't a major change happening to their bodies, to their entire lives. Tana amazed him, coaching her team, running a swim meet, creating a baby.

What man in his right mind would walk away from the miracle of her?

Maybe no man had. She and the father of the baby could have gotten back together. They probably had. They must have. No man could be that much of an idiot.

Another loud splat of a human body on the water surface jerked Caden's gaze away from Tana. That splat had the diving coaches halfway out of their chairs, but the diver surfaced and headed for the ladder with sure strokes.

I'm lifeguard certified, Tana had said. There were no ambulances parked outside during the workouts she must run daily, yet any sports injury that might happen on a playing field, like a concussion or a cramp, could be deadly underwater. Tana would be the one who'd have to jump into the water and haul an unconscious body out.

She was pregnant. Should Tana jump into the water to save one of her swimmers?

Caden watched her walk away. Another swimmer came up to her, talking a mile a minute with agitated gestures, and Tana put her arm around the woman's shoulders as they walked.

Tana would dive in for her team. Pregnant or not, Caden knew she would.

She doesn't have to today. I'm here.

But he couldn't be here all the time. He hoped she had gotten back together with her significant other. He hoped the man took good care of her. He hoped—

Caden scrubbed his hand over his face. That was as much as he could hope. Maybe they'd talk today, maybe they wouldn't. Tana was fine without him, and he was... doing okay without her.

Sarah was *very* nice.

He gazed around the swim meet, looking at nothing, looking at everything, looking for any distraction. He recognized one of the diving coaches as Shirley from the CPR class. Tana must be her boss, then. He looked at the banners that hung from the ceiling, declaring the years of the school's past glories in the NCAA, their regional and divisional championships. Painted on the wall, there was a list of Masterson swimmers who'd set pool records, school records, NCAA records. He looked at the blue water, at the bright red lane lines that—

Caden's eye went back to that list of records. *M. McKenna*, and *M. McKenna* again. And again. He read down the list. Another McKenna. Another. *Another.*

Montana McKenna had been their most prolific champion. Who better to coach the swimmers on a champion's winning mind-set?

Honest to—

Caden was never, ever going to meet another woman like Tana, and he was never, ever going to completely extinguish the torch he carried for her.

You have to put that loss behind you. That was a champion's advice.

He hadn't technically lost anything. They weren't in love. They'd never even kissed.

Caden just needed a little distance again, and he'd get back to the good life he'd been leading. Shifts at the fire station with his team. Days at the ranch with the rescued mare, with his niece and nephew, with his brother, who was even more in love with his wife as they raised their babies. Another date with Sarah.

Sarah *really* was very nice.

He just needed to get through the rest of this swim meet. The diving ended, eventually. Swimmers reappeared on the pool deck, slipping into the warm-up pool to do laps, or hanging on the lane lines to talk with their teammates. Tana sat once more in her canvas chair, a little bit closer to the pool than before. She'd never see him unless she looked back over her shoulder.

A relay must be next, because female swimmers clustered in groups of four around each starting block. The school-spirit chants ratcheted up as the first swimmer for each team dropped into the water and grabbed a silver bar on the starting block. Caden knew, from watching the Olympics on TV, that meant the first leg of the relay must be the backstroke. He saw the swimmer whom Tana had advised to focus on this race. She looked focused, all right. Fierce.

The cheers died into a silence so sudden, it was eerie.

"Swimmers, take your marks."

The buzzer cued an eruption of noise. Up and back—the backstroke leg was completed in thirty seconds. The moment the backstrokers touched the wall, the breaststroke swimmers dove in over them.

All the coaches were on their feet, including Tana. Each time a swimmer's head bobbed out of the water, the coaches gave a short whistle, setting a cadence. Tana had an impressive whistle. Caden found himself smiling a bit to see it, although he wondered how any of the swimmers knew which whistle was for them. The butterfly leg was next, then the freestyle leg, which had Masterson and their rivals neck and neck down to the finish. Everyone in the building was on their feet, shouting as the swimmers touched the wall.

Masterson won by a tenth of a second. The women, soaking wet, ran to Tana for a victorious group hug, soaking their coach in their enthusiasm. Tana was laughing, high-fiving, slapping her girls on the back, and Caden was assuring himself he was not falling in love with her.

Then the men took their places for their relay. Another moment of utter silence, another buzzer, another close race. Caden was almost too caught up to notice that Tana was a little winded after whistling her way through the breaststroke lap. He definitely caught the way she set one hand on her belly as she fist-bumped the victorious men's team, pushing them toward the cool-down pool. He got worried when she flopped into her chair. She reached toward the ground with one hand without taking her eyes off the busy pool scene, then waved her hand around a little bit, until it landed on a stainless-steel bottle. She picked it up and took a drink.

Good girl.

She was taking care of herself. Caden didn't need to

watch her like a hawk. He was not her rescuer, because she didn't need rescuing. On a dance floor at Thanksgiving, he'd seen that she was a successful woman who didn't want to be coddled. She was wildly successful, he realized now, and she didn't need to be coddled at all. Good for her. Really.

There was some discussion taking place between the referee and another person with a stopwatch around his neck. The next set of swimmers, women again, were keeping their jackets on and jumping in place behind the starting blocks to keep themselves warm. And Tana? She was nearly bent in half in her chair, patting the pool deck because her water bottle had rolled under her chair. Her clipboard went clattering from her lap to the pool deck. She picked it up fast, but the deck was wet, and Caden figured her papers were now, too. He heard her little growl of frustration.

He could keep his distance again after the meet. Right now, he wasn't going to watch a woman struggle to bend over her pregnant belly to reach the floor, no matter how cute her little growl had sounded. Caden pushed himself off the wall and headed toward her. She'd just snagged the handle of her water bottle with one finger, when her pen dropped off her clipboard and started to roll away.

She grabbed for it and missed. With a curse instead of a growl, she dropped the clipboard and abruptly sat up, smacked the arms of her chair to push herself to her feet, then whipped around, ready to crouch down and retrieve her things—but she staggered.

"Tana."

She looked at him, surprised, then her eyes rolled back in her head, and she fell to the pool deck.

Chapter Eleven

"There you are."

Tana squinted up at the silhouette of a man. His face was hard to see, because the industrial ceiling lights were bright beyond him. Why was she looking at the ceiling lights?

"You fainted," the man said.

She knew his voice. She'd recognized him, just before she'd—oh, crap. She had fainted again, hadn't she?

Her fireman was here again. Cradling the back of her head again.

She tried to smile. "Hi."

"Hi. We've got to stop meeting like this."

Very cute, that. She appreciated his warm hand cushioning her head, but her head didn't hurt. Her tailbone did. She must have landed hard on her butt. Water drops plopped onto her from above, one right between the eyes. She blinked.

"Coach McKenna!" Cindy stood above her, dripping wet and shrieking. "Oh, my God, Coach McKenna."

Tana made a calm-down gesture with her hand. "Shh…"

More girls arrived, their swim caps and clean faces blocking out the ceiling lights. "Oh, my God! What happened? It's Coach! What happened?"

"I'm fine." Tana made the effort to speak, because they were well on their way to freaking out. "Just dizzy. No big deal. I didn't hit my head or anything."

"Coach!" More water drops rained onto her face as young men crowded over her, too, their bare chests and shoulders blotting out more of the light. "Coach M!"

She looked at her fireman. They were stuck at the bottom of a dog pile, practically, a dog pile that was raining drops of water on them. She thought it was funny.

Caden Sterling wasn't laughing. There was no crinkle at the corner of those blue eyes.

"I'm fine," she said to him. Just to him.

"What hurts?"

Half her team was around them. She wasn't going to talk about her butt. "Nothing. I'm fine. I just stood up too fast." She'd better get up, so her team would quit worrying.

Caden kept her down with a firm hand on her collarbone. "Whoa. Let's not make the same mistake twice."

"Let me stand up slowly, then."

"Nope." He let go to hold her wrist and take her

pulse. His other hand continued to cup her head, a pillow for her instead of concrete pool decking. The bulk of his shoulders blocked most of the dripping water.

Someone set a heavy black gym bag next to him. Caden looked up at their audience. "I want everyone to step back. Two big steps." Ceiling lights came back into Tana's view. Caden jerked his chin at one of her six-foot-tall boys. "Give me your towel. Roll it up like a pillow." He lifted her head and tucked it under her, so he had two hands free to unzip the bag.

He took out a stethoscope, looked up at someone else. "Ref, how about a little privacy?"

The referee shooed the swimmers away.

The referee? That meant the whole meet had stopped when she'd fainted. Everyone in the building was waiting on her before they could get going again.

"Okay, I'm fine." She started to sit up.

"Nope." Caden put the stethoscope on her chest and pushed her back down with it as he listened for whatever medical people listened for.

Tana made eye contact with the ref, who was the only person left hovering over them. "I'm really fine. We can start the 400 medley in just a minute."

"Stop talking, so I can hear." Caden sounded a little pissed off. He moved the stethoscope a few inches, listened, then slid it around her rib cage to listen to her back, a sensation she suddenly remembered from before, at the CPR class. Then he placed the stethoscope on her belly, his fingers resting lightly on the rounded firmness of her baby bump.

That was a new sensation. His eyes were closed as

he concentrated. The fetal heartbeat—he was listening for the baby's heartbeat.

Suddenly, the swim meet could wait.

She was fine, she knew it, but now she wanted Caden to tell her she was, officially. Medically. She watched his expression, looking for any sign that he was hearing something abnormal, so she was staring right at him when he opened his eyes and stared right at her.

That warm, tropical blue—the loveliest water to sink into—she was so glad he was here. "Is everything okay?"

He nodded and moved the stethoscope to the side of her baby bump without looking away from her. God, those eyes. Everything about him was so calm. Calm and big and safe, a protector. Her personal protector, at the moment.

He took the stethoscope out of his ears but kept the part in his palm cupped against her belly. "Sounds strong. Do you want to hear?"

"I—I believe you."

A little crinkle appeared at the corner of his eyes. "You should. But you might want to hear for yourself, so you can breathe easier. You hold your breath a lot."

She put the earpieces in. It took a moment for her to sort out the unfamiliar sounds, but then she heard it, the rapid *whoosh, whoosh* of her baby's heart.

"Little hummingbird in there," she said, and Caden's professional calm eased into a genuine smile.

She handed him the stethoscope. He put it in his bag and took a radio off his belt, then turned to wrap his large hand around her ankle. She jerked her foot away without thinking. He held fast.

"What are you doing?"

"Checking your pulses." He let go and took her other ankle. She felt his fingertips seeking a specific spot, stopping, pressing.

"You never did that before."

"Pregnant ladies get special treatment." He winked at her, but into the radio, he said, "Michelle, we're going to need the gurney on the pool deck."

"What? No. My ankles are fine."

"They are, but you have to go to the hospital."

"*I'm fine.* I bent over too long, then stood up too fast. It makes me dizzy even when I'm not pregnant. My doctor knows about it. Orthostatic hypotension, okay? It has a name."

"I know what orthostatic hypotension is. You're still going to the hospital."

In a flash, she remembered the last time they'd spoken. On the dance floor, they'd started out just like this, all friendly. They'd ended up speaking to each other in quiet, angry tones.

"That's not up to you." She spoke through gritted teeth now, keeping her voice low. "Remember when you said I always have a choice in medical decisions? That glucose monitor? I'm making a choice now. I'm staying for these last two races."

"You have a choice, but there is a right answer. Go to the hospital."

"This is my *job*."

"Tana."

"I'm working."

Caden looked around. The ref was still hovering. Every eye in the place was directed toward them. With a sigh, Caden bent over her and slipped an arm under her back. She had the crazy idea that he was leaning in to kiss her, like she was Sleeping Beauty and he was a prince. Instead, he lifted her, so he could speak privately, quietly in her ear. "Your pants are wet. I don't know what's making them wet."

For a moment of mortification, Tana feared she'd peed her pants, but she hadn't. Blushing furiously, she whispered back. "Lying in a puddle on a pool deck, that's what."

"There's no way for me to tell whether it's water or amniotic fluid."

Her breath left her.

"You landed hard on your rear end. There's a very small chance you could have ruptured a membrane. Amniotic fluid could be leaking out."

No, no, no. But her tailbone did hurt, like it had when she was a child on roller skates that slipped out from under her, landing her on her butt on the hard floor of the roller rink.

Her heart pounded with fear, but she'd fallen that hard a half-dozen times in her life without any problem. Caden shouldn't be scaring her like this, over nothing.

"My shirt's wet, too," she said impatiently. "Only my pants would be wet if—if that was it. You're wrong. Your pants are wet, too, you know, from kneeling on the pool deck."

"You're probably right, but you need to go to a hospital."

"Half of my team is in tears already. They need to focus on their race, not on their coach being carted off on a stretcher. Can't you tell that it's water?"

Those warm, blue eyes could turn icy, after all. "No. Obstetric exams on a pool deck are beyond my pay grade. Stop fighting me on this."

A woman in a blue uniform came out of the locker room, pulling a massive yellow gurney behind herself. "Sorry it took so long. Had to figure out how to get out here."

"Nothing's wrong. It can't be. I'm only at twenty—" Tana gulped. "Twenty-six weeks. It's too soon. It would be too soon, if—"

"Tana." Caden placed his hand on the side of her face and turned her toward him, a touch that felt entirely personal. Entirely caring. "This is just a precaution. There's a ninety-nine percent chance that you're right, but I can't ignore that tiny one percent chance. You'd pay too high of a price if I let you walk away, and I was wrong. Go to the hospital. Prove me wrong. Please."

She didn't really agree, but he must have thought the way she was blinking back unwanted tears was a yes, because he lifted her to her feet. The uniformed woman pushed levers and lowered the gurney, so Tana turned and sat on it.

"My clipboard," she said flatly.

Caden handed it to her, then buckled a seat belt across her hips, under her baby bump. "Do we have to go out through the women's locker room?"

Tana pointed toward the door that led to the offices. "That hallway goes out to the parking lot."

Caden looked around. "Who is coming with you?"

"Aren't you?"

He introduced her to the woman. "This is Michelle. She's got you now. I have to stay on site."

Tana didn't want to be wheeled away from him. Everything in her protested. "But—she could stay. You could take me to the hospital."

"She's with a private ambulance company. I work for the city. We can't switch places." He looked around again. "Is there no one here to go with you?"

Caden was sending her off without him, and she felt scared, maybe sad. Nothing made her angrier than feeling sad and scared. She glared at Caden. "My assistant coaches have to stay because the meet isn't over, remember?"

"Are we ready?" Michelle sounded chipper as she raised a bed rail.

Caden started pushing the gurney. "I can call someone to meet you at the hospital. A friend? Your boyfriend?"

She was outraged that he'd even ask that. She'd told him at Thanksgiving there was no one. Since Michelle was speed walking with them on the other side of the gurney, Tana just glared at Caden in silence.

"How about your family?" His voice had changed to pity.

She hated this.

"What about your parents? Don't they come to your meets?"

Her parents hadn't come to anything for the past ten years. It was overwhelming, the loss she felt at the sudden memory of her parents' faces in the spectator seats, supporting her with their presence. Tana wanted to cry, but she couldn't, not now.

She hung on to her anger desperately. "Can you stop with the personal questions? My whole world is watching me."

The crowd started applauding as if she were an injured player being carried off the field. She waved with her best smile plastered on her face, the one that should have sold soup as she wore a gold medal.

The gurney stopped. Caden disappeared behind Tana's head. She couldn't see where they were going, but Caden must have been getting the doors while Michelle pushed her along with a too-cheerful smile. "Almost there."

They rolled outdoors. The asphalt rattled the gurney. She heard what had to be ambulance doors opening behind her.

"Hi, there." A man appeared at her other side. His uniform matched Michelle's, not Caden's. He pushed more levers, raising the gurney, bumping her into one of the ambulance's open back doors.

"There's no one, Tana?" Caden asked quietly, back by her side. "No one? How is that possible?"

She crossed her arms over her chest, warding off his pity. "I have people. They just aren't at this swim meet, so you can stop looking at me like that."

The gurney and Tana were pushed into the brightly lit ambulance. Michelle sat on a little bench in the back with her. The new man jogged out of Tana's vision, but she heard him shut the driver's door and start the engine.

Tana pretended she wasn't afraid as Caden stood in the parking lot below her. She had to look past her feet to see him and his strong shoulders, the ones upon which she could never rest her head and give up. She'd been divorced by one man, left alone as an unwed mother by another. She knew better than to jump in with a third, especially with one who looked down on her with pity, even as he stood on the pavement, looking up at her.

With a smile of reassurance that didn't fool her and a touch of his fingers to an invisible cowboy hat, Caden shut the ambulance doors on the woman he felt sorry for.

The baby kicked her, a good, strong, healthy kick. Tana hunched over and wrapped her arms around her belly. She wouldn't cry.

The sirens wailed all the way to the hospital.

"Masterson Hospital, how can I direct your call?"

"ER nurses' station. This is Lieutenant Sterling from MFD." Caden was put through directly. When a nurse answered, he gave his name and rank again. "I'm checking on a patient I sent there an hour ago. Montana McKenna, screening for preterm membrane rupture after a fall."

"Yes, no rupture. No fetal distress of any kind."

Thank God.

Caden cleared his throat. "Could you give her a couple of messages for me? I wanted to let her know her team won the relay races she missed at the swim meet. Men's and women's, both."

"She was discharged already, but great. Go, Musketeers."

"Discharged? How is she getting home? If she's waiting on a ride—"

"Her friend came rushing in here right after she did. She seemed really surprised to see him, but there were lots of happy tears, and they left together maybe ten minutes ago. I wheeled her out to his car myself. What was the second message?"

Tell her I can come for her. Just got off my shift.

But the offer wasn't necessary. Caden said all the polite, expected things as he thanked the nurse and hung up. At least, he assumed he'd said them. He was staring at the phone in his hand, and the call had ended.

Goodbye, Tana.

It needed to be for the last time.

Caden flipped through the contacts until he found Sarah's name. He should take her out tonight. That would be the best thing he could possibly do.

Sarah really was very nice.

He stared at the phone until the screen went dark.

Chapter Twelve

Tana's phone vibrated against the nightstand as its screen lit up. The combination was enough to drag her awake.

She opened one eye. The phone screen was obnoxiously bright, because her bedroom was pitch-black. It hadn't been when she'd lain down for a quick cat nap, exhausted from her cross-country car trip.

The vibrating stopped as the call went to her voice mail. Tana didn't raise her head off the pillow as she groped for the phone to check the time.

"Crap." She'd been asleep for five hours. Beneath the time, her phone screen listed one identical alert after another: *Missed Call: Coach Nicholls.*

Bob Nicholls was going to kill her. She'd promised to let him know the minute she arrived home, but she'd gotten to her apartment, walked straight to her bathroom—at thirty-seven weeks pregnant, she felt like she had to pee every thirty-seven minutes—and then she'd flopped onto her bed for just a quick minute, five hours ago.

She needed to call him, pronto. Driving home from the NCAA Championships in Indianapolis hadn't been as easy as she'd assured everyone it would be. One thousand miles in a rental car had been uncomfortable at best, even broken up over two days, but she'd done it.

She'd had no choice.

The airlines that flew where she'd needed to go were the ones that wouldn't let pregnant passengers fly after thirty-six weeks. Missing the men's NCAA championships wasn't optional for a coach who needed her one-year contract to be renewed. She'd flown to Indiana on Monday at thirty-six weeks. She'd had to rent a car to drive back to Texas on Sunday, at week thirty-seven.

She called her former coach. "I am so sorry."

"The last time I talked to you, you were in Arkansas. I was seriously going to call the highway patrol to put out an APB on you. What happened?"

"I got home and fell asleep. I'm fine. Just tired."

Actually, her ankles were swollen, for the first time in her entire pregnancy, from so many hours of sitting immobile. She hadn't been able to work out for the two weeks before all this travel, either. Tana had flown to Georgia for the women's championships the week before the men's. Tomorrow, she'd get back in the pool and swim some laps. That would put everything to rights.

Not really. Getting back in the pool and then getting a renewed coaching contract—*that* would put everything to rights. She hadn't heard anything from the athletics director yet. Her baby was coming, but her paychecks were ending.

"Well, you probably need the sleep," Bob said. "Congratulations again on your showing at the NCAAs."

"We didn't bring home the trophy." The trophy wasn't everything, but it sure would have helped impress her boss. He was big on trophies. Football trophies, especially.

"Appelan set a new record. Masterson swimmers were up on that winners' podium again and again. Don't underestimate the impact of all those second- and third-place finishes. Your school colors are in practically every podium photo. You'll have your pick of recruits next year."

Tana could practically hear her parents: *Silver and bronze don't get soup commercials.*

But Bob Nicholls wasn't her parent. He was her mentor and, this year, her guardian angel. He'd been in the spectator's gallery the day she'd fainted on the pool deck, unbeknownst to her. He maintained he'd come to see Shippers and Appelan compete, but Tana knew he'd come to watch her coach her team and run a three-college meet. As her parents had emphasized, he'd put his reputation on the line for her.

When she'd fainted, he'd apparently been frantic to get from the gallery to the deck level, but she'd been taken to the hospital within minutes. He'd followed, not as her former coach, but as the man who'd basically raised her from age sixteen to twenty. When he'd walked into the emergency room, she'd been so relieved to see a familiar face, she'd burst into tears.

In the months since the fainting incident, she and Coach Nicholls—Bob, now—had talked plenty. Tana had been right: he wanted her to coach future Olympians, not be one.

Unless you're driven to compete again, Tana. If you are, I'll bring you back to Colorado. You wouldn't be the first Olympian to win a medal after having a baby. I know you're tired of your parents comparing you to her, but Dara Torres—

I know, I know. DT had a baby between Olympics. Honestly, I'd rather coach.

Then Bob had said the one thing she'd most wanted to hear: *That's because you're a great coach. You've always thrown yourself wholeheartedly into what you're great at. I'm so proud of you. We're peers now, fellow swim coaches. It's time you started calling me Bob.*

Redemption.

No one at the international level bore her a grudge, although they did toward her ex-husband, according to Bob, for fraternizing with her. Her parents would realize she wasn't the black sheep of the swimming world that they thought she was. Someday.

In the meantime, Bob was doubling as her mother hen. "You're going on maternity leave now, I hope?"

"I only have office work this coming week. It won't be demanding." Her entire future rested on how well she wrote up her reports on the team's performance and her plans for next year. "I don't have a maternity leave.

My contract ends on graduation day, May fifteenth, and I'm due April twenty-third, so unless they renew me..."

She'd be jobless with a three-week-old newborn. Homeless, too. She lived in the junior-faculty apartments on campus. She needed her job to be eligible to continue living there.

"They'd be crazy not to keep you. I'd hire you."

"I'd work for you." But she'd have to leave Texas. Leave Masterson. Turn her young swimmers over to some unknown replacement. Say goodbye to the friends she'd spent a year getting to know, friends like Ruby. Friends like... Caden.

If she left Masterson, she would never run into a blue-eyed fireman again. She looked for him every time she went to the grocery store, every time she went out to eat with friends. She wanted to strike up a friendly conversation, like she had when she'd been dressed as a witch. Their last two emotional encounters were not the impression she wanted him to have of her, but she never saw him.

If Caden Sterling had wanted to see her, he could have volunteered to work another swim meet. He had not. Their friendship had been too new to take so much stress, perhaps. She might as well move to Colorado.

"I may have to take you up on that," she said.

"My budget wouldn't let me pay you for more than a measly part-time."

"Part-time pays more than no time." She put just the right note of humor into her voice.

"Don't worry. Masterson will renew you."

"Sure. I'm fine."

She'd survived the dreaded month of March. That was something. Tomorrow would be April first. Twenty-three days and counting until she had this baby. Twenty-three days to convince the university to extend her contract.

Tana hung up, then lay in the dark and worried about her future, until exhaustion pulled her under, and she dreamed about floating without a care in a tropical blue sea.

There it was, parked outside the diner: the swim-mobile.

The swim coach was here.

Caden put his pickup truck in reverse with a tired sigh. He'd just wanted to order a cup of coffee and a sandwich to go. He needed to get to the station a little early, because he was still in his civilian clothes. He kept a spare uniform in his locker for days like today. A meeting at his brother's ranch with a rescue group had run long, so he didn't have time to go to his house, get into uniform and make himself a dinner. The Stream-liner Diner was on the way into Masterson from the Sterling ranch. Its food was almost as quick as a hamburger drive-thru, and less greasy.

But Tana was here, so he shouldn't be.

Distance. A little distance was all he'd needed this spring to keep a healthy perspective on his relationship with Tana McKenna—or the lack of it. He thought he'd been doing well, too, but a couple of days ago, an April Fools' Day prank had forced him to stop kidding himself.

Javier's wife was expecting, for real. Javier had thought it would be a great prank to bring in a fake sonogram and announce it was triplets. Since triplets were usually born around thirty-five weeks, Javier had set a new due date that just so happened to be the exact date three of their coworkers were leaving for their annual hunting trip. Department policy gave paternity leave priority over vacations, so one of the guys would have to cancel his trip to fill in for Javier. The joke had been watching the three as each one hemmed and hawed and stalled, hoping one of the other two would step up and volunteer to take one for the team.

By the time Javier had said *April Fools'*, the coworkers had resorted to rock, paper, scissors, and Caden had calculated the due date for the director of aquatics at Masterson University. If she'd been twenty-six weeks at the swim meet in January, then she was due the last week of April, which meant she was probably around thirty-six weeks now, so if she'd been pregnant with triplets, they would have been born already, but she would have told him as he'd treated her on the pool deck if she was pregnant with multiples, plus she would have looked much bigger than she had, instead of having that cute little soccer-ball bump, and if Caden thought avoiding her all spring had made him forget about her, he was the fool on April first.

He threw his truck into Park again and shut off the engine. It was April third, distance was a failed tactic and he was on a tight schedule. He just needed a sandwich to go. If Tana was in a booth with her back to the door, she'd never see him standing at the counter. He wouldn't have to smile and wave and pretend he wasn't dying to see how she was doing.

He shoved his hands into the pockets of his jeans and crushed gravel under his boots with each step toward the stainless-steel doors. Tana fainted too easily. Some people just did, and it worried him. One glance, and he'd know if she looked healthy. He didn't have to talk to her.

He saw her right away. She was in a booth, facing the door. She could have seen him if she'd looked up, but she was absorbed in a conversation with the two people sitting across from her. She was all smiles, animated as she spoke. She looked good. Radiant. Beautiful.

He sighed at himself. "Just healthy."

The cashier tapped her pen on the counter. "I didn't catch that, honey. You want the health plate? That's a tomato stuffed with cottage cheese and dry toast. I'm an expert on what a growing boy like yourself needs. That ain't it." She winked at him suggestively. She was old enough to be his grandmother.

Who was he to judge what was inappropriate? He was practically drooling over someone else's pregnant girlfriend. Tana's hair was in a ponytail that bobbed a little with every enthusiastic gesture she made with her hands. She had a sporty kind of femininity, even pregnant.

He shouldn't be noticing things like that. "Turkey and provolone to go, hot peppers, no onion, and the largest cup of coffee you can sell me." He paid and stepped aside for the next person.

From this angle, he could see the two men she was

talking to. They looked related, a father and son, but the son didn't look old enough to be at Masterson yet. The father was talking, so Tana's ponytail was still.

Her hand suddenly went to her side, a motion that he'd report as *guarding* in medical lingo, the human instinct to put a hand on some part that hurt.

He watched her face. She was still smiling as she listened, but it was taking her some effort. After a moment, she relaxed.

"How many creams do you want, sugar?" the cashier asked.

"None, thanks."

Stop staring at Tana like a stalker.

He leaned against the bench by the door while he waited, but he didn't sit. If he sat, he wouldn't be able to see Tana.

I'm not staring at her. I'm glancing her way. Often.

She handed a booklet across the table to the teenager, a college catalog, or something similar in the university's colors. She was a coach. It didn't take much to figure out she was recruiting a prospective student.

It shouldn't be hard. Her swim team had killed it at the national championships. It had been in the paper, way in the back of the sports section. Swimming didn't get the attention of football or baseball. It ought to, though. As sports events went, the swim meet had been more exciting in person than he'd expected.

Then Tana had fainted, hitting the ground so hard, he'd been frightened for her and her pregnancy.

He glanced her way for the hundredth time. Something in her eyes told him she was concentrating on something going on internally, not on what was being said across the table. It couldn't be too bad, though. She was able to keep her smile fixed in place.

Real contractions were more serious, at least the ones he'd responded to as a paramedic. Those women had called 911 when they were too far gone to drive themselves to the hospital, unable to speak during the contractions, soaked in sweat. A few had screamed in pain as his team had whisked them off to the hospital, racing against Mother Nature. Those women couldn't have begun to sit in a booth at a diner and conduct any kind of student interview.

Tana wasn't in labor.

The paramedic training made him do it, anyway: he opened the calendar on his phone. Accuracy mattered in medicine. He'd only estimated her due date before. He flipped back to January and the Saturday of the swim meet. Week twenty-six. He started counting.

Tana laughed. He glanced up from his phone. She wasn't in pain, and he was a little too obsessed with her.

He finished counting, anyway, to today's date. Week thirty-seven. Still early to go into labor. There were probably plenty of other things that caused women a minute of discomfort in the ninth month. Once, he'd watched Abigail push on one side of her own belly with both of her hands to make the baby move, because she'd said he was kicking her right in the bladder.

TMI, dear sister-in-law.

But there went Tana, off toward the ladies' room, so her baby had probably been doing the same type of thing. Caden put away his phone as he watched her walking away. She was so much bigger than she'd been in January, it was stunning. How did women do it?

"Here you go, hon. Coffee, black, and a turkey-provolone. Have a good evening."

Perfect. He could leave while Tana was in the bathroom. She'd never know he'd been creeping on her. He'd gotten what he wanted, reassurance that she was well. She was still the successful, confident woman she'd always been. Good for her. Really.

He picked up the white paper bag. "How about a slice of apple pie, too? If you're not too busy."

"You got the money, honey, I've got the time."

Tana didn't return until Caden had paid for the apple pie and a second paper bag had been brought to the register. She hesitated, halfway between the restroom and her booth, and put one hand on her side. When she got to her booth, hands were shaken, words exchanged. The father and son passed Caden on their way out. The kid was too young to shave, but he was as tall as Caden, and he had that same lanky build as the swimmers on the pool deck in January. Definitely, Tana was recruiting, still working, three weeks before her due date.

Heck, the nationals had just been last week, and they'd been held across the country. It seemed like a lot of traveling for a pregnant woman, but what did he know? When Abigail had gone into labor with little Abby, she'd gone out to the barn and fed her horses before she'd let Edward drive her to the hospital. His brother still hadn't gotten over that.

Tana sat alone. Caden didn't bother trying to talk

himself out of it. He picked up his paper bags and walked over. "There you are."

She did a double take and stared at him.

"Mind if I sit down?"

"Hi. No. Go right ahead."

He sat and pushed the father's plate off to the side. "Long time, no see." *I stayed away as long as I could.*

"Yes. It's nice to see you again."

"You, too."

She seemed a little embarrassed to be talking to him, as she'd been at the pub over Thanksgiving. Sometimes former patients were that way when they saw him later. A broken arm never seemed to make anyone shy, but some other ailments might. Leaking amniotic fluid, for example—which she hadn't been doing. Thank God, again. He'd been so damned scared for her. He doubted he'd been able to hide it the way an emergency provider should.

He knew why it had been so difficult to stay professional. It was because the patient had been *her*, someone he felt too much for.

She spun her water glass slowly. "Can I say something serious?"

"Shoot."

"I apologize for my attitude at the swim meet."

"What attitude?"

"After I fainted, I was so mad. I told you to stop asking me questions, when you were just trying to help. I yelled at you to 'stop looking at me that way,' out in the parking lot, do you remember?"

Caden didn't know what he'd expected when he'd sat

down, but it wasn't this. "I remember, but you weren't yelling."

"I wasn't?"

"Not even close."

"I was so afraid I was going to cry. I couldn't, not in front of my team and my staff, so I couldn't let you give me any sympathy. It would make me feel weak when I was supposed to be leading a team. I hope you'll forgive me, because we started off friends, you know, back at the CPR class, but I've been so…really, everything's been so… I didn't mean to take it out on you. I just didn't want to cry in public."

"Tana, are you crying now?"

She was. An actual tear spilled from the corner of her eye.

He felt terrible for her. "There's nothing to cry about. You didn't yell at me. We're good, okay? Everything's good."

"Right when I'm trying to say that things don't have to get so super-emotional every time we meet, I cry." She wiped away the tear with one hand. "I cry at the drop of a hat now. It's the weirdest thing."

"You said a different pregnancy thing was weird at Thanksgiving." He wanted to remind her of more friendly conversations. They'd laughed, before.

She laughed now. "Oh, the bra budget is astronomical at this point. Frankly, every single thing about pregnancy is weird."

"Except the end result."

"A baby is a good thing. It meant a lot to me when you said that."

"Just stating a fact. I've got a niece and a nephew that are cuter than anybody has a right to be."

It felt good to be with her, so much better than trying not to see her, not to talk to her. She was a nice person. He should have let their friendship develop instead of being so damned scared that he'd fall in love with her. He'd thought so during that first waltz, thought he could be friends with the original while he prayed for her clone to come into his life.

If it felt a little too good to see her, he didn't dwell on it. He couldn't stay long, just a few minutes before he had to head to the station. What harm could this little talk do to his heart?

She wiped away fresh tears. "See? Even laughing makes me cry. It's weird, I'm telling you." She barely finished *you* as she sucked in a sudden breath.

Caden knew pain when he saw it.

She looked at the saltshaker, or in the vicinity of the saltshaker. She looked a little unfocused. Her grip on her water glass was so tight, her knuckles were white.

He set his hand on her wrist, trying not to be too obvious about checking her pulse.

She released her breath. Blinked. Relaxed her grip.

"What was that about?" Caden asked.

"Are you taking my pulse?"

"Busted. Compulsive pulse-taking is kind of an occupational hazard. Are you having contractions?"

"No." She seemed confident, but he'd seen what he'd seen.

"You sure about that?"

"I just saw the doctor on April first. He said these

were Braxton-Hicks contractions. Practice contractions. The baby's playing his little April Fools' trick on me. Or she is."

Caden relaxed a little. She'd seen her doctor two days ago about this. "He or she? You were serious when you said you didn't want to find out the gender on the sonogram?"

She hissed in another breath. She grabbed his wrist instead of the water glass this time. This grip, he recognized. A woman who'd been screaming with every contraction had grabbed him like that once. He'd been so relieved to pull into the ER and hand her off to the hospital. He'd heard she hadn't had the baby for another three hours after that. He couldn't imagine anyone being in pain like that for three hours. Abigail said it had been twelve for her. How did women do it?

Tana relaxed her grip. "The doctor said Braxton-Hicks can come and go like this from now until my due date."

She was supposed to go through this for three more weeks? That didn't seem possible. "But you're only at thirty-seven weeks."

She looked at him sharply. "Yes. How do you know that?"

Busted. "Just doing a little math from January."

"The baby might not come for two weeks after my due date. I might have a May baby. Five more weeks of this. Oh!" She sucked in another breath.

Caden let her cut off the pulse in his wrist as he casually looked at the watch on his other wrist. He knew what Braxton-Hicks contractions were. False alarms were a big part of emergency medicine. One caller had informed them after they arrived that she'd had a single contraction—an hour prior. They'd sent her to the hospital, anyway. He and his team were firemen, EMTs or paramedics, but they were not ob-gyns. If a woman thought she was in labor, he wasn't going to tell her she wasn't and then leave.

Caden wasn't going to leave Tana, either. He'd be late to work, but he could stay a while longer. They had their own station rules, a pirate code among themselves, and one was that a firefighter could be late by up to an hour for his shift if something urgent came up, but he had to buy a six-pack for whichever firefighter on the outgoing shift got stuck working that extra hour. More than an hour, though, and Caden would not only be screwing over a teammate, he would also be required to give the chief a damned good reason for being a no-show. No-shows got fired.

"The doctor said they're unpredictable. I had some this morning that were one right after another, but that stopped. So far, I think the longest I've gotten is maybe a twenty-minute break between them. I haven't had a decent night's sleep in—"

"Three days? You've been having contractions every twenty minutes for three days?" For the first time, Caden felt a frisson of fear. "You need to call your doctor's office."

"I was just there. April Fools', remember? Oh!"

Caden looked at his watch. The contraction lasted less than thirty seconds, but still…

"There's no such thing as a three-day-long April Fools' joke. Call your doctor."

She didn't look too pleased with his advice. "I thought there was always a choice in medical care. The glucose stick, remember?"

"There's also a right answer. Call your doctor. I'll wait."

Chapter Thirteen

Tana felt better, now that she'd walked out of the diner.

Caden had been insistent, so she'd called her doctor while standing in the parking lot. It was seven in the evening, so an answering service had taken her number. She'd paced in front of the diner, waiting for the doctor to call her back. Caden had paced with her. They'd both stopped when her phone had rung a couple of minutes later.

"What did the doctor say?" Caden asked when she hung up.

The call had been pretty useless. "He said it was unusual to have so many in a day, but not concerning. He asked if I tried changing positions to make them go away. You probably heard my answer."

Caden must have heard it. He'd kept a respectful

distance, but Tana had said *I've been sitting, stand-ing, driving, going to work and trying to sleep. Do you think I've been sitting in a chair in the same position FOR THREE DAYS?*

"It was a good answer," Caden said.

That made her feel a little better. "He said if it hasn't been worse than it was two days ago, then it's not likely to change tonight, either, but he'll check me tomorrow when the office opens at eight. If I want to get checked now, I could try going to an emergency room."

"Go to the—" He stopped himself in mid-command. "I think you should go to the ER."

"All they do is check to see if you're dilating. If, you know, things inside are…dilating."

This was the most mortifying conversation with Caden yet. At her appointment, the doctor had gloved up to reach inside her and poke at her cervix. It had hurt. He'd said she'd be dilated ten centimeters when she gave birth, but she was currently at a total zero.

If a fingertip pressing on a zero-dilated cervix hurt that much, she couldn't imagine how painful a baby's head pushing through a ten-centimeter cervix would be. She didn't want to find out. She had an appoint-ment on Thursday at the hospital to preregister for the delivery, including the optional epidural. As far as she was concerned, it wasn't optional.

She started pacing again, just so she didn't have to stand still and look a male acquaintance in the face and discuss *checking*. "I think I'll just go home. I haven't had a Braxton-Hicks since we walked out here."

Caden checked his watch. "That's only five minutes, so far. Do you live alone?"

Alone sounded so pitifully lonely. "I have my own place. I've got one of the faculty apartments on campus." She had paced the perimeter of her living room last night for hours, by herself and in pain. She wished they gave epidurals for Braxton-Hicks contractions.

"Would you like to have someone spend the night?"

She stopped. "You want to sleep with me?"

He blinked at that.

"Never mind," she said to the gravel at her feet. He was trying to be friendly with an acquaintance as she waddled around a parking lot, yet she'd reacted as if he'd propositioned her at a bar, acting offended—and a little flattered.

He was nice enough to ignore her goof. "Could your mother come? How about Ruby?" He paused. "The baby's father?"

The damned tears started again, and she dashed them away with her sleeve. "Let me guess. This is one of those things you'd do for your ex-girlfriend. You'd sleep on her couch for three weeks before her due date, just in case she goes into labor when she's home alone. Seriously?"

As soon as she asked it, she realized it was exactly what he'd do. Lieutenant Caden Sterling would have been the most wonderful ex-boyfriend in the world, but he wasn't her ex-boyfriend. He wasn't even her friend. She'd finally gotten the chance to apologize to him, but acquaintances didn't become friends in fifteen minutes.

She wished she'd run into him sooner, like in January. They'd be better friends by now, and she wouldn't keep putting her foot in her mouth—or at least they'd be able to laugh when she did.

Neither of them was laughing now. Her throat felt tight and her nose felt clogged, because, for once, the tears weren't some hormonal anomaly. She genuinely felt sad, because she didn't have him, or anyone. "I told you there is no father. I've told you and told you. Please quit asking me that."

"I thought… Okay, but who came and got you at the ER back in January? Could he stay with you?"

She sniffed in as hard as she could, so that she wouldn't cry, and her nose wouldn't run. "That was my old coach. He's in Colorado. How do you know about that?"

"I called to check on you that day. See if you needed a ride home. I was glad to hear you were right, and I was wrong."

That did it. A huge sob escaped, then another, and she had to slap her hand over her nose and mouth. "I need a tissue."

Caden pulled a napkin out of his to-go bag and tried to get her to smile. "Ta-da. A friend in time of need is a friend…"

"Indeed." She scrubbed the napkin under her nose.

She felt weird. Antsy. She wanted to be moving. Walking. Anything.

She headed to her car. "I'm going home. I'll call 911 if anything changes."

Caden matched her strides easily. She wouldn't win any speed-walking prizes with a ninth-month baby bump.

"Do you know what will happen when you call 911?" he asked conversationally. "I'll show up at your door with two other firemen, because we usually beat the ambulance, and we'll have this exact conversation again. Javier and Keith will not be thrilled."

"You're working tonight?" She gestured toward his plaid Western shirt, the cowboy kind with the pearlized snaps up the front. "You look like you're going to a ranch."

"I'm coming from one. I stopped here on my way to the station."

"I didn't realize firefighters did the…" She started to wave her hand toward the crotch of her black leggings, then thought better of it. "You check to see how many centimeters…if, uh…?"

"I don't. I provide transport to the hospital, where they *do*. Let's save ourselves all the hassle and go to the ER now. I'll drive."

The contraction hit her then, right as she was walking. It was big, a force that was pressing down so hard it was a struggle to stay standing. Caden caught her close with his arm around her, a crazy waltz position, right here in the diner's parking lot. She clung to his strong shoulder as the pressure tried to send her to her knees. It was so intense, relentless—and then it stopped.

She gasped for breath.

"This time, you don't have a choice," Caden said.

She nodded. "The right answer is *yes*."

As he drove, Caden looked at the endless stretch of empty road ahead, at the clock on his truck's dashboard, at Tana as she sat beside him. She looked serious, but she wasn't in pain at the moment. It had been four minutes since the last contraction.

Caden kept one hand on the steering wheel, but he held out his other, just in case she wanted to hold it. He wished his pickup truck had lights and sirens. He wished the hospital wasn't halfway to Austin. He wished County Road 89 didn't wind through empty cattle country.

Don't panic. She had just one big contraction, almost five minutes ago. You have plenty of time. Hours and hours.

Tana took his hand. "The baby can't come today. I'm only at thirty-seven weeks. It's not ready yet. It can't come for twenty more days."

"It's okay if he does. Or she does. Thirty-seven weeks is far enough along. Everything is good." Caden remembered that from his training. The survival rate for babies born after thirty-six weeks was very high.

The survival rate. His heart squeezed in his chest.

Tana squeezed his hand and braced her other hand on the window, palm flat, as if the contraction was trying to knock her sideways in her seat. Caden counted silently until she relaxed. Fifty-five seconds. Four minutes apart.

"I think this is real labor," she said. "I'm scared."

You and me, both. "Why don't we call your Lamaze coach? It might be less scary if you could talk to them. They should start heading for the hospital now, too."

"I don't have one yet." But the next contraction was already building, so she rushed the rest of her words, pain sending her pitch higher and higher. "I'm doing the all-in-one-day Lamaze class on Saturday."

I doubt that.

"I don't know who to ask. My mom lives too many hours away, and Ruby's not into babies—" By the time she got to Ruby, her voice was a squeak. "I should have asked Shirley. She's had babies, but I didn't want to bother her, because she's got babies that need her and oh, my God, this is—"

When the contraction ended, she wiped at her eyes with the napkins from his apple pie, and she began to cry in earnest.

His heart broke for her.

"I don't have anyone. I'm scared."

"You have me. Do you hear me? You have me. Everything's good."

He paid attention to the road, but he could feel the way she was staring at him.

"You're not dropping me off?" she asked, sounding surprised. "You're staying this time?"

This time. Caden hadn't meant to let her down in January, but there'd been no way to go with her.

"Please stay. I want you to stay."

His heart gobbled up those softly spoken words, greedy to hear that she wanted him by her side, if only as her friend. Right now, being her friend felt more important than anything else.

"I'm staying. We'll tell everyone I'm your Lamaze coach, so they won't ask me to leave. I won't leave you, even if they do."

"Promise?"

"Promise."

"I can't imagine how a Lamaze class could possibly prepare you for this. This—*oh!*—is—so—intense." She squeezed his hand. This time, she gave a short shout with the contraction, not a scream, but the sound of exertion, like an athlete hurling a javelin, a volleyball champ spiking the ball. *"Haa."*

She gulped some air as the contraction ended. "How much farther? I want an epidural."

I would, too. He couldn't be the first man to both admire a woman's fortitude and simultaneously think *Thank God, I don't have to go through that.*

"We're halfway there. We have lots of time. Your water would break before you could actually push the baby out." When responding to an intrapartum call, they were to put sterile absorbent pads on the gurney before seating the patient.

Tana was silent for an eternal minute. He took his eyes off the road for a quick glance at her face.

As another contraction built, she spoke in bursts of quick words, taking little breaths between them. "Maybe it did. At the diner. In the bathroom. I didn't know. I thought—it was a lot—a lot of—pee. Just pee—just weird. More weirdness. Sorry."

Caden drove on, forcing the fear down. They had time. If not, he had some experience. He'd gotten to a caller's house minutes after a baby had been born. Once. The baby had been breathing and crying. The mother had been talkative and happy, the father had been in a daze, but Caden hadn't been there during the delivery.

They had time.

Tana braced her hand on the ceiling and gave a javelin-throwing *haa*.

Or not.

"Are we going to make it to the hospital?" he asked her, a respectful request for information. It was time for him to focus.

She shook her head wildly. "No. I think it's coming out. It can't. It can't—*haa*."

"Okay. Good. Everything's good."

Caden pulled off the road. He got out of the truck, so that he could yank his go-bag from behind the bench seat. Everything seemed to be moving in slow motion, in a good way. He felt focused, able to think. *Don't drop the baby.* That was the most important principle they'd been taught, years ago. The baby would be slippery. They were to instruct the woman to lie on the floor, so there was no way the baby could fall and jerk the umbilical cord, tearing placenta free.

He wasn't going to have Tana lie in the dirt on the side of the road, that was for sure. He'd catch that baby before it could slip off his truck's leather bench seat, as if his life depended on it.

It did. If Tana's life and her baby's life depended on it, then his did.

"I can't have a baby in a truck," Tana said breathlessly. "I have an appointment next week for the hospital preregistration. It's not real labor."

"Okay, baby, but can you turn sideways for me? Put your feet right here where I was sitting." He didn't know why he was calling Tana *baby* when she was having a baby, but he wanted to get her away from the edge of the seat.

"It's coming," she cried. She sat sideways on the bench with her back against the door, one hand braced against the dashboard. She only had one hand free to tug on the elastic waistband of her stretchy pants. "Help me."

"Okay, baby. There you go."

Ironically, he had baby wipes in his go-bag, because they were good for decontaminating the skin after fighting a fire. Every fire released toxic particles, so their policy was to wipe off their skin before they drove back to the station to shower more thoroughly.

He opened the wipes and cleaned his hands. They were shaking, but he felt pretty calm, considering he didn't know what the hell he was doing, and neither did Tana.

"*Haa.* The head, oh, my God, I feel the head."

Damn, this was it. He wanted to wipe off the seat first. It couldn't be clean enough for a new baby, but the wipes left the leather more wet. More slippery. "Wait! I have a blanket."

"Wait?" Tana glared at him while panting. *"Wait?"*

He dug behind his seat for the blanket he kept in case the truck broke down in winter weather. Firefighters tended to be overprepared like that. The baby wouldn't go sliding across a blanket, he hoped. "Lift your hips a little, baby. There you go."

Tana was silent now. With her eyes closed, she concentrated as she pushed. Caden stood on the running board and leaned into the cab. He wrapped his hand around her ankle, just to hold her, not to take her pulse. He didn't need to; she was as alive as a human could be. He watched her face and felt humble.

"The head," she breathed.

Then he had a baby's head in his hands, warm from its mother's body, a surreal feeling.

Tana was silent, so he spoke softly. "Keep pushing, baby. Let's find out if it's a girl or a boy."

In a rush, the whole baby slipped out, right into his hands, the most incredible thing that had ever happened in the universe.

"The baby." Tana no longer sounded frightened. She was incredulous. "Look. There's the baby. The whole baby. It's out."

The baby looked so peaceful. Caden hated to wake it, but newborns were supposed to cry, and he was supposed to help. He held the baby chest-down in his palm and rubbed its back briskly.

The baby took its first breath and cried its first cry, and Caden knew that if his own life ended at this second, he would feel he'd lived long enough.

The baby sounded so indignant. Caden laughed in relief, laughed in gratitude that the birth had gone like it was supposed to—except they were in his truck.

He relished his role as the announcer: "It's a boy."

"He's so beautiful. He's perfect. Oh, let me have him."

"He's slippery. Here." It was an awkward reach to place the baby on Tana's chest, because Caden was only halfway in the cab, but she settled her baby onto herself as she told Caden to look at his eyes, look at his face, look at him, look at him. It was unbearably sweet, that litany of motherly love.

Caden hated to interrupt, but he had to. "We need to dry him off. He'll get cold."

Baby wipes wouldn't do the trick, and Tana was sitting on the only blanket. Caden backed out of the cab, unsnapped his plaid shirt with a quick yank, and shucked it off his shoulders. "Here we go."

"Get in. Shut the door." Tana struggled to sit up and move her feet off his seat.

Caden stopped her with a hand on her ankle again. "You stay put. Stay just the way you are."

He was aware the umbilical cord was still attached. There was something about keeping the baby and mother above or below or beside each other, but that clear sense of focus had fled, and he was lucky he could think of his own name right now. Tana and the baby seemed to be as comfortable as possible in the situation. He didn't want to move them.

"I want you to be in here," Tana said, and he was amazed she could sound so normal and speak so clearly after performing a miracle. Even more amazing, she was thinking about him. "Don't stand out there and shut me in here. I can move so you have room."

"Stay as you are. I'll come around to your side."

That was how Caden found himself with Tana in his arms once more. He sat with the hard door against his back, so Tana could rest her back on his bare chest. The baby rested on her chest. The plaid shirt was tucked all around the baby to keep him warm. Caden finished his call to 911 and dropped the phone onto the floor, so he could wrap his arms around them both, woman and baby, keeping them warm, keeping them safe.

They were his. At this moment in time, they were his to have and to hold, in the cab of a truck on the side of a road. He didn't want the ambulance to come.

"Are you okay?" Tana whispered.

"Everything's good."

"It really is."

They were quiet for a moment, and then Caden ducked his chin to see her, and she turned her face to see him, and the moment their eyes met, they started laughing, really laughing, big, genuine laughs. Caden wasn't sure why, but they laughed like they were little kids who'd gotten away with some crazy candy caper. They'd fooled all the adults and pulled off some wacky stunt.

"We did it," Tana said. "Can you believe this? We did it."

"Yeah. Let's not do it this way again, though."

She rested her head back on his chest, so she could keep looking at her baby, but she talked to Caden. "You didn't fool me, you know. You kept saying *everything's good* when everything was out of control. What a funny thing to say."

He rested his cheek on top of her head. "Everything was good, though, or we wouldn't be sitting here right now. It wasn't as funny as you telling me it was a baby, like you hadn't expected a baby to come out. 'A whole baby,' you said."

"I still can't believe it. He's here. He's a real baby.

Look at him. Look at his little ear. Look at the tiny nose…"

Caden listened and fell completely, deeply in love. She was the woman of his dreams, and he'd known it from the first. He wasn't going to wait for a woman like her to come into his life, because that would never happen. There was no other Montana McKenna.

She'd insisted she didn't need a man during her pregnancy. She'd started that pregnancy without a relationship, deciding she wanted a baby without a man at all. She didn't want romance.

But she'd wanted to be friends with him, apologizing over nothing so he might like her better. Friendship was what she needed, for now. He loved her, so he would be that friend for her.

But someday soon, Caden was going to try to win her heart.

"Oh, look, Caden. Look at his little mouth. It looks like he's smiling."

She already had his.

Chapter Fourteen

The baby was sleeping.

The nurse had wrapped him up in a blanket like a little burrito, and the baby seemed to be most content that way. Tana was most content when she held him, which was why she hadn't let him go, not since Caden had left them in their hospital room.

Firefighters couldn't skip work or call in sick, she'd learned. Another firefighter who'd already worked for twenty-four hours had covered for Caden until midnight, though, a woman firefighter who had her own children to go home to, and Tana was grateful for her generosity. At midnight, like some kind of firefighting Cinderella, Caden had left the hospital to go to the station.

Tana had made her first attempt at breastfeeding,

then fallen asleep for a few hours, but she was up now, feeling like she had enough energy to swim ten miles and set ten world records while she was at it.

Ruby had come early, before work. She was tiptoeing around, filling the room with balloons and flowers.

"You don't have to be so quiet," Tana said. "He's sleeping pretty hard. You, um, you didn't want to hold him, did you?"

"He looks cute, but I don't want to wake him. They aren't so cute when they cry."

Tana was relieved. She'd barely been able to stand it when the nurse had taken the baby out of her arms to take his temperature.

Ruby sat on the foot of the bed. "Now tell me everything. I want every gory detail."

"So, I was at the diner, the one outside of town, interviewing this scholarship candidate from Dallas. He's got a fantastic backstroke. I think he could fill the gap when Appelan graduates."

Ruby made a *hurry up* gesture.

"He left, and then Caden Sterling just walked up out of nowhere and sat down."

"Caden Sterling? As in, Mr. Hot Buns at the grocery store? As in, Mr. Waltz-with-only-you-all-night?"

"As in, the paramedic who has treated me twice now for fainting. I think he was checking on me to make sure I wasn't on the verge of fainting again."

"Huh. Okay."

Tana told Ruby everything, every detail she could remember, because it made it seem more real. If it weren't for the baby in her arms, she'd think it had been a crazy, vivid dream.

Ruby's jaw dropped open and stayed open as Tana finished her tale. "Caden Sterling delivered your baby? On the side of the road, in the middle of nowhere? Good gravy on a biscuit. He was already the world's hottest CPR instructor. Now he's…" Ruby waved her hands around, at a loss for words. "It's enough to make a girl think about having a baby. Almost. Not quite. But still… there's something very sexy about a man who can handle any kind of emergency."

Tana rolled her eyes. "There was nothing sexy about it, believe me. Not for a moment."

She meant it, but her brain instantly popped up the image of Caden stepping back and ripping off his shirt for her baby. It had a vibe like Clark Kent ripping open his shirt to reveal he was Superman. She might want to think about that later, when she wasn't feeling all bloated and swollen.

Then he'd climbed halfway into the truck, leaning over them with his shirt in his hand. He'd been bare chested, a very masculine body in motion. She'd been aware of that aura of strength as he'd held himself above her, taking his time as he used his own shirt to dry her baby. She'd felt so grateful that he was sheltering her when she was so vulnerable. *Sheltering.* Not sexy.

When she'd wanted him to stay with her, he'd walked around the hood of the truck to her door, bare-chested in low-slung blue jeans in the golden light of the setting sun…

Eye candy. She hadn't thought about it at the time. Leave it to Ruby to point it out.

Tana was in a new phase of her life now. Sometimes, a man with a bare chest in blue jeans was just a man with a bare chest in blue jeans.

Not when it's Caden.

Her parents arrived.

"I can't believe you're here," Tana said, which made Ruby look at her funny. Of course, her parents were here, but it was only eight in the morning. They must have left Houston before dawn and rushed here to see her, like normal, proud parents.

Ruby left, and Tana sat, propped up in her hospital bed, beaming at her parents. They were supporting her, they were interested in what she was doing, they were *here*. And, for once, she hadn't failed them. She was holding a real baby. She'd done it!

As she told them the story, they seemed a little appalled at how she'd done it, though. Her mother sank slowly to perch on the hospital's vinyl rocker-recliner. Her father stayed standing in the corner, but he didn't say anything. He looked a little seasick, actually.

There was a quick knock at the open door, and Caden himself walked in, wearing the dark blue uniform he'd been wearing at Halloween. Her already-happy heart just about burst with extra happiness to see him, her friend, *the* friend who'd been there during the most amazing part of her life.

He stopped short when he saw she had company. "Sorry. I can come back."

"No, come in. These are my parents." And to them,

"This is my friend, Caden. He's the one who delivered the baby."

He came in with a polite nod to her parents, but he was too far away, and she was too excited to see him. She kept the baby snuggled close as she reached out her hand for Caden, wiggling her fingers as if he couldn't see it. He didn't have much choice except to put his hand in hers. She tugged him to sit on the wheeled stool right beside her bed, then let go. She was so excited, she needed her hand to talk.

She spoke to her parents as she gestured toward Caden, ticking off his roles on her fingers. "He was my Lamaze coach, my labor nurse. The doctor and the chauffeur. The baby catcher. The blanket provider. My personal recliner while I tried to come back down to earth and let everything sink in. He was my every-thing."

By the time she'd ended her list, she was looking at Caden, not her parents. He was leaning toward her and she was leaning toward him over the bed rail, and she could have bumped noses with him, if she'd wanted to. She felt so giddy, she was just barely adult enough not to do it.

"You were a very calm cheerleader," she said. "I was pretty freaked out, but we did it, didn't we?" She tilted her head and studied him closely, this man who had been there for her.

He looked happy. A little tired, perhaps, but the over-head lighting was harsh. It revealed his five-o'clock shadow at eight in the morning. He'd been working all night, but he was happy to see her. He'd come here just to see her.

"Thank you," she said. "I would have hated to do it without you."

"I'm thanking you. I'll always thank you." His voice was as warm as it had been last evening. "I got to witness a miracle, up close and in person."

"You did have a front-row seat. Your front seat, literally. You couldn't witness anything any closer than that." It was a silly thing to say, but she felt too bubbly to be serious for long.

Caden grinned at her. "Everything was good."

"Everything was good," she agreed, and then they laughed, because their little inside joke was hysterical.

Her father made a choking sound.

Everyone looked at him.

He coughed and choked some more, turning his back to them.

"Dad? Are you…are you crying?"

"I just—" He lifted his head and took a deep breath, then turned around and headed toward Caden with his hand stuck out for a handshake.

Caden came to his feet while her dad pumped his hand up and down. She'd never seen her father so emotional. Never, not even when she'd set that world record in Singapore. Her parents had been there, halfway around the globe, although they hadn't made any of the meets in Houston or Masterson in the ten years since then. But they were here now, and her dad was clearly losing it, which meant he loved her despite his disappointment in her.

"Thank you. She told us her intention had been to drive herself home. I can't stand the thought that she could have been alone, behind the wheel, stuck in traffic. God knows what could have happened. She could have passed out or crashed or any number of horrible things, but she wasn't alone. Thank you. Thank you."

Caden let her father keep pumping his arm up and down. "She would have done anything she needed to do. You should have seen her. She was so focused. She was amazing."

Her father shuddered. "No, thank you. I'm not good when I see things like that. When she said her friend was cool, calm and collected, I didn't expect you to be such a man's man. A fireman. Real men pass out during childbirth, right? I did, anyway. Hit the floor. God bless you for not passing out. You must be very tough." He pumped Caden's hand some more.

Caden glanced at Tana, a little helpless, a little amused. "Well, I'm a paramedic, as well, sir. Nothing medical has made me pass out yet. Certainly not a healthy new baby."

"God bless you for being a paramedic. God bless every paramedic. God bless you for taking care of my little girl in her time of need. Thank you." He placed his other hand over theirs and started a two-handed sandwich handshake.

"Dad, you're being so sweet. Let go of him now, okay?" Tana patted the bed rail where Caden had been a moment before, wanting him to come and sit beside her again, so she could talk to him without her parents listening to every word. "Are you off work now?"

"Not until seven tonight. I'm here on official business." He showed her a folder of paperwork that he'd kept unwrinkled in his left hand. "I have to submit the birth certificate. I just need a few pieces of information and your signature. My team is downstairs. We're going to deliver the paperwork to the registrar in style, in the engine. They're claiming him as a firehouse baby, because he was born during their shift. I didn't have the heart to point out that you and I were nowhere near the station."

"But you *are* a fireman. My dad sure is glad about that."

Caden leaned in closer to her and turned his head to look out the window. "Good, you can see the parking lot from here. When we leave, we'll come around this side of the building and flash the lights. It'll be my team's way of saying hi to the baby."

"That sounds so fun." They were cheek to cheek again. That seemed to happen one way or another, every time they were together.

Her dad asked her mother when she wanted to get lunch. Tana hoped her dad would keep talking to her mom, so she could keep Caden all to herself.

"I didn't know firemen filed birth certificates."

Caden stopped looking out the window and looked at her, instead. "Rarely. Since I delivered him, I get the honor. The form gives me a bigger signature block than you, I'm afraid. Smack in the center. Everyone wants to give me credit. You did all the work."

They grinned at one another again. If this was a postpartum endorphin high, she was all for it. "So, what do you need to know for the certificate?"

"The baby's name, for one thing."

"Oh, yes." She sat up straighter and scooted back on the bed, still holding her baby close. Just hours ago, the baby had been inside her, part of her for months. It seemed only right to continue keeping him against her now. "Dad. Mom. It's time for the big reveal."

Caden looked at her parents in surprise. "She hasn't told you the name, either?"

"Is everyone ready for this?" Tana held out the baby bundle, just a little distance away from herself, and she pulled the blanket away from his chin so they could see him better.

He squiggled a little bit and got his fist out of the blanket, his tiny, wrinkly, adorable fist, and set it against his own cheek. It was an amazing thing for him to do. Tana snuggled him in again, to kiss his forehead. "He's so perfect."

"That's an odd name," Caden murmured softly, but his eyes were glued to that tiny fist, too.

She watched him watching the baby. "His name is Sterling."

"Sterling?" her mother asked, but Tana only had eyes for Caden.

His reaction was so him. No punching a victory fist in the air, no cracking a boastful joke. He simply looked at her, calmly…amazed. Could one be calmly gobsmacked? Caden was.

"You don't have to do that." His voice came out all

husky, almost a whisper. He cleared his throat. "You really don't have to."

"It's a perfect name for a perfect baby. Sterling Montana McKenna."

"Well." He cleared his throat again. With one finger, he pulled the blanket away from the baby's face himself. "Hey there, Sterling."

"That's such an...unusual name." Her mother managed to make her mouth smile while her eyebrows were drawn together in a frown. "Unexpected. People will wonder where you ever came up with a name like that."

Tana felt so clever. "If they see his birth certificate, it will be pretty obvious when they see Caden *Sterling's* name on it."

She winked at Caden. They'd done it. They'd had a baby without anyone else. It felt like such an achievement. They were superheroes.

"Oh, thank the Lord above!" Her mother threw up her hands, then collapsed back in her chair. "You do know who the father is. 'Sperm donor' was so ugly. So unnatural. I couldn't stand it."

"Mom."

"Who wants to have to explain to everyone that your grandchild came from a mystery man your daughter knows nothing about? Thank God, he's not that kind of baby, after all."

That kind of baby? Her mother had been sitting in this hospital room, convinced that Tana's perfect Sterling was *less than*.

Tana's joy disappeared in an instant, a soap bubble

that had been beautiful one moment and popped the next, gone as if it had never existed.

Tana had believed, she'd hoped, that her parents had adjusted to the idea since Thanksgiving, that they were even looking forward to a grandchild. She'd been delusional. Her parents had been disappointed from the moment she'd announced her pregnancy until this moment, when they'd assumed Caden was the father and their disapproval had instantaneously lifted.

There was nothing Tana could do right by herself. Her baby wouldn't be good enough for them unless it had a father. Any father would do. A man they'd known for five minutes? Fine. Any man would make the baby more acceptable—*better*—than what Tana could do alone.

It was humiliating to have a witness, to have Caden, of all people, see what her own family thought of her. She was the girl who'd wasted her talent. She'd blown her shot at glory. The reason they never acted like normal parents was because she was not a normal daughter. She was the biggest failure of their lives.

Caden stood. He spoke with an unruffled authority as he clarified the legalities. "My name goes on the certificate where the doctor's usually goes, as the birth attendant. Tana's name goes on it as the mother who performed a miracle, and the baby's name goes on it as the reason we're all here. The reason we're happy."

She knew he was looking down at her, but she couldn't look up at him. She felt too heavy, sinking like lead under the facts of her life. She'd made bad decisions ten years ago, and she made bad decisions still.

She'd gotten knocked up by a man who didn't care if she existed. Her parents would think she was an even bigger failure if they knew.

Caden set his hand on her shoulder as he stood by her side. "Texas has no requirement for a second parent to be named. No explanation is required. No explanation is given. Not now. Not ever."

Then he bent down to speak to her, just to her, and the bulk of his shoulders blocked out the harsh overhead light that was making her eyes sting. "So why don't you sign this now? I'll give you my pen, if you let me hold this miracle baby."

She didn't move in any way, not even to breathe, because the only move she wanted to make was to bury her face in Caden's shoulder and cry.

Caden spoke so quietly, only she and the baby she was clutching like a life preserver could hear it. "Hey, Tana. Everything's still good. I want to hold him again. He and I share a name. We've got things to discuss. You and your parents have a few things to discuss, too. May I?" With hands that were strong and sure, Caden took the bundled baby from the crook of her arm. He carried him over to the window and turned his back to give her some imaginary privacy with her parents.

Tana could hear Caden talking to the baby, not what he was saying, but the way he was saying it, the voice of a man who was innately positive. The man who believed that the worst situation could only get better. The man who believed miracles could happen when people had a fierce determination to try their best.

A fierce determination. Tana had always been able

to summon it, and it came back to her now, more fierce than it had ever been before. The feeling when she'd been poised on the starting blocks, determined to break a world record? That was nothing compared to this, because she was a mother now, and Sterling was her baby, and no one, absolutely no one, not even her own parents, would ever harm him.

She took a breath and raised her chin. "You've been disappointed in me for a long time, but Sterling is not a disappointment. He's a new person, tiny and perfect in every way. I wouldn't change a thing about him or about how he got here. I'm *happy* he's here." Or she had been, before they'd made it clear that she was still a child to be ashamed of. How natural it was for them to think her new child was someone to be ashamed of, too.

Fierce determination. You can't make the situation worse.

"There is only one parent on his birth certificate, and I wouldn't change that, either. You don't have to understand why I am okay with it, but that's the way I feel. So, starting today and for the rest of our lives, if anyone presses you for details that are none of their business, you can say, 'Our daughter is single.' That's it. Don't start the habit of apologizing or sighing or acting like this baby is lacking anything in his life. He won't be a baby forever, and if you ever, ever say words like 'mystery man' around this little boy, you will hurt him, and I cannot let you hurt him."

She drew her finger across the empty line on the birth certificate form. "If this blank line is a showstopper for you when it comes to your grandchild, if you decide the relationship is not worth trying your best for, then I—I—"

She remembered Caden's words on a dance floor and followed his lead. "Then I'll be pretty damned sad. I will never be your enemy, but Sterling is not going to be raised in a family that makes him feel like he isn't quite good enough, no matter how hard he tries. Maybe he'll screw up in the future even worse than I have, but my goal is to be the mother who loves him unconditionally, because a baby is a good thing."

She picked up the pen and the folder Caden had set on the bed, and she signed her name with a flourish. "My baby is the greatest thing."

Her parents had become two statues, locked in their poses, one seated, one standing.

Tana felt sad, but she'd done her best. Behind her, Caden was still murmuring to her baby, and she twisted around to look at them, instead of the stony faces of her parents.

The baby's eyes were open as Caden spoke to him, soft and low. The expression on the baby's face was priceless. He'd only known a dark, quiet world until a few hours ago, so now he focused on Caden in consternation. *What in the world is going on?* The baffled look on his tiny face made him look as calmly gobsmacked as Caden had, a few minutes ago.

Caden thought he'd witnessed a miracle. As Tana watched him talking to that miracle, another one occurred.

Her mother came over to the bed, took both of Tana's hands, then sat on the stool where Caden had been. "Oh, my darling girl. You remind me so much of myself. I never wanted anything bad to happen to my baby, either. I did everything I could to make sure you had the opportunities you deserved, so when you turned your back on them, I just… I feared for you. I feared for your future. It made me angry when you took needless risks instead of doing the safe thing, so angry that I haven't stopped being angry. But seeing you with your baby is making me miss my own precious baby. I was so worried about her, but she created her own opportunities when the ones I gave her died, and she's doing well. She's so happy, holding her baby, and I hate to think—I hate knowing—that the only bad thing in her life right now is me."

With real tears in her eyes, her mother leaned in to give her a kiss on her forehead.

Caden had been right. There was nothing to lose by trying. Sometimes, a miracle could happen.

Tana felt absolutely gobsmacked.

Chapter Fifteen

"I brought my suitcase, like we'd planned."

Caden heard Tana's mother behind him, but there was no response from Tana.

Her mother tried harder. "I still want to stay and help my baby and her baby. My grandson is perfect. His mother is single, and that's that. I'll say that from now on. Will you give me a chance?"

Caden heard most of it as he kept up his monologue with the baby. "That's you, my friend. They're talking about you."

So far, he'd been able to hold the baby's interest. Caden was trying to stave off the next cry for attention. He wanted to give Tana as much time as he could.

He'd guessed long ago that her parents weren't very supportive. He felt badly for Tana that he'd guessed right. Since the baby was here now—*Sterling* was here now—there was no time like the present for Tana to set the record straight. Caden could only listen with half an ear because he needed to keep talking to the baby, but Tana had definitely laid down some ground rules, and her mother had apologized.

"Sounds like they're making up over you, little guy. Way to go. Not even twenty-four hours old, and you're already making the world a better place. Pretty boss of you, Sterling. Pretty boss."

Sterling fussed. Not an outright cry, but it wouldn't be much longer before Caden couldn't keep distracting him.

"I hope you like your name, Sterling. It's kind of weird to call a little baby by my last name. Your mommy says everything about having a baby is weird, so there you have it. I'll tell you a little secret, but you gotta keep it between me and you. I've got plans to make this more of a permanent thing between us. Me and your mom and you, right? It's going to be pretty funny if we end up as Mr. and Mrs. Sterling, with our son, Sterling Sterling."

The fussing became a cry.

"No need to get loud about it. It'll be okay. We'll figure it out."

But the cry had done its job and gotten the attention of all the other adults in the room, especially Tana. She held out her hands for the baby, and Caden set him in her arms for the second time in their lives.

"Do you think he's hungry?" she asked Caden. Him, as if he knew anything more about babies than she did.

"I don't know. He's furious about something, though, for sure. Maybe it was something I said."

Tana grinned a little, even with a crying baby in her arms, but her mother was the voice of experience. "He's hungry. At this stage, they're either hungry or asleep."

"He's been wide-awake for Caden." But Tana's protest was mild. She probably didn't want to test their fragile truce. "So, um…if he's hungry…we're trying to figure out the whole breastfeeding thing, so…"

Her dad left the room like it was on fire.

Caden managed not to laugh outright as he checked with Tana. "I'll be going, then?" It was a question, because he'd promised her last evening that he wouldn't leave her when she wanted him to stay.

She nodded, blushing profusely. Kind of adorable, after what they'd been through together. "I'll watch for your fire truck out the window."

"Fire *engine*." The baby was wailing, and Tana was sort of patting the collar of her hospital gown, looking distressed. It was a really bad time to realize he didn't have her number, and she didn't have his. He spoke while backing out of the room. "If you need anything, just call the station. Anything at all. Anytime."

"Oh—yes, I don't have your number. My address is on the birth certificate. You should come see the baby."

Her mother shooed him the rest of the way out of the room. "Come in a couple of weeks. Mothers and babies have a lot to figure out. People always give new mothers a couple of weeks before they start expecting them to receive visitors. Don't visit if you have a cold, even then."

It sounded so reasonable, but Caden hated it instinctively. Two weeks seemed like a very long time. He looked back at Tana to see if two weeks sounded right to her, but she'd untied the top of her gown and was holding a screaming baby, and she looked a little desperate for him to go, so he left.

Two weeks. Fourteen days. He could make it.

Ten days later, Caden couldn't wait an hour longer.

He stood outside Tana's apartment door with the tiniest pair of cowboy boots he'd been able to buy, one of the plastic toy fire helmets they gave kids at the station, which was still bigger than the whole baby, and flowers. He figured he could give Tana flowers even if they were just friends, because Ruby had left flowers in her hospital room that first day.

Caden knocked.

He felt like a little kid about to tear the wrapping paper off a gift to see what it was, only he knew the gift was Tana. The door couldn't open fast enough for him. He would have been here at eight days, but he'd gotten forced at work, which was their slang for being assigned to work back-to-back twenty-four-hour shifts without notice. *Forced* was an even more accurate term than usual, since he'd had plans to come see Tana.

Ten days was his absolute limit. Her mother would just have to understand. He hadn't laughed in ten days the way he laughed with Tana.

He heard a dead bolt sliding open.

Everything's good. That's what he'd say when the door opened. He couldn't say *I love you*. Not yet. Someday.

Then the door opened, and Tana stood before him, and he couldn't say anything at all.

She wore nothing but a man's shirt.

His.

He'd last seen that shirt when he'd tucked it over her baby in the truck. It sure looked different now. The snaps were open at the top, exposing her throat and collar bones. The tails ended high on her thighs, making her long legs look longer. His gaze dropped to her bare feet, to the slender ankle he'd held more than once. That seemed intimate, suddenly, to know the feeling of wrapping his hand around her ankle. Her hair was coming undone from a ponytail, the way it would look if it were messy from a pillow. Messy from his hands, the night before.

She looked like she'd spent the night in his bed, and she'd raided his closet for something to wear for breakfast.

She looked like sex.

That wasn't what she was supposed to look like. Not yet. They were friends for now. He was here to enjoy talking to her. *Everything's good.*

"Caden. Hi."

"Hi." He nodded toward the mother-of-pearl snaps in the middle of her chest. "That's my shirt."

What a stupid thing to say. His brain had run away with his imagination.

"I'm so sorry." She snapped two buttons up, standing right there in the doorway. "I was going to go to the fire station and return it. I washed it, but the baby spits up a lot, and I'm running out of things that button up the front, because—" She pressed her hand to her cleavage. "This. I needed something that wasn't too tight, because—" She brushed her hand over her stomach. "That. I couldn't find anything else that was clean, because I haven't gotten any laundry done. Not the baby's laundry, though. His stuff is all clean. I wash all the baby's stuff, and I'll wash your shirt again and return it. I just—I just needed it today."

Somewhere in the middle of that explanation, Caden's brain did a 180 and came back. Tana's explanation was too long, almost babbling, and wholly unnecessary. He paid attention to her face, her eyes. She might be dressed like a girlfriend who'd spent the night, but she was a new mother, and her eyes looked tired.

His hands were full of gifts. He reached out to nudge her with the tiny cowboy boots. "Are you okay?"

For one unguarded moment, he saw how miserable she was.

Then she swallowed and stood up straighter and smiled at a spot somewhere in the hallway behind her. "The baby's better than okay. He's doing great. He eats a lot, every two or three hours. He's supposed to. I got a book on it." Then her gaze came back to Caden, brown eyes shining. "He's so amazing, Caden. I stop what I'm doing and go watch him sleeping sometimes, because I love him so much. You should see him."

"I'd love to." He waited a beat. "Can I come in?"

"I have to warn you, the place is a mess. These boots are so cute. Thank you. I'll put the flowers in water in a minute. I'm sorry the place is such a mess."

He glanced around as she shut the door and locked it

behind him, dead bolt and all, as if someone might intrude on their visit. There was a lot of clothing draped over the usual furniture. Nice couch, ladder-back chairs around a dining room table, everything piled with baby blankets and shirt after shirt after shirt. Some glossy junk mail stuck out from under a pile of towels on the coffee table, and several bouquets were lined up on top of a bookcase, all of them wilted and shedding petals.

He shrugged. "I've seen worse."

"Where? At a fraternity house?"

Even when she was exhausted, she made him smile.

"You don't have potato chips ground into your carpet." He put the plastic hat on her head. "You should see my place after a poker night."

"The hat's for me?"

"It's for Sterling. That's the smallest I could find. I don't expect you to save it until he grows into it. Could take a decade or two." He shouldn't have put the hat on her. She looked too much like a firefighter's flirty girlfriend.

"The baby's not awake yet, so here, sit here." She started pulling clothes off a chair for him, piling them higher on another one. "Most of these are baby clothes and blankets. My neighbor gave them to me, since I hadn't really done a lot of shopping yet. That was supposed to be last Sunday's activity. Lamaze on Saturday, baby shopping on Sunday. Anyway, I washed them. I just haven't put them away. I should have found something of my own to wear, but your plaid shirt was easy to spot in all these pastel baby things, so…"

"Tana, I'm not too worried about your laundry. I'm

a dude." He sat in the chair she'd cleared, so she would sit at the table, too.

"You don't have to be so nice. I know it looks a mess. It's afternoon, and I haven't gotten around to a shower yet. I will, though, I hope. I need to wash my hair. I keep throwing it up in a ponytail. Maybe I'll just keep this fire hat on from now on."

"Seems practical. The house looks fine. You look fine, too. You look…" *You look like you're mine. My shirt, my hat, my sexy forever-girl.*

She waited for him to finish his sentence. "I look indescribable?"

"You look cozy in plaid." He was pretty proud of himself for coming up with that one. "Like a lumberjack tucked in a log cabin."

She stared at him for a moment, and then she groaned and buried her face in her hands, but she was laughing, a real laugh, and it made his heart happy. "Now I know why you have ex-girlfriends. Never tell a woman she looks like a lumberjack."

Caden knew that. He'd just wanted to make her laugh, and he'd succeeded.

She took off the hat and looked around. "I lost my water cup. I'm supposed to be drinking all this extra water. There's a lot of things to do. The books are very clear on counting diaper changes, and… I forget the other things. Would you like a glass of water?"

While Caden was trying to decide if she was so chatty because she was exhausted or because he was making her nervous, he followed her to the kitchen. Like much of the university campus, this building was historic—which, in Texas, meant nineteenth century—so the kitchen and, living room weren't one open, modern space. He was too big to fit in the kitchen with Tana, so he stayed just outside the doorway. Dishes were piled up on every surface.

He was having a hard time trying to keep things light and friendly. His gut feeling was that Tana was normally the neat and tidy type, all clipboards and khaki shorts with crisp seams. Sure enough, she started apologizing for the mess again.

He interrupted. "Where's your mother?"

"She left, um, sometime last week. What day is today?"

Mrs. McKenna had left her daughter. She'd told Caden to stay away, and then she'd left? Damn it, he should have listened to his gut. He shouldn't have waited one day, let alone ten.

"What happened? You made things pretty clear at the hospital. Did she say something negative about Sterling?" The possibility made him so mad, so quickly.

"I didn't kick her out. Everything stayed good between us with the baby. He wants to be held all the time, and it's really hard to do everything one-handed, so she held him a lot. I got the laundry folded and put away. I cooked hot meals, too. But..."

Shouldn't Tana have gotten to hold the baby while her mother did the laundry?

"What was I getting? Oh—water. My cup's probably in the other room."

He trailed her back to the living room. "But?"

"She said I was a good mother. That was nice to hear, *but* I apparently still don't know how to load my own dishwasher correctly. Towels should be folded in thirds, and you shouldn't top off the flower vases with water, you should dump it all out and then start with fresh water." Tana wrinkled her nose, sending Caden right back to a September night and a patient he'd thought looked too cute when she wrinkled her nose. "She might have been right about the vases."

She was even cuter now, obviously exhausted and going through big changes, but she was still hanging in there, still trying to find the humor in her situation. She still reminded him of his mare, the one they'd rescued on Thanksgiving. He'd officially adopted the horse in January, shortly after the swim meet. He hadn't been able to stand the possibility that he'd go out to the ranch and find her gone, not after he'd let Tana go.

Since women didn't take kindly to being compared to ranch animals any more than they did to lumberjacks, he kept the thought to himself.

"I felt good, so when Mom mentioned her book club meeting, I said she shouldn't miss it. Everything was under control." Tana picked up a huge plastic mug. Tick marks for the ounces were marked down the side, along with the hospital logo. "See? I'm drinking a lot. You don't even have to ask."

"Your mother left, so who's been helping you out instead?"

He knew the answer was no one. He wanted to be wrong.

"Ruby?" he asked.

"She came over and gave me a new bathrobe. It's around here somewhere." Tana tugged a few inches of blue satin out from under a pile of terrycloth, then gave up. "It's pretty. Needs to be washed on delicate and line dried. I'll get it done. This isn't as disorganized as it looks."

Caden tried to remember who else she'd mentioned as a possible Lamaze coach. "Shirley?"

"She brought me a casserole when my mom was here."

Shirley must have assumed Tana's mom was staying longer, too. He was so angry at himself for assuming the same.

"You should have called the station."

"There was no fire."

"You know what I mean, Tana. You can call on me for help. Anytime."

She turned away and started brushing dead petals off the bookcase into her palm, acting as nonchalant as if she were a hostess in high heels and a dress, instead of a woman with bare feet, wearing the last clean shirt she could find. "Why do you think I can't handle this? I know the house has exploded, but I'm doing better than I look. I'm even writing a postseason summary for my performance review. It'll go in the alumni magazine, too. Hopefully, we'll get some donations to the swimming program. I can do this. The baby wakes up and I nurse him, and then he sleeps for two or three hours, so I have time to get my work done. Piece of cake."

"Every two or three hours? For ten days?" Caden was shocked. No wonder she looked so exhausted.

There was nowhere for her to put the petals in her

hand, so she put them back on the bookcase, a neat, pastel pile on one corner.

Through an open bedroom door, a newborn's wail of distress pierced the silence.

"He's awake," Tana said, and she burst into tears.

Chapter Sixteen

The baby was crying.

Tana opened her eyes, but it was pitch-black in her bedroom. Was this the midnight feeding? The three a.m.? She couldn't remember what time she'd gotten into bed. She usually just slept on the sofa between midnight and three, if she couldn't keep her eyes open any longer. The bedroom was for that brief, heavenly nap between three and seven-ish. If it were seven, though, it wouldn't be pitch-black.

This was so hard. She'd already lost track of the days of the week. Now she was losing morning and night.

She rolled over, ready to stick her hand in the bedside bassinet to pat Sterling and let him know she was there for him. If he didn't cry too furiously at first, she'd be able to grab a granola bar, so she could eat while he was nursing. How many meals in a row could she eat granola bars before nutrition got to be an issue? Did the book say anything about that?

Her hand met air. Nothing. No bassinet.

She bolted out of bed, tripping over the bed sheets. The baby's cry was coming from another room. What— who—how—?

It clicked: Caden. He must have rolled the bassinet out of her bedroom. He'd stopped by this afternoon with a pair of tiny cowboy boots, and he'd stayed. After she'd burst into tears, he hadn't believed anything she'd said about everything being under control.

He was right. It wasn't. But it could be. She just had to figure it out how other single mothers did it.

A little sleep was all she needed, and that was what Caden had tempted her with to let him stay. Nothing major—he could pick up Sterling when he cried, change his diaper, then bring him to Tana. She could stay horizontal, if not asleep, for more than two consecutive hours. If she showed him how to change a diaper, he'd be her butler, bringing her a baby who was freshly changed and ready to nurse.

A baby butler? She'd given in to the temptation.

Just once, she'd said, for the midnight feeding. He'd pushed her toward her bedroom around ten. He'd brought her the baby after midnight. She'd fed Sterling and then put him in the bassinet by her bed without having to stand up and walk around, changing a diaper, and it had been much more restful than she could have guessed.

She'd assumed Caden would leave. Midnight was

when bars were closing, movies were over, people were going home. She hadn't expected him to change the next diaper and bring the baby to her the next time, too. Why would he do that? He wasn't her ex-boyfriend.

He's so into you, you lucky witch. Ruby had always maintained that Caden had the hots for Tana.

The possibility scared her. Love made people put on rose-colored glasses, so they couldn't see the truth until it was too late. She hadn't seen her husband's manipulation until it had derailed her swimming career. Jerry's carelessness had derailed her coaching career—nearly. Not quite yet.

When will you learn? Why couldn't once be enough?

Sometimes, her mom was right. Tana had to rely on Tana. She couldn't withstand the whole love-him, change-your-life-for-him, lose-him routine, not again.

It seemed unlikely that Caden had romantic intentions toward her, no matter what Ruby said, but why else would a man be so thoughtful and caring at a time like this?

Because he was her friend?

Ruby was her friend. Shirley was her friend. Bob Nicholls was her friend. They weren't watching over a bassinet for her in the middle of the night. Caden must have a different motive. He must.

Tana stopped just outside the baby's room. The nursery had a diaper changing table and a rocking chair. The crib was still in its box, but it was neatly sitting in a corner. The nightlight had a soft pink tint to it. Unlike the chaos in the rest of the house, everything was calm and lovely for the baby.

So was Caden. As he changed the baby's diaper, he kept up a gentle monologue. His deep voice would have lulled her back to sleep had she not been standing up.

"Shh, let your mommy sleep. Be patient for just another minute. This is only my third diaper change. It's not like you're an old pro here, either, little fellow."

Tana watched from the hallway. Caden's Texas drawl was more pronounced when he crooned to the baby. Little fellow was *liddle fella*.

But Sterling was making fussy mewls more earnestly now. The baby hated having his arms and legs free. He had no muscle tone to control them, so they waved around like he was falling.

"All right, all done. See? We survived. Let's swaddle you up. You'll be happier that way. Then, I'm gonna lay you down next to your mommy, and everything will be right in your world." Caden crossed the baby's arms over his chest like a little Egyptian mummy and kept them secure with one hand, but when he started to pull the bottom of the baby blanket over Sterling's legs, the baby kicked his little foot into Caden's palm, *pat, pat, pat*. Caden stilled it by cupping it in his hand.

Caden went still, too. He looked at his hand. Tana looked at the expression on his face and held her breath.

Then Caden bent his head, lifted his hand and kissed that tiny, perfect foot.

Why was Caden here at three in the morning, taking care of the baby she'd named after him? Because he was falling in love with the baby.

Not with her. He and she were friends; he'd given her the shirt off his back. They were close friends, but just friends. It was the baby with whom he was falling in love.

That, she could handle.

Her sigh of relief was so great that Caden must have heard it. He turned his head toward her as he tucked the baby blanket around Sterling. His gaze roamed over her lightly, quickly, from her hair to her feet. She couldn't help but remember a Halloween night, Ruby's confidence: *He looked you over from head to toe. He liked what he saw.*

She had bedhead from her pillow. She'd pulled on some black maternity leggings, but she still wore his shirt, which had absorbed a little baby spit-up during the evening. He couldn't like what he saw. She was safe from any complicated, romantic intentions.

"You're supposed to be in bed," he said. "Butler service is on its way."

"I thought you'd want to get back to your own house at midnight."

He seemed serious in the gentle glow of the nightlight. "I told you ten days ago that I wouldn't leave you, not if you wanted me to stay."

It was easier to look at Sterling than at Caden. "I better feed him before he gets too wound up, or else his nose starts to run, and it's harder when he's stuffy to get him to…"

As if amniotic fluid and cervical dilation hadn't been personal enough, now she was about to discuss a baby latching on to her nipple? No. No, she was not.

"I'll just sit here in the rocking chair," she said, "since I'm up."

Caden placed the baby in her arms and left the room, pulling the door shut. Just before it closed, she was seized by a moment of blinding panic, a terror that she wouldn't see him again.

"Caden."

He paused.

"Are you leaving?"

"I can hit the road if you want me to."

Don't leave me. I can't walk out of this room and be all alone again. "I don't have a guest bedroom anymore. Just this nursery."

"You've got a big enough couch. I won't leave you, not if you want me to stay."

She could do this alone. She could.

The baby wailed.

"Stay. Please."

"Good. That's the right answer."

In the dim light, she saw him smile to himself as he shut the door.

The baby fell asleep with his mouth open and still full of milk.

When Tana snapped her top back up, Sterling made a little sucking motion with his perfect bow-shaped lips, swallowing the milk while somehow staying deeply asleep.

Tana carried him into the living room quietly. She didn't want to disturb a sleeping Caden, but he hadn't put the bassinet back in her bedroom.

The only light in the living room came from the

kitchen. The bassinet was next to an empty couch. Tana laid the baby down.

Caden stuck his head out of the kitchen and saw her. "There you are."

He disappeared into the kitchen for a moment, then came out with two plates. "I thought you could use a little midnight snack at four in the morning."

"You made scrambled eggs?"

"We ordered that pizza ten hours ago. You've got to be at least a little hungry."

She heard a hum in the kitchen. "Is the dishwasher running?"

"I made sure to load it incorrectly first." He winked at her, a flirtatious kind of move that looked damn good on him.

He was taking care of her, keeping her company, sharing a little meal in the cozy dark. A man was coming into her life and taking over, handling everything for her. *When will you learn?*

She ate the scrambled eggs, because she was hungry. She kept her eyes on her plate, because she was older, wiser, and she knew better than to look into a firefighter's too-handsome face.

"Are you okay?" he asked.

She had to make herself ask questions. "Why are you doing this? It's four in the morning. Why are you here?"

"Because we're friends, and you needed help."

"It's too much to expect from a friendship. A friend shouldn't have to give up everything, even their bed, to help out."

He finished his last bite, put down his fork and

leaned back in the chair, but she didn't look up. "Fire-fighters work twenty-four-hour shifts. Sometimes we sleep three hours, even six in our bunks. Some nights, we can only catch naps on the couch or recliners in the station's game room, because we're getting calls every couple of hours. I'm used to this. Out of all of your friends, I'm the best one to call when you need a little help at night."

"I didn't ask you for help."

"No, but I offered it. If Shirley offered to wash some dishes and change a diaper or two, would you be fighting yourself this hard to not accept your friend's help?"

"Shirley is a woman."

"Ah. So, that's it."

Tana kept her head down, kept moving forward. "There's no chance Shirley and I would…misunderstand one another." She ate her eggs determinedly, eyes on her plate.

"Do you think it's impossible for me to be your friend because you're a girl and I'm a boy?" He asked it with a gentle humor, but when she didn't respond, he turned serious. "What do you suspect my ulterior motive is here? That I'm trying to rack up points, hoping you'll invite me into your bed for a little *thank you* sex, sooner or later?"

She felt embarrassed for thinking it. Her body was flabby in the stomach, instead of hard, and hard in the breasts, instead of soft. She couldn't have sex for six more weeks, anyway, according to the hospital discharge instructions. Caden, with his medical background, probably knew that. It made his motives all the more baffling.

He shifted in his chair, leaning toward her now. "You asked me why I'm here, so let me answer you. I am sitting here, right now, because that baby is important to me. I held him before he took his first breath. He's named after me. I can't do a whole lot for him right now. Only you can, so I figure the best way I can take care of my namesake is to make sure his mother isn't exhausted and hungry."

Her plate kept going out of focus. She couldn't blame tears, because she was not crying. Her eyes were simply too tired to focus.

"That ties into the second reason I'm here. You are my friend, and friends don't let friends stay exhausted and hungry."

He was the kind of man who jumped in to help, even if the situation was dangerous. Did he know how dangerous love was? Had any of his real-life ex-girlfriends made him as *pretty damned sad* as her ex-husband had once made her?

He stood. "Finish your eggs and go to sleep. This isn't about men and women and sex. I'm just cooking you scrambled eggs. Don't make more of it than it is."

He picked up his plate and hers, then walked toward the kitchen.

She addressed the table where her plate had been. "Are you leaving me now?"

He stopped. "No."

"Is everything still good between us?"

"Everything's good."

She picked up her head. She was tired of driving herself forward.

"You're the nicest man I've ever met. I'm lucky to have you as my friend."

"I'm the lucky one. I get two of you. You only get me."

It was one of the nicest things she'd ever heard.

Tana wiped her eyes on her—his—sleeve.

"Go to bed," he said.

She did.

Chapter Seventeen

Caden was ready for a nap.

Sterling wasn't.

Caden had gotten off work at seven this morning after a night that had been busier than usual, but he hadn't gone home to crash. He'd had a date to keep—with a baby.

Tana needed to go to campus for an awards event involving her athletes. It would take her out of the house for a good four hours, at least. Caden was the only person she felt comfortable leaving her newborn with. They'd tried it with shorter trips, like her last doctor's appointment. Sterling would take a bottle of breastmilk from Caden happily enough, as long as Tana wasn't around. But if his mama was in the room? Forget it. He wanted Tana, not a bottle, and there was no fooling him. Caden hadn't realized a baby could be so down-right stubborn.

Since Tana was at her luncheon, Sterling had guzzled down the bottle, but he was still awake. That had to be a Murphy's Law of babies. The one time you were counting on their nap, they didn't pass out in a milk-drunk stupor.

"Not sleepy yet, Sterling? I am." Caden stretched out on the couch with the baby on his chest. Sterling fell asleep like this, usually. Hopefully.

Caden held out his phone and pinged his sister-in-law for a video chat.

"Look who I've got here." He angled the phone down, so the baby's little face and wide open eyes were on the screen. They were still that otherworldly blue Caden had first seen on the side of the road, but they were turning indigo now, well on their way to being brown. Tana had brown eyes.

And the donor?

Caden didn't give a damn what color eyes he had.

"Oh, what a sweetie. That's a really young one. He's so teeny-tiny." Then she got all high-pitched. "Hello, little cutie patootie, sugar dumpling, pumpkin pie."

Caden snorted. He'd known Abigail would totally lose it over the baby.

"Whose baby is this?" she asked.

Mine.

"Is it the fire inspector's? What's her name?"

"Nah, Christyne's baby has gotta be at least three months old now. This is my little guy, the baby I delivered. Sterling." He put the camera back on himself.

"You couldn't forget that name. It was in the papers, if you did. I got a lot of credit for standing there while he was born."

"Oh, wow. That's Sterling? The college coach's baby?"

"Yes, not to be confused with all the other babies named Sterling that I delivered."

"What is he, four or five weeks now?"

"Thirty-four days."

Abigail raised an eyebrow. "Pretty specific there. I take it you're still checking up on him."

Caden shrugged, which jiggled the baby a little. "I come over and give his mother a break now and then." Every third night, like clockwork, for the past three weeks. He worked one night, spent one night at Tana's, then spent one night in his own bed.

He was waiting for Tana to ask him to stay more than a night. It was so much nicer to eat dinner with her than alone. So much better to crash on her couch with a movie they paused for diaper changes. The hell of it was, she wanted to spend more time with him. She was always reluctant to say it was okay for him to leave, and that wasn't his wishful thinking. He didn't know why she was so hesitant, but since she had a thirty-four-day-old baby, he wasn't going to push. Not yet.

"And the baby's father is cool with this?"

"There's no father. I wanted to pick your brain a little bit. What do you know about those strollers that are made for parents who run? Really athletic parents who can run fast?"

"Jogging strollers? They're expensive. Are you guys at the station going to chip in and buy one for the baby?"

"No, we already chipped in and got him a swing. That's one of the greatest things ever invented. If Sterling doesn't go to sleep soon, I'm going to put him in it. It's naptime for me."

"You sound very domesticated. You're a thirty-two-year-old bachelor. Pretty good-looking, if not quite as handsome as your brother. You should be driving fast cars and chasing loose women."

"I need to drive something that'll pull a horse trailer."

"Still, your bachelor's card is going to be revoked."

Not fast enough to suit me. "Can we focus here? Mother's Day is Sunday, so I was thinking about getting Tana a jogging stroller. Did I tell you she used to be on Masterson's swim team when she was a student? I saw her name on the pool wall. She set some school records. Anyway, the doctor won't let her in the pool for another couple of weeks, and she's stressed out because she can't swim. I thought maybe she could go for a run, instead. Is that a good gift?"

"Caden…she isn't your mother. Why are you buying her a Mother's Day gift?"

Caden pointed the camera at the baby again, mostly to see if his eyes were still open. They were. "You don't expect him to buy one for her, do you?"

"It's just that you shouldn't—"

"Check this out. He's got a grip that'll keep him on the back of a bucking bronco." Caden wiggled his finger into Sterling's fist. Five tiny fingers clutched him tightly.

"*Caden*. Yes, he's adorable. Now look at me."

"Edward buys you a gift from Abby and Max. Same thing."

"No, it isn't. Edward is my husband. My children are his children. Be careful here. You're not related to this baby. You've got no claim on this child at all. The real father could show up any day, and I don't think he's going to like having you spending all this time with *his* baby."

"Not going to happen."

"Yes, it could. Don't let yourself get too attached to him."

Caden wished he could tell Abigail the truth, but if Tana didn't want her own parents to mention sperm donors, she wouldn't want him to, either. He had to stick to her script. "Tana is single."

"She wasn't always, obviously. I've known you since you were twenty-two. You're the kind who plans to settle down. You want Miss Right to come along, so you'll have the white picket fence and the children and the dog."

"And the horse. I'm keeping my horse. That picket fence better be tall."

"You can't find any of that while you're playing house with someone else's woman and child."

Playing house. This was no game. He couldn't cool his feelings for Tana no matter how hard he tried—and he'd tried, for almost nine months.

"You need to be out there dating, not babysitting. Find a woman without a history. Someone who hasn't been with a man in a way that's going to keep her tangled up with him for the next eighteen years. Someone with a clean slate."

Caden did it all: took a deep breath, counted to ten and reminded himself that his sister-in-law cared about him.

"So, I'm looking for a virgin who hasn't done anything with her life yet? Sounds great. Just a big ball of fun."

"I'm being serious."

Caden got serious, too. "Tana is a friend. She's in a tight spot. She doesn't qualify for maternity or family leave, because she hasn't been at MU for twelve months yet. She asked me to come over because there's an event on campus that she's supposed to be part of. Don't make more of it than it is."

But, honest to God, he wished there was so much more to it than there was. They'd get to laughing, and she'd tilt her head or duck her chin or do something a little flirtatious, some body language that would have given him a big green light to ask for her number and invite her to dinner if they'd just met at the pub or a costume party—or a CPR class. But since they were usually sitting on her couch with a baby in one of their laps, she would catch herself flirting, her eyes would get big and round, and she'd act embarrassed while he pretended not to notice.

It sucked.

"Exactly," Abigail said. "Don't make more of it than it is, but I have a bad feeling that you are. By the way, that baby is way too young to be put in a jogging stroller. No neck muscles yet. He should be five or six months old before you take him for a run. Bye."

"Bye. And, by the way, happy Mother's Day, in advance. You're a nosy sister-in-law, but Abby and Max lucked out and got a real good mom."

"Aw. I love you, too. Bye."

They disconnected the call. Caden kept his phone pointed toward Sterling's face, hoping to see those indigo-blues closing. No such luck.

He wasn't one for singing lullabies, but he was pretty good at talking Sterling to sleep. "Looks like I know what you'll be doing in September, my friend. You'll be feeling the need for speed out on the jogging trails. I'll run with you and your mom. I'm not bragging or anything, but there's no chance I'll embarrass myself on dry land. Your mom would kick my butt in a pool for sure, but you already know that. She's only ridden a horse a few times in her life, though, can you believe it? So, I'll teach you to ride, she'll teach you how to swim, and the three of us will go for runs together. Doesn't that sound like a nice life? You go ahead and sleep easy now. September will be here before you know it. The future is pretty sweet."

The future sucked.

Tana was going to lose Caden.

She'd thought nine months of *not* knowing her future had been bad. Would being pregnant be hard? Would she let down the kids who'd come to the university to swim? Was this one-season contract going to be her last?

She'd kept moving forward, hoping the answers would be good ones.

This morning, out of vacation days and sick days, she'd checked her work email and her voice mail, and she'd gotten her final answer. The athletic director had not responded to any of her requests to discuss a contract extension. His administrative assistant had, but only to say their calendar was too full to schedule a meeting. It was a gutless way to let someone go, but being let go was the result.

She wished she could go back to not knowing what the future held.

Her van crawled along with the graduation-week traffic jams. The student-athlete awards were today. Sunday would be Mother's Day, then Masterson University would graduate its latest batch of Musketeers, and Tana would be officially unemployed. Her faculty apartment lease ran out in two weeks. Tana was going to move back to Houston, back into her parents' house.

She had no choice.

She dreaded telling Caden after the awards. He was going to be shocked; she hadn't even hinted to him that her time was running out. The very worst part of her very near future was that she was going to lose her very best friend.

Caden loved her baby. When she left Masterson, he would be devastated to lose Sterling. Then Tana would lose Caden, because who could be friends with someone who caused them so much pain?

She pounded the steering wheel. *Damn* her boss. Her heart was breaking, but he wasn't sparing her a moment's thought. The only thing the athletic director thought about was football. Every other sport only mattered if it won a national championship.

In one season, Tana had taken Masterson's program far. Having swimmers finish second, third and fourth in multiple events was a greater achievement than having a single superstar place first, while the rest of a college's swimmers finished so far down the list, the school might as well have not brought them to the meet. To Bob Nicholls, it was so obvious that he couldn't imagine her contract not being renewed—but that wasn't how the Masterson athletic director's mind worked.

Tana had flown thousands of miles and driven a thousand more while pregnant, hoping for that one big trophy she could plop on her boss's desk, but she hadn't gotten it. There was no other athletic director she could appeal to, no other channel to use. The only person her boss answered to was the president of the university.

Tana gripped the steering wheel as a crazy, daring idea threatened to knock her sideways.

The president would be at today's awards. Tana's swimmers were going to be raking in the recognition. There would be socializing afterward, the polite meeting and greeting that normally took place at any banquet. What if she spoke with the president in that environment, when her biggest coaching achievement, the athletes themselves, would be celebrated? Could she go behind the athletic director's back without making it look like she was?

She was already dressed for battle. She was wearing the one non-maternity skirt in her closet that had an elastic waistband, the one blazer that looked good, although she couldn't button it yet. For the first time in thirty-four days, she'd styled her hair and put on her makeup and high heels. It wasn't as empowering as cat eyes and a cape, but Tana looked as much like a successful director and coach as she possibly could, thirty-four days after having a baby.

At last, she reached the event center. She pulled in to a faculty parking spot and checked her makeup in the rearview mirror. It was time for the coach's pep talk.

"I think you can do this. You have nothing to lose, and your whole life to gain."

She was far from fearless, but she was going to try.

Chapter Eighteen

Tana slapped the steering wheel.

She'd needed one of Caden's miracles, and she'd gotten it.

Tana hadn't had to maneuver herself into the president's vicinity. He'd come up to *her* by the dessert buffet, with the athletic director at his elbow. The president had been impressed with her team, not only with their podium count, but with their attitudes as they'd accepted their individual awards.

Tana hadn't planned on speaking to him in front of the athletic director, but she'd gone for it, anyway. She'd shaken the president's hand and told him how much she was looking forward to developing more Masterson student-athletes in the next two years, although three would let her see this year's freshmen through to their senior years.

The president had insisted on three years.

The athletic director had taken the easy route and agreed, although Tana had practically seen him desperately flipping through his internal files, trying to remember if he'd ever bothered getting around to offering the director of aquatics any contract at all. Regardless, if the president wanted three years, the director would have his assistant write up a contract for three and be done with it. On to next year's football prospects.

Three years. Tana could stay here in Masterson. She could keep all of her friends, especially the man who'd taught his CPR students to try, even when success seemed impossible.

The man who'd held her baby before he'd taken his first breath.

Oh, Caden—she wanted to see him. She wanted to *be* with him, with Caden and Sterling, both.

At last, she reached the apartment building. The ancient, creaky elevator was too slow, so she started running up the stairs to the third floor. Excitement could only carry her so far. She hadn't swum since before the championships in March, so she was overheated and out of breath by the second floor. By the time she got to her door, she was walking, carrying her pumps in her hand and her blazer over her arm, but she was home.

Nobody else was. There was no man stretched out on her couch, no man cooking in her kitchen. The baby swing was empty. The bassinet was empty. Her apartment felt like it had before Sterling had been born.

Lonely.

She dropped her shoes and hurried to the baby's room, but the changing table was empty and the rocking chair deserted. She backtracked to the living room, but she didn't see any note from Caden. Her bedroom door was cracked. She pushed it open, hoping, even though Caden never spent time in her bedroom, never, she was hoping—

"There you are," she whispered in relief.

Her bedroom blinds were drawn, making the room as dark as night in the middle of a bright Texas afternoon, but in the daylight from the hall, Tana could see the unmistakable shape of a man stretched out on her bed, sound asleep, with one sculpted arm thrown over his head. Her baby slept on his chest, held in place by Caden's sure hand, even as he slept.

She willed her silly heart to slow down. Of course they were here. Caden wouldn't leave her. He'd promised.

She wouldn't leave, either, for three years. That would be triple the length of her marriage. Double the amount of time she'd wasted with Jerry. No man had stayed in love with her for anywhere close to three years, but Caden wasn't in love with her. He was her friend. She couldn't keep a man for three years, but she could keep a friend forever.

She watched him sleep. It didn't matter how handsome his face was. It didn't matter how appealing his solid, strong body looked on her bed. She wouldn't hope that she'd catch a hint of his aftershave on her pillow tonight. This was not about men and women and sex, he'd said, and she needed to keep it that way, so that she could keep him in her life.

She sat on the mattress carefully, her hip by Caden's. She and Caden would never split up, never divorce, as long as romance never changed their friendship.

He must have come into her bedroom for the darkness, either to help himself or Sterling fall asleep more easily. Probably himself, after a twenty-four-hour shift. He'd done her a huge favor by coming over so early. Friends took care of their friends, and he always took care of her.

She wanted to take care of him. She should carry Sterling out to his bassinet, so Caden wouldn't be disturbed when the baby got hungry. She slipped her fingers between the warm baby blanket and warm, muscled man, but Caden pulled Sterling more tightly to him, a little reflex. He mumbled in his sleep. "Itsababy."

Well. Tana didn't want to wake anybody with a tug of war. The baby looked as peaceful as Caden, so she slipped her hands free again. Now what?

There was nothing she had to do. She hardly knew how to feel, now that the fear that had been hanging over her head was gone. So relieved, so happy, so tired, all three.

It was a little bit like the way she and Caden had felt after Sterling had been born. The three of them had stayed close together in the truck, locked together in an embrace that made her warm every time she remembered it. To feel that again, even for a few minutes...

Gingerly, she lay on her side and put her hand on the baby's back with Caden's. She watched Caden's chest rise and fall, and she breathed in time with him, an easy breath with every stroke, a lazy way to swim.

She was nearly asleep when she realized she was slow-blinking into Caden's tropical-blue eyes.

"Had a long night?" she whispered.

He nodded slightly, a little rustle on the pillow. "Your day?"

"I'm home. I'm so glad I have this home. I'm so glad I have us, like this."

But Caden had closed his eyes and drifted back to sleep.

She closed hers and followed his lead.

Caden checked his watch.

Fifteen minutes until his shift started. Tana was cutting it close this time. The school year had begun, and she was juggling a new schedule this September. Sterling slept through the nights now, so Caden no longer had an excuse to sleep at Tana's place. But, between the daycare center's hours and Tana's coaching schedule, Caden still had plenty of excuses to see her and Sterling. It was babysitting, not dating, friendly meals and laughter, not passionate nights, but it kept them in his life.

Caden sat on the massive chrome bumper of Engine 37 and waited. Sterling sat in his lap, facing out. He loved to see what was going on in the world.

"What's up, my dude?" Keith was speaking to the baby, of course. Everyone spoke to the baby, and Caden couldn't blame them. He thought Sterling was one of the most interesting people he knew, too.

Tana rounded the corner of the station, calling to him from down the sidewalk. "I'm sorry I'm late."

And there was the most interesting woman he would ever know.

She was as athletic and graceful as ever. Her face was still beautiful and her eyes were deep brown, but she had something extra now. Motherhood had put a permanent glow about her, one that came from loving her child and being loved in return.

Sterling was never stingy with letting his mother know how much he loved her. When Tana walked into a room, the baby would kick his feet in enthusiasm, babble or laugh, and generally light up like a Christmas tree.

As Tana got closer, Caden stood Sterling on his thighs, so the baby could bounce in joy. "I feel you, little fella, I feel you. She's pretty awesome."

Caden wished he could be so open with his feelings. He couldn't go striding out of the engine bay to eliminate the distance between them faster, couldn't scoop Tana off the sidewalk and kiss her hello like she was the woman of his dreams.

Not yet.

"Hello," she said, smiling as she came right up to him, as if she were going to greet him with a kiss—but she dropped the kiss on top of Sterling's head, inches from Caden's mouth.

Caden smelled orange blossoms. "Someone got her laps in today. Must be why she's in such a good mood."

"How do you always know?" She scooped up Sterling with an unconscious toss of her hair. More orange blossoms.

It had taken Caden a few weeks to figure it out,

once the doctor had given her the go-ahead to resume her swimming. She used a regular shampoo at her apartment, but she showered at the pool with a special chlorine-removing shampoo that smelled like orange blossoms.

He'd first smelled flowers in her hair when he'd given her a ride to the Tipsy Musketeer after the CPR class. He knew now that she'd been swimming the day he'd met her. He knew a lot of things about her now—except the reason she kept him so firmly in the friend zone.

Caden stood to say goodbye. He stepped close to Tana and the baby, so close he could have wrapped them in his arms, his to have and to hold. His gaze dropped to Tana's lips as they curved into a smile, soft and invit-ing, and he willed her to meet him halfway. She wanted to, he was certain, because she started to lean toward him, but she caught herself. Again. Always.

Not always, he corrected himself. *Just not yet.*

Caden brushed his kiss over Sterling's baby-fine hair instead, because that was all Tana could handle.

"Bye. I'll miss you." He said it to Sterling, but his gaze was locked with Tana's.

"We'll miss you, too."

We. Not her, the woman, missing her man. *We* meant her and her baby. It was nice. It shouldn't make the space between his shoulder blades tense with irritation.

"I'm dropping him off at your place tomorrow, before Javier's CPR class, right?" She leaned around Caden to smile at Javier. "You're not planning to keep us more than an hour, I hope."

"I want to get home as much as you do," Javier answered.

It struck Caden that her smile for Javier was different from her smiles for him. Tana and Javier were just friends.

He and Tana were not. They were more, so much more, and tomorrow would mark a year since he'd met the woman of his dreams.

Not yet needed to become *now*.

"Bring Sterling to the classroom with you," Caden said. "I'll meet you there."

He watched her walk away until she rounded the corner and was out of sight, not even trying to kid himself that he wasn't checking out the legs that her khaki shorts revealed. It had been a long time, a long, long time, since he'd held her ankle in his hand. The sensation was burned into his mind, all the same.

He turned to Javier. "Ever think to yourself, 'If I could do it over again, knowing what I know now…'?"

Javier raised a brow in question.

"Do me a favor," Caden said. "Let me teach that CPR class for you tomorrow night."

Javier raised both brows. "I don't think you know what the word *favor* means."

Caden breathed in the lingering trace of orange blossoms. "I met a woman named Montana McKenna at that CPR class. I've waited a year to have a chance for a do-over."

The CPR class was being held in the same building as last year.

Tana waited by the vending machines, pushing the

stroller back and forth to keep Sterling asleep. He'd zonked out during their walk across campus, which was exactly why she kept his car seat clipped to the stroller more often than she buckled it into the swim-mobile.

The indefatigable Granny Dee was peering into the car seat. Tana was afraid she was going to poke the baby, so he'd wake up and she could play with him. She wouldn't really, of course. Probably not.

"Oh, joy. Oh, rapture." Ruby was the center of attention. "It's that time of year again. The annual CPR recertification. Nothing says autumn like the scent of alcohol wipes and a plastic dummy."

Shirley giggled. "Maybe the instructor will be another hot bachelor. Since Tana didn't want the last one, maybe she'll have better luck this year."

"Not want him?" Tana objected. "We're best friends."

"That's not the same thing as wanting a man," Ruby said. "I have no idea why you haven't let Caden out of the friend zone, but if it's not going to happen, then I guess it's not going to happen. What kind of guy would make you want to hire a sitter and go out for some adult fun?"

Strong arms, but holds babies like they are precious. Whips up the fluffiest scrambled eggs before you even know you're hungry. Sets your parents straight without being a jerk. Dances like a man who knows what he's doing. Looks hot in a uniform, coming and going.

In other words, Caden Sterling. The one man she couldn't have, because then she wouldn't have him as a friend. It made sense to her, but she'd given up trying to explain to Ruby why she needed a friend more than a lover.

Tana pulled the stroller closer to herself. Granny Dee was trying to wake the baby, darn it.

Ruby bit her lip in consternation. "You're not bringing the baby to class, are you? That is not going to help you catch a guy. Walking in with a stroller and a diaper bag is kind of a boner-killer."

"Ruby...please. There are innocent ears here."

Ruby rolled her eyes. "If Sterling's first words are *boner-killer*, then he really will be the most impressive baby ever born."

"I think she meant my ears," Granny said. "But I know all the lingo you kids use."

Behind Tana, a masculine voice addressed the milling group of people. "All right, CPR time. Let's get started."

Tana smiled before she turned around, because she knew Caden's voice. "Hi. How was work?"

"I'm still working. There's been a change in plans. I'm teaching this class."

"Oh." Sterling was sleeping like an angel. She doubted it would last for another full hour, though. "Then I'm so sorry, but my childcare arrangements just fell through. I'll have to bring my baby to class. If he cries, I'll just slip out. I'll still be able to pass the test, if you let me take it."

"You have to do what you have to do, Coach. We'll work it out."

"I'm getting that déjà vu feeling."

"We've got to stop meeting like this."

Ruby huffed past them, rolling her eyes. "You two need to get a room. Please, please, get a room. I can't take another year of this."

Ruby held the door open and gestured for Caden to go in, so he could set the dummies down at the front of the classroom. Tana followed, pretending not to admire the fit of a firefighter's navy uniform slacks, the way she and Ruby had at a grocery store last Halloween.

Granny followed them all. She kept her voice pitched just under the squeak of the stroller wheels as she poked Tana with one finger. "I cannot believe you're keeping that hunk of bacon in the friend zone."

Tana watched Caden as he tossed his bags into the back of his truck.

"I can drive you over to the Tipsy Musketeer," he said.

Except for the fainting, this night was going like it had last year.

Tana played along. "We have someone new with us this time, but I let Granny Dee give him a bottle while you were testing the rest of us. He should be good for a little while."

Caden put the stroller in the truck bed while Tana buckled Sterling's car seat in the center of the leather bench where he'd been born.

They drove toward the Musketeer in silence, which wasn't how it had been the year before. "If we're reliving last year, then I think you should be telling me to keep drinking until I have to pee."

Caden smiled briefly as they stopped at the one traffic light between campus and the pub. He put his hand on Sterling's chest and gave him a wiggle. "How're you doing there, little fella?"

Sterling looked at him with a perfectly serious expression and answered by blowing some slobbery bubbles. Satisfied with that communication, he went back to work on getting a giraffe-shaped teether into his mouth.

Caden parked across the street from the pub. It was the same spot he'd parked in one year ago, the exact spot where he'd congratulated her on her pregnancy. *Babies are a good thing.*

She hadn't expected to feel emotional about a parking spot. "Why are we doing everything the same tonight?"

"When I look back, it was one of the most significant nights of my life. I met you. But if I could go back and do it again, I would do it differently."

"You would?" She sounded a little breathless, but those three little words, *I met you*, had sounded almost as significant as the romantic three little words that changed lives. They'd changed hers when other men had said them, and not for the better. It was irrational for her to wish she could hear them from this man.

"Last year, things were going well up to this point," he said. "So far, so good, right?"

On the other hand, men could be so dense. Even Caden.

"Maybe good for you. I'd *fainted*."

"Which is how I found out you were pregnant. If I hadn't known, I would have asked you out after class."

"What?" But she'd heard him.

"You wouldn't have given me your number or let me buy you a drink, but I wouldn't have known why. It would have hurt my pride. I might have done something stupid, like giving up on getting to know you. Or I might have tried even harder to get you to go out with me, and you would have shut me down, and that would have been the end of us."

The end of us. It sounded frightening, a loss she didn't want to contemplate.

Caden turned off the truck and sat back. "I'm kind of glad you fainted, because here we are."

"That's...something I've never thought about. I didn't know you'd been planning to ask me out."

He jiggled the giraffe in Sterling's mouth affectionately, then shifted in his seat to face her full-on. "The first time I saw you, you had your back to me. That's my defense for immediately checking out your legs. I couldn't see your personality or even your face, but you had and still have the sexiest legs I've ever seen, bar none."

Tana gaped at him. He thought her legs were sexy? She walked on them all the time around him—well, duh—but he never checked them out, not that she'd noticed.

"I looked away to talk to someone. When I looked back, you were facing me with this expression on your face like..." He shook his head. "I don't know. Like you were looking to see if I was who you thought I was? The bottom line is that I saw your serious brown eyes, and I thought, 'I have got to get her name and number. I need to know her.' Simple as that."

Tana looked away, out the windshield. This was really dangerous. He was saying things she wouldn't be able to forget, things that would forever color their relationship differently. She should stop him, say something bright and friendly and change the subject, but much too much of her was deeply flattered, drinking this in like it was what she'd always wanted to hear.

"You were talking to Granny Dee," she said. "I was thinking that you were very respectful and kind to her."

"That was it? I've wondered about it for a year. I moved your certificate to the bottom of the stack, so you'd be the last to leave and I could ask you out, did you know that?"

"But then I told you I was pregnant, so that threw a wet blanket on everything."

"No, it didn't." He touched her face.

He never touched her face. They sat next to each other a lot. They bumped shoulders to get each other's attention, and they put the baby in each other's arms when he was sleeping or screaming, but she'd never run her fingertips over Caden's cheekbone or under his jaw, like he was doing to her now, tracing the lines of her face.

"By the time you told me, I'd already seen how smart you were, how much other people liked and respected you. I'd already seen you force a CPR dummy to come back to life with a vengeance. You told me you were a lifeguard and the new director of aquatics, and I thought you were so interesting. I liked you. Being pregnant didn't change any of that."

He put his hand back on the steering wheel and

looked toward the pub. His profile was serious in the town's lights. "But this is the point I wish I could do over, Tana. Right here, this moment. This is when I watched you walk across the street and disappear inside that pub."

"Nothing bad happened to me."

"I was so sure you were starting a family with another man, that there was a boyfriend who was about to hear the biggest news of his life, some guy in Houston."

Tana caught her breath.

"I know," he said, as if she'd argued. "There was no man, but I was certain you had someone. A boyfriend, a lover. You wore no ring, so I assumed there was no fiancé or husband, but there would be, if the man had any kind of a brain. Now I know it was your parents that you were going to tell in person, in Houston."

That much was true. She hadn't really lied about that. She hadn't really lied about anything. Ruby had misunderstood her analogy of Jerry being no more involved than a sperm donor, and Tana hadn't said anything to correct her. Everything had snowballed from there. She hadn't known one could make a snowball out of things that were never said, but it was huge, and it was chilling.

Caden shook a plush rattle toy for Sterling, then waited patiently as the baby concentrated on grabbing it. "Aren't you going to ask me what I would do differently, if I had it to do over again?"

She really shouldn't.

But she did. "What would you do differently?"

"I was the only person who knew you were pregnant.

I told you that you should have your friends toast you with cranberry juice, remember?"

She nodded.

"If I had it to do over again, I would get out of this truck and go drink a glass of cranberry juice with you."

It sounded so simple, yet he sounded so remorseful.

"Since it was a secret, I would catch your eye and raise the juice in a silent toast. You'd know what I meant. If I could, I'd go back and add a little celebration to your night, because you had something to celebrate, but no one else to celebrate it with."

The expression on his face was one she'd never seen before, not in an entire year. Regret? Sorrow.

She didn't fight the impulse to smooth her thumb over the tiny wrinkles at the corner of his eye, although there were no tears for her to wipe away. He closed his eyes as she touched him in this new way.

"It's a lovely thought, my friend, but please don't be so sad. You barely knew me."

He opened his eyes, and she pulled her hand back at the intensity she saw burning in them.

"Imagine it, Tana. If I'd chosen that path a year ago, your friends would have become my friends so much sooner. We would have tailgated together at some football games last fall. You would have made friends with the guys at the firehouse in January instead of May, because I would have asked you to be on our team for the station's pancake fundraiser. I would have volunteered to be the medic at every one of your swim meets this season. All of that could have happened, even if you were married and pregnant with your third baby. Our lives would have been better, if we'd been friends."

Friendship. He was talking about friendship. Sexy legs and serious eyes were thrilling, but thrills didn't last. The baby chewing on a giraffe in between them was more important than the way her heart had pounded as Caden had traced her face. Friendship gave her child stability. A passionate night with Caden would disrupt everything.

The dangerous part of her wanted it, anyway.

"Instead, since I couldn't have you the way I wanted to have you, I felt so sorry for myself that I pulled out of this parking spot and drove home. I ended up not having you in my life at all."

"Everything's good. We are friends now."

"Yes. But if I'd walked into that pub a year ago, we would have already been friends when we waltzed to that Christmas carol at Thanksgiving. I would have known you well enough to believe you when you said you couldn't work things out with a sperm donor, instead of assuming you were just really pissed off with someone in Houston. I could have talked with you later, maybe caught lunch at the diner with you one day, to try to understand why you'd chosen to have a baby on your own."

He cupped her face fully. No light touch, this. His hand was strong, his palm was warm, the same hand that had taken her pulse on a pool deck, the same palm that had caught her newborn's kicking foot. "And then, Tana...then I would have asked you out on that date, because I've caught you looking at me the way I look at you. We would have been dating for four months before the baby came. You would never have wondered who would be your ride home from the ER. You would never have cried over not having a Lamaze coach—"

"Caden. *Caden*."

"And I would not have had to wait an entire year to kiss you."

Caden pulled her close and claimed her with a kiss that held nothing back. He reached for her with his other hand, too, cupping the back of her head, tumbling her hair forward, stirring up the scent of orange blossoms.

Tana grabbed a fistful of his shirt at his shoulder. She kissed him with all the pent-up passion she'd kept so carefully hidden, but not because he was the type of man who could inspire her to hire a sitter for some adult time. Not because he was a handsome man with a firm backside and a confident, masculine walk. Not because he was the man with the bare chest and low-slung jeans in the golden light of sunset.

She kissed him because he was her everything.

The baby between them kicked his feet and babbled "da-da-da-da-da" in delight.

Chapter Nineteen

She had time.

Tana's apartment was only minutes away, but the baby forced them to pause, to think things through, to cool off. A diaper had to be changed. Footed pajamas had to be snapped over chubby legs and soft arms.

I shouldn't do this. If we start something, there will be an end to it, someday.

She placed the baby in the crib that Caden had assembled for her this summer. He'd offered to do it last Thanksgiving, when they'd been dancing at the pub. He'd offered to do so many things as an ex-boyfriend, with no expectation of sex. After a romance died, he'd said he'd still do everything he could for his baby, and that included taking care of its mother.

She'd wished, as she'd waltzed, that he was her ex-boyfriend.

If she took him to bed tonight, she would get that wish, sooner or later. Boyfriends became ex-boyfriends even more easily than husbands became ex-husbands. Her heart would break, but if the man who broke it this time was Caden, then her son would not suffer. Sterling wouldn't be cut out of Caden's life with a phone call, then forgotten as if he'd never existed.

Caden walked up behind her. In the soft pink light of the nursery, they looked into the crib together, cheek against cheek. She kept her hand on the baby, her other on the safety rail.

Caden pushed her hair to the side, baring the nape of her neck, and placed his mouth on her skin.

She let go of the baby and held on to the safety rail with both hands. She wanted to touch Caden, to have the right to touch him, everywhere and in every way. She wanted to feel his hands on her.

Caden tasted his way to her ear, where he bit her ear lobe lightly, as she listened to the way his breathing changed with arousal. Not with anticipation, but with purpose, for this was it. She didn't want to keep resisting this.

"Tonight?" he asked in a hushed tone.

"Stay. Please."

Caden lifted the edge of her shirt and smoothed his palms over her stomach. His fingertips slid under the waistband of her khaki shorts, under the elastic of her underwear, and he pulled her back against his body, away from the crib.

Nearly six months of wanting and wishing were over for her. Incredibly, a year was over for him. Because Caden would be the perfect ex-boyfriend in the future, she could make him her boyfriend.

Now.

She let go and fell into Caden. They pushed each other far enough away to grab for buttons and zippers, they pulled one another close to kiss in greed and need, and they tripped their way out of the nursery and down the hall. By the time they reached her room, she was naked except for her white cotton underwear. Caden had gotten out of his boots. She had taken care of his belt. As she backed up to her mattress, she pulled his navy firefighter T-shirt off over his head, a whoosh of fabric, a release of body heat.

Caden pushed her down firmly to lie on her back, and for once, she had no desire to get up. He stayed standing to pull out a foil square and drop the rest of his wallet on the floor, like the useless thing it was in a moment like this. Then he shoved his uniform slacks all the way off.

She pushed herself up on her elbows, wanting to see more of him. Instead, their gazes met and held, brown eyes into blue. He stood over her confidently, gloriously nude, and sheathed himself.

Time stopped for a breath as they looked at one another.

Then he was on her, pushing her up the mattress to where he wanted her, kissing and tonguing his way over her breasts and down her stomach, taking big, greedy mouthfuls of her body. It was so wanton, so uninhibited, it was hard to believe she could have conceived a child with the tepid sex she'd had before.

But she had conceived a child. She felt a flash of fear, a flush of guilt—she shouldn't do this, the baby was more important than her love life—but she could do this, as long as Caden became the ex-boyfriend that he'd described during a waltz. He just had to.

"You have to promise me something," she gasped.

"Yes."

He pulled her underwear over her hips, down her thighs, backing up on the mattress as he did, so that he could follow the cotton with kisses on her hip, her inner thigh, the side of her calf, all the way down the legs he found so sexy. He dropped her underwear on the floor, then his hand circled her ankle. He caressed his way back up her leg, smoothing his hands over all the skin he had kissed, until he was above her once more, his chest and arms beautifully braced as he looked her over from her head to her toes. The way the corner of his mouth cocked into a half smile meant he liked what he saw.

She was burning for him. As long as the baby was still loved when the passion cooled—

"Promise me," she panted.

"Anything."

Caden shifted all his weight to his left arm, so he could reach down with his right to take her ankle and wrap her leg around his waist. She felt the smooth, hard heat of him, pressing where she was so ready to have him.

"Promise."

"I promise," he said, and he sank into her body.

She wrapped both legs around him and held on all night.

* * *

Caden lay on his back, looking at the ceiling of Tana's bedroom as the morning light turned it from gray to white.

He'd never been playing, not once, not ever. But last night, she'd been his playmate, and the games they'd played had been intimate. *Turn all the lights on, I want to see you. Close your eyes, guess where I'll touch you next. Turn the lights off. Touch me everywhere.*

He'd made love to the woman of his dreams. She would be his forever, the mother of his children. She'd want more babies, since she'd gone to all the trouble of artificial insemination to have her first. But every one of Sterling's brothers or sisters would be born in a hospital or birthing center, not in a truck, so help him God. They'd watch those children grow up and have their own children. Tana would be the sweetheart Caden held hands with until the day he died.

But right now, he didn't know what to say to her.

He couldn't propose. Less than twelve hours ago, she'd been surprised that he wanted to be more than just friends.

She rolled onto her back with a rustle of sheets, and sighed. He couldn't see much of her face, not when she was using his shoulder as her pillow.

"Are you okay?" He picked his head up to look at her, but mostly he saw the tip of her nose.

"With what?" She sounded a little apprehensive.

"It might have been too much, after... We probably should have taken it easy the first night... I mean, it's been a while for you, after the baby and all." After they'd used his one condom, she'd opened a drawer and taken out a box, and the games had begun.

"I think we established that everything's in working order." She sounded like she was smiling now. "In fact, I feel fantastic."

"I think you feel fantastic, too."

"You're very funny."

He smiled into her hair as he kissed the top of her head. "It's been a while for me, too. After the baby and all."

He felt her go still in his arms.

"I dated a little, this past year," he said. "But I figured it wasn't fair for a man to take a woman to bed, when he'd only be wishing she was someone else."

I love you. We're going to marry and have a family and grow old together.

Tana propped herself up on her elbow. Her expression was thoughtful as she ran her fingertips over his eyebrow, down his nose and caressed his lips. Then she looked at him through her lashes, her brown eyes mischievous and flirty, now that she didn't have to try to stop herself from flirting with him.

And we're going to have a whole lot of fun while we're at it.

She feigned a concerned expression. "Are you okay? Did I wear you out?"

"I'll keep up with you, somehow. There are times in a man's life when he just has to cowboy up."

She liked that, grinning as she settled onto him, soft breasts against his chest. "Honestly, I've never lost my mind like that before. Never. Last night was…intense."

Well, damn. Here he was, trying to appreciate how

sacred and special sex was with Tana, and then she went and said a thing like that. He tucked one arm behind his head, as cocky and smug as a man could feel. "I lost my mind, too. I know you made me promise you something, at the very beginning. Tell me again what it was."

She struggled to keep her grin in place. He saw it, right before she turned to lay her cheek on his chest. "I might not have gotten around to any specifics. It doesn't matter."

He frowned a little. "There's not a whole lot that's going to embarrass me or scare me away. You can tell me. What promise did you want from me?"

"You'll do it, anyway. I know you will."

"That's mighty comforting, but tell me, so I'll know when I'm doing it."

She was silent.

"Tana."

She sighed. "Fine. Do you remember when we were dancing, and I told you there was nothing a man could do for me now that I was pregnant? You gave me a whole list of things you'd do for the mother of your child, even if you two were no longer in love."

"I remember."

"I thought that you'd be the perfect ex-boyfriend. I wished you were my ex-boyfriend."

He could only see the top of her head as she rested on his chest, toying with his arm, running her fingers up and over the curve of his bicep.

"Now that we're sleeping together, I'll get my wish, sooner or later. I don't want Sterling to be hurt. I know he's not your son, but he's attached to you. I wanted you to promise that you'll still see him sometimes, because he'll miss you an awful lot. I'm not worried, though. I know you'll still be good to him, when you and I are no longer sleeping together."

What the hell?

He rolled her over, pinning her so they were face-to-face, blue eyes into brown. "No longer sleeping together? Is that what you think this is? Some kind of occasional friends-with-benefits crap until we find other people? Tana, damn it, I love you."

"Oh."

He hadn't meant to say it quite that way, but it was out now. "I love you. I have loved you for a long time. We're not sleeping together. We are together."

"I'm talking about the future, when you're not in love with me. I know you'll need to leave me. I just don't want you to leave my baby."

He couldn't speak.

"Not too abruptly, at least, for his sake." She patted his arm in a soothing way. "That's all."

Caden shifted positions to brace himself on his forearms and hold her head in his hands, so he could study her face. So he could understand her, and she could understand him. "Nobody is leaving anyone. I already promised not to leave you. Haven't you noticed that I never leave, not until you tell me it's okay with you?"

She looked up at him with her eyes wide, looking more shocked than anything else. How could this be news to her?

"You were in labor when I made that promise. Maybe

that's why you don't remember. I'm not leaving you, not if you want me to stay, and I'm not leaving Sterling."

"I remember. That's why this is okay. If you wouldn't leave the baby then, you won't leave him even when you're my ex."

It hit Caden in the heart. She believed that he could love the baby, but she didn't think he could love her.

"Tana, sweetheart. The baby hadn't been born yet. I had no idea what loving a baby would feel like. I held your hand, and we drove toward that hospital, and I promised you I wouldn't leave you, because I already knew what being in love with you felt like."

"You loved me when I was waddling around the diner's parking lot?" She sounded skeptical.

"I did. I was trying so hard not to, but I did. In the truck, you cried because you didn't have someone in your life who could be by your side. I decided to be that friend for you then, because I already loved you then. When you love someone, you want them to have what they need."

She began to touch him, trailing her fingers up his side, down to his hip. "In that case, you should tell me what you need."

He touched his nose to hers in relief. "I need you in my life. It's as simple as that."

She smiled. It started small, even shy, but she ended up beaming at him.

Through the open bedroom door, Sterling's cry carried clearly.

"He's awake." Tana wrinkled her nose. "At least it's easy to guess what he needs."

She put on the blue satin robe that Ruby had given her as a baby gift. He pulled on his boxers, and they walked into the oasis of the baby's room, together.

"Everything's good," Caden said.

She nodded. "Everything's good."

The baby in the high chair didn't think anything was good.

Tana was working late, holding a team meeting after practice. That wouldn't normally make Sterling grumpy, not if Caden was with him.

After Tana had left for work, Caden had taken the baby to a couple of stores. He'd bought a high-speed jogging stroller in the first store, a diamond ring in the second. He didn't know when he'd offer Tana the ring. They'd moved from just-friends to lovers only last night, but Caden was going to have the stroller ready to surprise her this evening.

At least, that had been the plan. He'd started putting it together, assuming Sterling would be happy to scoot around on a blanket next to him, having some tummy time. Not tonight.

Caden offered him a spoonful of baby oatmeal. Sterling clamped his little lips together and turned his head. It was amazing how stubborn a seventeen-pound baby could be.

"Okay, let's switch it up here, little fella."

Applesauce met oatmeal's fate.

Caden let Sterling hold the empty spoon, but even waving that around didn't satisfy the baby for long. He squirmed in his high chair, fussing and unhappy.

"Let's mop you up, then we'll go for a bottle. You

need to have a nice, full belly, so you'll sleep tight to-night. Your mommy will be home soon, and she and I need a chance to…work on our relationship. I'll explain it when you're older."

It hit Caden that he would be there when Sterling was older, and he actually would have to explain the birds and bees to him. For the first time, he imagined it from a parent's perspective. How had his dad done it with a straight face?

Sterling objected with a little baby yell and a fierce frown.

"No, I'm not going to tell you now. You don't want me to, trust me. It's going to gross you out to find out how your parents make babies. Sorry about that, in advance."

The doorbell rang just as Caden put a toy on the high chair tray, hoping to buy a little time to warm up a bottle. Since the high chair was at the dining room table, Caden could keep an eye on Sterling as he opened the door.

A man stood there, obviously surprised to see him.

Caden didn't know him. He was around his age, dressed in hiking or outdoor-adventure clothes, although they looked pristine. The brand name was prominent.

"Who are you?" the man demanded.

"Apparently, I'm not who you were expecting. Wrong apartment." Caden started to close the door.

The man slapped his palm on it. "Hang on."

Caden switched gears in an instant, squaring off against the man, blocking him from coming in the door. Who the hell did this guy think he was?

"Where's Tana? Montana McKenna? She does still live

here, doesn't she?" He craned his neck to see past Caden. "Yeah, that's her couch. Come on, man. Let me in."

Caden didn't budge. "Who are you?"

"You're shacking up with her now, aren't you?" The man held up his hands in mocking surrender. "More power to you. I'm only here to see the baby."

"You mean Steven?"

Yeah, the wrong name was a test.

The man looked surprised. "That's a boy's name, right? It was a boy. Good."

Fail.

The man drew himself up tall. He still wasn't tall enough to look down his nose at Caden, but he sneered, anyway. "I'm Steven's father."

Caden knew better. What was this guy's angle?

The baby chose that moment to throw his toy and kick his chair, crying because he'd lost Caden's attention.

The man craned his neck again. "Is that him? Let me in. I want to see my kid." He tried to shove his way into the apartment.

Caden stiff-armed him, smacking his palm against the man's chest. No stranger was going to get near Sterling, full stop.

"Does he look like me?"

Caden was incredulous at the man's audacity, but one possibility explained it. Caden had assumed fertility clinics had airtight privacy policies. Maybe not.

He shoved the man back a step, out into the hall. "Are you the sperm donor?"

"Sperm donor, my ass. Tana and I lived together in Houston. I'm the baby's father."

Chapter Twenty

The door was locked.

Tana let herself in with her key. There were no lights on, although the sunset was over, and the last gray light of gloaming was all that came in the window. Her apartment felt like it had before Sterling had been born.

Lonely.

There was an opened cardboard box in the middle of her living room floor and a set of spoked wheels propped against it. She looked around for some sign of life. With a little start, she realized Caden was sitting at the dining table, watching her.

"Hi. I'm home." She turned on the lamp by the couch as she passed it, walking straight toward him, ready to greet him with a kiss. She could do that, now. They were together.

He didn't say anything. He didn't move.

"What's going on? Is the baby—" Her heart stopped. That was the one thing that could make Caden look so grim. "Oh, my God, the baby—"

"He's fine."

Something about Caden's tone of voice made her sink onto the hard chair next to his. "What happened?"

"Who is Jerry?"

She felt like she'd hit the water from the high-dive platform. Jerry—*whack*. That name shouldn't exist here.

"He came by, Tana."

She jumped up. "Where is the baby?"

Caden caught her wrist. "He's asleep. Do you think I'd let a stranger take him?"

Her heart was pounding so hard, Caden must have felt her pulse without trying.

Caden dropped her wrist. "Someone who was a stranger to me, but not to you, obviously. He said he was Sterling's father. It's true, isn't it? Your first thought when I said *Jerry* was that he came for the baby."

"Yes, but—"

"It's true." Caden cut her off. "*Artificial insemination.* You said you used artificial insemination."

"I called him a sperm donor. That's all he was. All he is." The point she'd thought was so important didn't seem as significant now, but she said it, anyway. "I was very careful not to say that I went through an artificial insemination procedure. I didn't lie. Not once."

Caden shoved his chair away from the table and stood. "It was a huge lie. You told me there was a sperm donor when we danced on Thanksgiving. I didn't believe you, at first. I thought you were just angry at your boyfriend. I should have trusted my gut. But ever since you went into labor…"

Every muscle in his body strained with the effort to contain the emotions that were tearing him up inside.

"Every day since then, I believed you, damn it. In my truck, just last night, you sat there while I poured my heart out to you. I told you I left you at the pub a year ago because I thought you were going to Houston to tell a man you were pregnant. I said I knew now it must have been your parents. You could have corrected me last night. You could have told me the truth. A hundred times, you could have told me. At the hospital, with the birth certificate. Your parents believe Sterling has no father. Ruby believes it. But it's all been a massive, massive lie."

Tana was horrified at the fury and agony in Caden's face. She was horrified, because it was her fault.

"My sister-in-law warned me. She said the real father would show up one day to raise his own child. He has. He does."

"Does what?" Tana desperately needed to make herself clear. "Wants to raise Sterling? He does not."

"He'll be back to talk things out with you." Caden grabbed his jacket off a chair, his truck keys off the table.

"You and I have to talk," she said, panic making her rush her words. "Us. We. Not him."

"It's not even the lie that kills me. It's not. It's the fact that you knew." Caden squeezed his eyes shut and pinched the bridge of his nose. His chest heaved with each breath. "My God, Tana. You knew this would happen. You let me love Sterling, anyway. Month after month, you stood by and *watched* me fall in love with that baby. How could you do that?"

He dropped his hand and headed toward the door.

She pushed away from the table and ran after him. "Where are you going?"

"Away from here. I have to step aside. The real father wants to be with his son. He has that right."

"Jerry isn't a father." Why would no one, not one person, believe her on this? "Did you know he could get the courts to order a paternity test? He could, but he won't. He's the kind who dodges responsibility. He always has."

Caden rounded on her. "You know damn well he is Sterling's father, but you'll force him to go to court to prove it? That's cruel. You have no idea, none at all, how much a child can mean to a man." Caden yanked the door open. "I wish I didn't know, either."

Her own front door was shut in her face.

She could barely get out the words. "Stay. Please."

It didn't matter. Caden was already gone.

Ten days.

That was all Tana could stand.

Caden hadn't been home—or he hadn't answered her knock—each time she'd tried to see him. She'd gone with Sterling, holding him on her shoulder so his little face would be visible through the peep hole. On Ruby's advice, she'd tried going alone, wearing Caden's plaid shirt and her shortest denim shorts. There'd been no answer to her knock then, either. Caden blocked her number. She couldn't even leave him a message.

She missed him every minute of the day.

So did the baby.

Tana might deserve to lose Caden, but Sterling did not. Ten days was enough.

Tana finished assembling the jogging stroller, buckled Sterling in it and ran to the fire station, right into the open bay doors. She parked the stroller next to Engine 37, wiped the sweat from her face with her exercise towel, and tugged on her ponytail to tighten it up.

Javier saw her first. "Hey...Tana." He looked nervously toward the door that led into their living area. "Stopping here for some water?"

"No. I'm stopping here to see Caden." She gave herself kudos for sounding confident when her stomach was in knots.

Keith joined them. "I can see if he's here. I mean, he's here, but he might be asleep. Let me go ask him. Check on him, I mean."

From behind her, a masculine voice addressed them all. "I'm here. I'll meet you guys in the office. This won't take a minute." Javier and Keith disappeared almost as fast as Tana turned around to face Caden.

Her thoughtful plan, a mature approach to a necessary conversation, flew right out of her head. *It's you, look at you, look at those eyes, I love you, I miss you.*

Caden crossed his arms over his chest. "Why are you here, Tana?"

She'd rehearsed this answer. "I came by to answer your questions."

"I have none."

She wished Sterling hadn't zonked out in the stroller. If he were awake, he would have dive-bombed from her arms toward Caden, and Caden would have caught him, rather than standing here like an angry bar bouncer.

"You had several questions," she said. "You asked how I could have watched you fall in love with this baby, when I knew you weren't the father."

"It was a rhetorical question."

He wasn't going to make this easy. She took a breath and kept moving forward. "I had no plans for anything when I went into labor. You must know that. But afterward, there we were, parked on the side of the road, the three of us. It felt like…that was it. That was the way it should be, it would be, from now on. The three of us."

He dropped his arms and turned to go.

She dragged the stroller along as she hurried to plant herself in his path. "So, yes, I hadn't planned it, but from that point on, I wanted you to love my baby along with me. Yes, I wished you were his father."

Caden looked disgusted. "No, you wished I was your ex-boyfriend."

"Well, now you are," she snapped in frustration. "And you're doing a lousy job of it."

He raised one eyebrow in disbelief.

She gestured toward the stroller. "I don't want to be enemies. This isn't about just me."

"This isn't about just me, either. You lied to everyone. Ruby thought there was a sperm donor. Your parents thought there was a sperm donor. You let the birth certificate go blank, because you didn't want your parents to know…what? What could possibly justify that? Are they some kind of religious fanatics, and you lied so they wouldn't think you'd had sex? I've been racking my brain, trying to think of any excuse for you, Tana. Any excuse."

"They weren't mad at me for having sex and getting pregnant. They were mad because I got pregnant when they wanted me to start training for another Olympics."

"Another—what?" He literally stepped back. "You were in the Olympics?"

Once more, she was forced to correct someone. "I was supposed to be, but I didn't go. My parents thought my old coach, the one that picked me up at the ER after I fainted, they thought he wanted me to start seriously training again."

"For the Olympics."

"Right."

"Not once did you mention the Olympics."

"Why would I? I never went. I set a world record, though. The one-hundred-meter backstroke."

He was silent. Had she thought he'd be impressed?

"It's been broken since then. It was broken the next year, just like my husband had told me it would be."

"Your husband? *Husband?*" He stepped back.

"Ex," she added hastily, in case he thought she'd been cheating with him. "Ex-husband. Sorry. Ex. We're divorced."

Caden paced away from her. "I don't know you at all, Tana. I thought I knew you, but you never shared anything with me. Anything." He punched his fist into his own heart, as if it had died and needed CPR.

She hadn't planned to talk about this. How had she swum so far out of her lane?

"I was twenty. It lasted less than a year, but during that year, he convinced me to skip the Olympics. My parents had invested everything they had, for years, to enable me to train. They'd gotten me an endorsement deal, a million dollars to hold a can of soup. Instead, I eloped. My parents have never forgiven me."

Caden kind of fell back against the wall, like standing was just too much.

"The hardest thing was that I'd let down the whole United States of America. We didn't medal in my event that summer. Not even bronze." She twisted her hands together. "For ten years, I thought everyone from my old life hadn't forgiven me, either, until my former coach recommended me to Masterson. This year was my big chance to redeem myself. My parents think I've wasted my talent, but I wanted to prove to them I'm using it. I'm valuable, still, in the swimming world. I'm coaching kids with the potential to be future Olympians."

Caden just looked up into the rafters, shaking his head.

"My coach and I got to be friends this year, after I fainted in January. He said no one had ever been mad at me. They blamed my husband, because he was one of the trainers, and he was older. Thirty-three. He should have known not to fraternize with a swimmer on the job."

"Thirty-three to your twenty?"

"I know. My parents are furious that I was such a sucker." She let go of her hands. "Anyway, that's the history with my parents. It's relevant, because they thought Jerry was a bad person, too, as selfish as my ex-husband. But when I told them I was pregnant, they demanded that I marry a selfish, bad person."

My parents were willing to sacrifice me to maintain their propriety. There was no bottom to humiliating conversations with Caden, still.

"Jerry said he didn't care if I had the baby or not, and he went off to Peru. He cut me out of his life like I'd never been there. So, when my parents started hammering me about how bad my judgment still was, I said Jerry had nothing to do with this pregnancy. It was true. He *had* refused to be part of it. But you're right, it was a relief when they jumped to the wrong conclusion.

"I think that answers the question on why I didn't tell my parents Jerry was the father. And Ruby..." She forced herself to chuckle. "I told her the truth this week. She called Jerry an ass and told me to wear my sexiest shorts and your plaid shirt to get you back. Pretty Ruby of her, huh?"

Caden only scrubbed his jaw with his palm.

"You also had a question about the birth certificate. How could I leave the father's name blank? That wasn't up to me. Texas law prevents me from naming anyone as the father, unless he's legally my husband. Otherwise, I can't name any other man, unless he signs a form first, acknowledging his paternity. When you told my mom and dad that I could leave the name blank without an explanation, that wasn't technically correct. I *had* to leave the name blank. But I appreciated having you on my side. Thank you."

Caden finally looked at her instead of the rafters, but he was looking at her like he'd never seen a creature before who was as bizarre as she was.

"I have no legal power to name Jerry as the father, but I also can't deny Jerry his paternity. He could go to court and demand a paternity test and have himself put on the birth certificate. That's what I meant, when I said he could do that. I didn't mean I'd make him do that."

Caden started scowling again.

Tana kept slogging forward. "I said that because I thought it would prove to you that he had no interest in being a father. If he really wanted to be Sterling's father, I couldn't stop him, even if I was as cruel as you think I am. But I'm not cruel. He came back, after you left. I told him I wouldn't dispute it if he signed one of those official declarations of paternity. They're online. He could just print one off and fill it out. I offered to file it for him to update the birth certificate."

"What did he say?"

"He left for Nepal. It's a two-year trip. His last words were 'I'm not stupid enough to sign that. Good luck collecting child support from the Himalayas.'"

"Why didn't you tell me this?"

"This is the first time I've seen you since that night."

"I mean all of this. The Olympics and the marriage and your parents. All of it. Any of it, at any time in the past year." Caden was furious, still. It was all aimed at her, in the way he frowned at her, the way his eyes bored into her. "We were friends, Tana. *Friends.*"

"I didn't want to lose you. If I listed all of the bad decisions I've made in my life, you wouldn't want to be my friend." She used the heel of her hand to wipe her cheek. "I was right. Now you know, and now you aren't my friend."

His expression went blank. She wished he would look at her with the expression he'd had ten days ago, when he'd held her head between his hands and told her nobody was leaving anyone.

"Is there anything else?" he asked, but the flat tone of his voice neither encouraged or discouraged any response.

"That was all of your questions."

He said nothing. He did nothing.

She needed every ounce of fierce determination she could muster in order to keep going. "You said that when you love someone, you want to give them what they need. I love you, even if that's not worth anything to you. I love you, and I love Sterling. You and Sterling need each other, so I want you to have each other. The answers to your questions might not be good ones, but I'm hoping you'll stop thinking of me as your enemy. I don't want you to avoid Sterling just to avoid me."

Buzzers sounded loudly overhead, followed by the dispatcher's voice over the loudspeakers in the bay. "Smoke reported. Kitchen fire at restaurant. Engine 37."

The sudden noise startled Sterling awake.

Caden was the only person who held still as the bay came alive all around them. The loudspeaker repeated *Engine 37* and added *Rescue 37*, too. Men and women in navy blue came out of the offices and the living quarters and headed to the vehicles.

Tana unbuckled the baby and picked him up. He was

so pitiful when he was tearful and scared. She kissed his cheek and held him close.

Caden finally moved, but only to pick up the stuffed animal that had been left behind in the stroller. "What's this?"

She'd made it herself, out of Caden's shirt. It was just a flat pillow, really. She'd cut the plaid into two silhouettes of a Scotty dog, stitched them together and stuffed them with cotton. It had killed an hour or two on a sleepless night, but she'd really done it because it had killed the temptation to wear Caden's shirt when she was feeling low. That would only make her feel lower now, a maudlin reminder of what she'd lost.

"I assumed you wouldn't want me wearing your shirt around town like I'm your girlfriend. I should have returned it, but I'd worn it out, honestly. Sterling is so familiar with it, and he misses you, so—"

Buzzers silenced her.

"I have to leave." Caden tossed the pillow into the stroller.

"Will you come by sometime? I'll leave, so you won't have to see me in order to see the baby, okay?"

"No, it's not okay. None of this is okay."

The disappointment was crushing, pushing her down, pulling her under. She'd failed, but dear God, she'd tried.

Sterling whimpered and her own eyes watered, but she held her head high. "I know I lied, and I know you're angry, but you lied, too. You said you'd never leave me. You may have been sitting at my table when I came in that night, but Caden, you were already gone."

In the middle of the rush around them, as engines

rumbled and loudspeakers blared, the silence between them was deafening.

Javier shouted for Caden. "Lieutenant."

The team kept the doors of the fire engine open at all times and their bunker gear by the doors, so they could be dressed and on the road in seconds. Keith already had his boots and turnout pants on.

Caden turned toward the engine.

Turned back.

"Are you going to be home tonight?" he asked.

The sudden burst of hope hurt. Maybe she hadn't failed to give the people she loved most what they needed most.

He started jogging backward toward his gear, waiting for her answer.

"Yes, please come see Sterling. He'll be so happy."

Caden nodded, but he looked more troubled than ever as he turned away. He stomped into his boots. While he pulled the yellow suspenders of his turnout pants over his shoulders, he shouted to Javier, who was already behind the wheel. "No sirens. Baby ears in the bay."

He climbed into the cab with his coat still unfastened. The flashing lights came on, and the massive wheels started to roll. Tana pressed her baby's head against her chest and covered his ear, but no sirens wailed until Engine 37 was down the street, because Caden had been taking care of Sterling.

Tana had gotten her wish. He was going to be the perfect ex-boyfriend.

She ran as fast as she could, but her tears started to fall long before she reached her apartment.

Chapter Twenty-One

Sometimes, where there was smoke, there was no fire at all.

Caden and his team, plus Rescue 37 and its team, had wasted their time on a false alarm at the restaurant. They headed back to the station, crawling through traffic without lights and sirens.

Caden couldn't stand the pace. He needed to be doing something, breaking down doors, releasing trapped heat before it could blow apart a building.

He needed to see Tana.

He'd screwed up. The smoke had been there, billowing, overwhelming. She'd lied about how she'd gotten pregnant. He'd been blindsided by a man claiming to be Sterling's father—a man who was actually Sterling's father. Caden had felt betrayed. He'd abandoned the scene, leaving it to burn itself out unattended.

But there'd been no fire. Tana had stood in the bay an hour ago, answering his questions one after another, and he'd realized that he'd completely blown the most important relationship of his life. Her parting words had cut him to the quick: *You lied, too. You said you'd never leave.*

Yet he'd walked out on her, ten days ago.

He ripped off his headset, then scrubbed his hand through his hair.

"You okay there, Lieutenant?"

"Fine."

But he saw the worried look Javier and Keith exchanged.

"I'm fine."

He would never be fine again. He'd done a damn good job at extinguishing every last flicker of trust Tana might have had in him. Trust couldn't be easy for her to give, not with the past he hadn't known about until today. All this time, she had believed he would want to be with her only if he never knew about her past mistakes. And damn it—damn him—he'd proved her right. Jerry—her latest mistake—had tried to walk in, and Caden had walked out.

It wouldn't be easy for him to earn her trust again. She'd given up trying to call him. She'd stopped coming by his house. She'd cut up his goddamned shirt. The relationship was dead.

He didn't know what to do, but he had to try something, anything. He couldn't live without Tana as part of his life. Tana and the precious baby she'd named—

Sterling.

They both loved that baby. Caden would start there. Tana wanted him to spend time with Sterling. When she offered to leave, he'd ask her to stay. They'd play with the baby together. Feed him in the high chair together. Have their own dinner together, one night. Go for a run together, one day. It would take time, but little by little, he'd earn the right to say *I love you* again.

Their engine's next call was legitimate, if boring. A minor car accident brought them south of town. While they got everyone out of the wrecked vehicles easily enough, a new report of smoke in town came over the radio. That would normally be their call, but since they were on this scene, Engine 23 from the next station north was dispatched to cover it.

Caden applied a little antiseptic to a few scrapes as Rescue 23 was called out on the radio. A minute later, Ladder 37 was sent from their house. He didn't have to tell Javier to wrap it up, but he got his rookie's attention as he headed toward the engine.

"Keith. Let's go. Sounds like it's going to be a second alarm." They left the police in charge and started rolling back to town.

It took them a minute to find the channel that all the responding units had switched to. The chatter was brisk. Fully involved structure, flames visible. Chief on the scene. As expected, the second alarm went out: more units requested. They hit their lights and sirens as the dispatcher gave them their destination. "Engine 37. Planchet Apartments, Felton Avenue."

Tana's address.

The whole team cursed, then they fell silent as they listened for evacuation reports. Caden's pulse was loud in his ears. Tana and Sterling. They were there, waiting for him to get off his shift and stop by. They'd ordered their lives around his stiff acceptance of their invitation to visit. They were in a burning building because of him.

Nobody spoke. The team on the Alpha side of the building—the front face—reported that the elevator shaft was the source of the fire. It was far too close to Tana's apartment, far too close to the stairwell she used.

Protocol labeled the four sides of the building, of any building, alpha, bravo, charlie, delta—*a, b, c, d*—so that fire teams could communicate their locations with less confusion. Tana's side would be the Charlie side of the building. Charlie tenants were being guided to the far stairwell on the Delta side of the building. Charlie and Delta were still evacuating as the building burned.

They could see flames as they arrived. *Tana and Sterling, my God, not Tana and Sterling...*

"Engine 37 on scene." Caden radioed their status, shocked that he could still speak at all as fear stopped his heart. One second later, he jumped out of the truck feeling so alert, so alive, he was ready to break down every door in the whole damned building, if that was what it took to get to Tana and Sterling.

The fire chief directed them over the radio. Caden's team was designated to be next on the roof to cut ventilation holes so the heat could escape. Ladders were already in place to scale the three-story building, set by the team that was up there now. Caden and his team grabbed their power saws and iron pikes, then moved to the front of the row of vehicles, where they were supposed to wait on bended knee, conserving their energy until they were called into action.

Firefighters could only last so long in the smoke and fire. It was exhausting work, so they had to tag team with other units, like a relay race. The initial team on the roof was coming up on twenty minutes of incident time. They'd be pulled out, and Caden's team would be sent up.

He keyed the mic on his radio. "Incident time?"

The dispatcher answered. "Incident time, fourteen minutes."

They'd go in at twenty. To hell with resting on one knee. Caden had six minutes to find Tana before he got sent to the roof. He left his chainsaw with Javier and strode down the lawn, parallel to the sidewalk where the residents and onlookers were congregated. With an air tank on his back and his helmet on his head, he headed for the Delta side of the building, where Tana would have been evacuated, if she'd been evacuated.

If wasn't good enough. He needed to know.

"Tana!" He bellowed her name every ten yards or so, until he reached the end of the sidewalk. She wasn't here. He headed back toward his engine as he radioed the mobile command post to ask if the third floor evacuation was complete. He listened to the reports so intently, he almost missed her cry.

"Caden!"

She was standing next to the fire chief's red SUV, she and Sterling both, the most beautiful sight he'd ever seen—so beautiful, Caden started to run. Tana met him halfway with the baby in her arms.

"I knew you'd be worried about Sterling," she said, raising her voice over the shouted commands of the fire-fighters and the high-velocity spray of water. "I wanted the chief to let you know he was safe, so that you could focus on what you have to do. You have to put every-thing else behind you, so you'll stay safe, too."

It was a champion's advice. Caden was in full gear, but he had to touch her. It had been too long since he'd touched them both. He started shedding his heavy gloves as he made himself heard over the noise. "I was worried about both of you. Both of you. Tana, don't you see? I hated everything you said this afternoon. I hated it."

She recoiled a step. Ladders and hoses were being directed all around them. She had to make her apol-ogy loud. "I'm sorry. I shouldn't have told you I loved you, not after you made it clear that you don't want—"

"I love you, too." He threw his glove on the ground. "I hate that you've been treated so badly. Your parents. Coaches. Jerry. Husband—I hate that you were taken advantage of by a man older than I am when you were just twenty. I hate that your parents blame you for it. I *hate* that the woman I love has been treated so badly that she's been scared for months to tell me about her life. I hate that she's come to expect people to let her down, so that she wasn't even surprised when I let her down,

too. And God, I did. I'm so sorry, I did. I should never have walked out that night. I was so sure I was right."

"You were right."

"But I was wrong. I should have stayed. You shouldn't have had to come find me today to make me listen."

Sirens joined the cacophony as more units arrived.

Tana was still keeping an arm's distance from him. She covered Sterling's ear with her hand and shouted over the sirens. "Do you mean—do you mean you'll give me a second chance?"

"You don't need the second chance, baby. I do."

"You don't need it, either."

"I'm so completely in love with you," he shouted back. "That will never change, even if you never forgive me."

"I love you, too. That will never change, even if I have to track you down again to tell you."

They were yelling at each other, laughing now. He chucked his second glove on the ground and came close enough that he could have wrapped them in his arms, but his gear was too coarse and bulky. Instead, he touched them the only way he could, one hand holding Sterling's precious head, one hand cupping Tana's beloved face. He kissed Sterling gently. He kissed Tana hard.

"Incident time, eighteen minutes," the dispatcher said.

"I have to go."

"I know." Tana kissed him again, quick. "Go save my apartment, or I'll have to move in with you."

"Move in with me, anyway. Forever. There was a diamond ring with that jogging stroller. I don't have it on me, but it's back at my house—"

This was insane. This wasn't how he'd meant to propose, but he couldn't go up on that roof without telling her his intentions. If anything happened, and she was left without knowing how he'd felt about her...

He couldn't wait another minute.

He dropped to his knee. He had to shove his face shield up farther, so he could see her from under the brim of his helmet. He held out his hand, and she gave him hers, palm against warm palm.

"I want to marry you, Montana McKenna. You have my heart. You always have, you always will, and I was a fool to try to live without it for even one day. I never want to be apart from you again. It's that simple. Will you marry me?"

His radio interrupted. "Incident time, nineteen minutes."

Caden squeezed Tana's hand. "I don't mean to rush you, baby, but you have sixty seconds to decide."

"Yes. Yes. Of course, yes." She tugged on his hand, putting some of her world-class muscle into it and pulling him to his feet.

Time was up. They couldn't kiss or cuddle or marvel at the miracle of finding their forever-partner. Instead, side by side, they headed for his team. The woman with the sexiest legs he'd ever seen matched him stride for stride easily, carrying the baby they both loved.

They reached the staging area. Caden moved close enough to speak into her ear, a brush of cheek against cheek. "When I get off this roof, I won't come near you and the baby. The smoke is toxic. Particles get on the gear. I won't touch you until I get showered at the firehouse."

"Then I'll be at the firehouse. I'll touch you anywhere you'll let me touch you. Unless you're too exhausted."

"Don't worry about that. I'll find a way to cowboy up."

She laughed. "There are innocent ears listening."

Caden dropped one more kiss next to the perfect little ear of his fussing, squirming baby—*his* baby, since that first breath.

Javier brought him his power saw. "You ready, Lieutenant?"

"Ready."

The announcement came over the radio. "Incident time, twenty minutes."

Caden lifted Tana's hand to his lips. He kissed her ring finger, where he would place a diamond before the day was through.

Then he pulled on his glove, dropped down his face shield, and started up the ladder toward the sky, although he couldn't get any closer to heaven than he already was.

* * * * *

Don't miss the next book in the
Masterson, Texas miniseries,
For This Christmas Only,
available December 2020 from
Harlequin Special Edition!

And for more swoon-worthy single parent romances,
check out these other great books, available now:

The Maverick's Baby Arrangement
By Kathy Douglass

The Last Man She Expected
By Michelle Major

The Matchmaker's Challenge
By Teresa Southwick

COMING NEXT MONTH FROM

⟨H⟩ HARLEQUIN
SPECIAL EDITION

Available September 15, 2020

#2791 TEXAS PROUD
Long, Tall Texans • by Diana Palmer
Before he testifies in an important case, businessman Michael "Mikey" Fiore hides out in Jacobsville, Texas. On a rare night out, he crosses paths with softly beautiful Bernadette, who seems burdened with her own secrets. This doesn't stop him from wanting her, which endangers them both. Their bond grows into passion... until shocking truths surface.

#2792 THE COWBOY'S PROMISE
Montana Mavericks: What Happened to Beatrix?
by Teresa Southwick
Erica Abernathy comes back to Bronco after several years away. Everyone is stunned to discover she is pregnant. Why did she keep this a secret? And what will she do when she is courted by a cowboy she doesn't think wants a ready-made family?

#2793 HOME FOR THE BABY'S SAKE
The Bravos of Valentine Bay • by Christine Rimmer
Trying to give his son the best life he can, single dad Roman Marek has returned to his hometown to raise his baby son. But when he buys a local theater to convert into a hotel, he finds much more than he bargained for in Hailey Bravo, the theater's director.

#2794 SECRETS OF FOREVER
Forever, Texas • by Marie Ferrarella
When the longtime matriarch of Forever, Texas, needs a cardiac specialist, the whole community comes together to fly Dr. Neil Eastwood to the tiny town with a big heart—and he loses his own heart to a local pilot in the process!

#2795 FOUR CHRISTMAS MATCHMAKERS
Lockharts Lost & Found • by Cathy Gillen Thacker
Allison Meadows has got it all under control—her home, her job, her *life*—so taking care of four-year-old quadruplets can't be that hard. But Allison's perfect life is a facade and she has to stop the TV execs from finding out. A lie ended former pro athlete Cade Lockhart's career, and he won't lie for anyone...even when Allison's job is on the line. But can four adorable matchmakers create a Christmas miracle?

#2796 HER SWEET TEMPTATION
Tillbridge Stables • by Nina Crespo
After a long string of reckless choices ruined her life, Rina is determined to stay on the straight and narrow, but when a thrill-chasing stuntman literally bowls her over, she's finding it hard to resist the bad boy.

**YOU CAN FIND MORE INFORMATION ON UPCOMING HARLEQUIN TITLES,
FREE EXCERPTS AND MORE AT HARLEQUIN.COM.**

HSECNM0920

Mikey's fingers contracted. "Suppose I told you that the
hotel I own is actually a casino," he said slowly, "and it's
in Las Vegas?"

Bernie's eyes widened. "You own a casino in Las
Vegas?" she exclaimed. "Wow!"

He laughed, surprised at her easy acceptance. "I run it
legit, too," he added. "No fixes, no hidden switches, no
cheating. Drives the feds nuts, because they can't find
anything to pin on me there."

"The feds?" she asked.

He drew in a breath. "I told you, I'm a bad man." He
felt guilty about it, dirty. His fingers caressed hers as they

neared Graylings, the huge mansion where his cousin lived with the heir to the Grayling racehorse stables.

Her fingers curled trustingly around his. "And I told you that the past doesn't matter," she said stubbornly. Her heart was running wild. "Not at all. I don't care how bad you've been."

His own heart stopped and then ran away. His teeth clenched. "I don't even think you're real, Bernie," he whispered. "I think I dreamed you."

She flushed and smiled. "Thanks."

He glanced in the rearview mirror. "What I'd give for just five minutes alone with you right now," he said tautly. "Fat chance," he added as he noticed the sedan tailing casually behind them.

She felt all aglow inside. She wanted that, too. Maybe they could find a quiet place to be alone, even for just a few minutes. She wanted to kiss him until her mouth hurt.

Don't miss
Texas Proud *by Diana Palmer,*
available October 2020 wherever
Harlequin Special Edition books and ebooks are sold.

Harlequin.com